Saturday Night at San Marcos

ABOUT THE AUTHOR

William Packard has published several collections of poetry and prose, including *The Condition for All Poetry*, *Genius Is Desire*, *Whales & Tombs*, and *First Selected Poems*. His plays include, *From Now On*, *Once and for All*, *The Killer Thing* (directed by Otto Preminger in 1980), *The Funeral*, and *War Play*. He has translated numerous works including, *Femmes/Hombres*, the erotic poetry of Paul Verlaine, and has edited a number of anthologies including, *Do Not Go Gentle*, and *The Craft of Poetry*. He is founder and editor of The New York Quarterly, and teaches acting and playwriting at H.B. Studio in New York City where he currently lives.

SATURDAY NIGHT AT SAN MARCOS

A NOVEL BY

William Packard

THUNDER'S
MOUTH
PRESS
NEW YORK

Copyright © 1985 by William Packard

Published in the United States by

Thunder's Mouth Press, Box 780, New York, NY 10025

This is entirely a work of fiction so its

characters and events and story lines are

wholly imaginary and any similarity or

resemblance or likeness to any past or

present or future characters or events or

story lines is entirely coincidental.

Design by Loretta Li

Grateful acknowledgment to the New York State
Council for the Arts and the National Endowment
for the Arts for financial assistance.

Distributed by PERSEA BOOKS

225 Lafayette, N.Y.C. 10012, 212-431-5270

Library of Congress Cataloging in Publication Data

Packard, William.   Saturday night at San Marcos.

I. Title.

PS3531.A2162S2   1985   813'.54   84-24083

ISBN 0-938410-25-3

Over the past twenty years William Packard has
attended or taught at or been co-director of
the following writer's conferences:

THE BREAD LOAF WRITER'S CONFERENCE, Vermont

THE CAPE COD WRITER'S CONFERENCE, Massachusetts

THE COOPER HILL WRITER'S CONFERENCE, Vermont

THE HOFSTRA WRITER'S CONFERENCE, New York

THE SUFFIELD WRITER-READER CONFERENCE, Connecticut

THE WESLEYAN WRITER-READER CONFERENCE, Connecticut

THE RHODE ISLAND WRITER'S CONFERENCE, Rhode Island

for Marjorie Finnell

one/Friday

I began writing this lousy novel at a corny boring writers conference out in California where a lot of lost souls go to be told how to write their own writing and I hadn't been really writing anything myself for the last 5 years but that didn't seem to bother anyone else out there so long as I taught the fiction classes and gave the individual manuscript conferences and helped the conferees write their own writing then nobody gave a good god damn whether I was really writing or not but I gave a good god damn because I can tell you it's hell to be a writing teacher at a writers conference when you're not really writing anything yourself because it feels like your whole life is a lie but thank god that's all over now because here I am writing this novel that you're reading right now although you don't have any idea where it's all going to go so maybe you're not even sure you want to keep reading the whole thing all the way through to the end and maybe you'd rather be reading some phony longwinded book review of this novel from some crummy Sunday book review section that would print a large photograph of me showing my shaggy hair and my crumpled coat and the dislocated look in my eyes and underneath the photo of me there'd be some book review that would go something like this:

> *Saturday Night at San Marcos* is an interesting novel but parts of it are so grotesquely overwritten and anecdotal and other parts are in such monumental bad taste that no one will want to keep reading the whole thing all the way through to the end because it's about this writer who is not really writing anything so the whole book is filled with all the illness and silliness that writers go through when they're trying to get back on the track of their own writing and Eliot Morrison is the narrator and chief character of this novel and he has all sorts of sick excuses for why he's not really writing like he gets these weird dizzy spells and he also gets these obscene phone calls from his crazy ex-wife and he also has this on again off again affair with a christ awful beautiful dumb actress and he also has to read his way through mountains of stupid student manuscripts at a lot of corny boring writers conferences so it's no wonder this Eliot Morrison character is such a fishy mishmosh of paranoia and thank heaven there are a few other characters who have a little more life to them like Ted Wylie who is a best selling novelist with a beady eagle eye who is writing a new novel about a writer who is not really writing and guess who Ted Wylie decides to write about and that's right it's our friend Eliot Morrison and then there's also Esther Martin who wears these bright canary yellow dresses and she hears these angel voices that tell her to go drown herself in the Pacific Ocean and then there's also Sylvester Appleby the kitchen boy whose hair is always falling all over his eyes and he is enormously likable in his unassuming stupidity and most of the other characters are pretty much caricatures but then who knows maybe that's what writers conferences do to most people and *Saturday Night at San Marcos* is written in this nonstop writing style that keeps heaping up all these run on sentences and endless paragraphs one on top of another until the reader gets so giddy with dizziness he doesn't know whether he wants to keep reading the whole thing all the way through to the end.

Well that's the phony longwinded book review of this lousy novel that you're reading right now and before we go any further I ought to tell you that part about how I'm such a fishy mishmosh of paranoia is nothing but a lot of shit bitchiness on the part of that book reviewer and as for my getting these weird dizzy spells it's true I do get them but I've never used them as a sick excuse for why I'm not really writing and besides they're not dizzy spells so much as they are blackouts and a dissolving of consciousness like a lozenge as I go collapsing backwards into hee haw country and how the hell am I supposed to be really writing when I keep hatching a lot of black holes inside my head and as for my getting these obscene phone calls from my crazy ex-wife it's true that Clara does phone me and when she starts shouting out at me it gets to be pretty gross going but that doesn't mean Clara is any crazier than any of the other characters in this novel and as for my having this on again off again affair with a christ awful beautiful dumb actress it's true I do have a thing with Cindy Stevens and she is awfully beautiful with her bright gold hair and her loose full breasts and her 2 ice blue tiny iris eyes but Cindy isn't really that dumb because she just comes across that way and as for my having to read my way through mountains of stupid student manuscripts it's true I do have to do that but it's no worse than driving a cab or being a doorman or picking up garbage or whatever the hell else one does to earn a living and I've never used any of these things as a sick excuse for why I'm not really writing and as for my nonstop writing style that's such a cheap shot it's not even worth answering because that phony longwinded book reviewer is just trying to talk you out of reading this lousy novel all the way through to the end and anyway he completely missed the most important point about this novel which is that it almost didn't even get to be written because I almost didn't go out to the San Marcos Writers Conference this year because on the morning of the day I was supposed to fly out to California I began to go into one of my desperation panic states and that was when I knew I had to see Cindy Stevens one last time even though I knew Cindy was busy rehearsing the female lead in a sick play called *The Cardboard Carton* by Ted Wylie which is based on Ted Wylie's best selling sick novel of the same name and it's about this zombie author who keeps peeking into a cardboard carton to see how different animals are killing each other off inside and all Cindy is supposed to do is hang around onstage and watch this zombie author as he keeps looking at these poor trapped animals and then in the third act Cindy has to fuck this guy right there onstage in front of an enormous mirror and like I say it's a pretty sick play but then it's based on a pretty sick best selling novel and don't ask me how such a christ awful beautiful actress like Cindy Stevens ever got stuck playing such a fruity part because I don't even know how she got stuck having an affair with a failure like me but she did and we've been seeing each other on again off again for the last year and we've even tried breaking it off about 17 times and every time we broke it off we agreed we would never see each other again not ever after that but then I'd begin to go into one of my desperation panic states and I'd have to phone for Cindy to come down and see me one last time and we'd go through a long fierce phone call fight and after about 15 minutes Cindy would agree to come see me one last time and she'd grab a cab and come down to my place and I'd meet her at the door and I'd put my arm around her and I'd lead her right on into the bedroom and I'd take off all her clothes and I'd put her down on the bed and I'd make love to her once or twice or 3 or 4 times before we'd both lie back and collapse and fall asleep but then next morning all hell would break loose because Cindy would begin yelling and screaming at me so I'd begin screaming and yelling right back at her and we'd both end up shouting out about how we never wanted to see each other again and we both knew it was all a lot of illness and silliness but that's the way it was and that's the way it happened on the morning of the day I was supposed to fly out to the writers conference in California because around 1:00 AM Friday morning I began to go into one of my desperation panic states so I phoned for Cindy to come down and see me one last time and she didn't sound too pleased when she answered the phone and found out who it was calling and she said:

"Jesus Christ Eliot Morrison and we both agreed last time that this time it was final and we would never be in touch with each other not ever again."

6

And I said I knew all about all that but this time it was urgent because this time it was an emergency because I was beginning to go into one of my desperation panic states because I was on my way out to this writers conference in California and I needed to see Cindy one last time before I left and I pleaded with her please to come down and see me please for one last time and when I said that Cindy said:

"Eliot Morrison you're always saying you need to see me one last time and you know damn well if I came down there tonight we'd just keep this sick thing going and we've both agreed it's no good for either of us because you're not really writing and my own show opens in 3 weeks and I don't even have lines yet and my christ this is such a sick play I don't know what I'm supposed to be playing because all I do is stand around and watch this zombie author as he keeps peeking into this cardboard carton to see how 17 chipmunks kill 45 guinea pigs and then in the third act I have to fuck this guy right there onstage in front of an enormous mirror and I don't even know what I'm supposed to be playing in this sick play."

And I told Cindy if she'd only calm down I might be able to help her because I said Ted Wylie was going to be at the same writers conference I was going to in California and I said if Cindy came down to see me one last time tonight then I'd ask Ted Wylie what she was supposed to be playing in his sick play and when I said that Cindy said:

"Nice try Eliot but no dice because you just want to get me in the sack one last time before you go off to California and the fact is I already met Ted Wylie when this sick play was being cast and I asked him then what I was supposed to be playing but he just asked me a lot of questions about what other roles I'd ever played so I told him I'd been in a couple of other Broadway shows and I told him once I played Lady Macbeth in Detroit and he wanted to know all about how I had played her so I told him I had this idea about how Lady Macbeth didn't only wash her hands in the sleepwalking scene but she was washing her hands every time she was onstage she kept going scrub scrub scrub all the while she was talking to Macbeth or Duncan or Banquo and when I said this to Ted Wylie he just smiled this vicious cynical smile and he said I was exactly right to play in his play but he didn't tell me anything about what I was supposed to be playing in his sick play.''

And there was a long pause so I said I thought Cindy should come down to see me one last time tonight and when I said that she said:

"Listen to me Eliot Morrison and do you know what we're both doing to each other I mean do you realize that we are just bullshitting each other into thinking that we have a relationship whereas actually all we have is an obsession and that's what my analyst calls it and she says we should always call things by their right names and she says the right name for what we have is a obsession.''

And I said I thought Cindy's analyst was absolutely right and I'd never been very good with words myself so that's why I appreciated her analyst telling us the right name for what we have with each other and I said I'd also be interested in knowing what her analyst said was the right name for how Cindy always ended up screwing everyone in every show she was ever in and I said that included the stagehands and the other actors and half the audience and for all I know she probably goes out into the alley afterwards and she sucks off a lot of stray dogs and I asked Cindy what her analyst would say was the right name for that sort of behavior because I said the only word I could think of was dumb and when I said that Cindy began shouting out into the telephone:

"*You shut your fucking mouth Eliot Morrison because you think you're such a smart ass artist but my analyst says I shouldn't pay any attention to anything you ever say because you're such a fishy mishmosh of paranoia and she also says that when you phone me up like this in the middle of the night and tell me you're going into one of your desperation panic states I should just hang up on you because all you want is for me to come down there so you can*

get your hot rocks off and my analyst says you should just jerk
yourself off and go to sleep."

And I began speaking very gently and very tenderly and I said I
couldn't do that because what I really needed was to hold Cindy in
my arms one last time and make love to her bright gold hair and her
loose full breasts and her 2 ice blue tiny iris eyes and I said if I
couldn't do that then I'd call the airport and I'd cancel my reservation and I wouldn't even go out to that writers conference in California so then I wouldn't get to talk with Ted Wylie and I wouldn't
find out what Cindy was supposed to be playing in his sick play but
I said if Cindy did come down to see me one last time then I'd go
off to California and I'd never ask to see her not ever again and
there was another long pause and then Cindy said:

"Is that a promise Eliot?"

And I said god yes it was a promise on my life and on my future as a writer and there was another long pause and then I heard
Cindy whisper into the telephone:

"Oh shit."

And I asked her did oh shit mean that she was coming down to
see me and she said she'd be there in half an hour so I got off the
phone and I spent the next half hour pacing up and down in my
apartment until I heard the doorbell ring and I ran over and I
opened the door and there was Cindy standing there with her bright
gold hair and her loose full breasts and her 2 ice blue tiny iris eyes
so I put my arm around her and I led her right on into the bedroom
and I took off all her clothes and I put her down on the bed and I
lay down next to her and I began playing with the stiff little tips of
her nipples and then when I got on top of her and I eased myself on
into her she suddenly threw her arms around my neck and she cried
out aloud:

"Oh god darling I've missed you and I've needed you and I've
missed you so fucking much!"

And suddenly there I was looking down into her 2 pinpoint pupils that opened out onto another universe as I kept thrusting away

inside of her and she began to let out these small whimpering puppy noises under me and I kept pumping and pumping and pumping away inside of her until suddenly I felt myself beginning to let go and that was when I thrust as hard as I could thrust on in and up and ah god I was gone in an explosion of composure and it was like an ocean flowing over me and then I felt myself collapsing backwards in a blackout as I rolled over on my side beside her and I went swimming in an underwater duckpond where there are these centuries of sand and large dark shapes that keep darting in and out in their slow motion going and for a long moment I was floating all alone down there in the sweet peace of sleep and then when I came back up for air I saw Cindy was lying on her side beside me and she was smiling a sexy wet smile at me so I rolled over and I eased myself on into her again only more slowly this time as I told her how much I needed her not only for tonight but always and Cindy said she would be there for me always and I felt myself come again inside of her in an endless frenzy energy and then I rolled over on my side again and I went off in a quiet twilight sleep and when I slowly rose to knowing where I was I saw Cindy was sitting on the side of the bed so I reached out for her to get on top of me and I slipped myself on into her again and we began a rapid rocking back and forth until my cock was so raw it felt like a live writhing wire inside of her and when I came this time it felt like a bolt of bright blue steel had passed right through my body parts and Cindy fell forward and we both lay there like two kids who had just taken a hot bath together and now we were trying to dry out in the wide open air and after a while I opened my eyes and I asked Cindy to come to California with me and when I said that she laughed out loud and she said:

"Oh sure you just want me to walk out on my show so I can follow you around out there at your corny boring writers conference in California and hand you a piece of ass whenever you decide you're going to go into one of your desperation panic states is that it and Jesus Christ do you have any idea what a selfish asshole self you are Eliot Morrison I mean does it ever occur to you?"

And I began nibbling away at the stiff tip of her left nipple as I said I could phone the airport right now and book another reservation on the same plane I was taking later on today and Cindy said:

"Good god and you really do mean for me to go out there with you don't you and what the hell do you think I'd do all day all by myself while you were off screwing around with all your students?"

And I began nibbling away at the stiff tip of her right nipple as I said she'd have her hands full making love to me 17 times a day in between all my classes and my individual manuscript conferences and Cindy said:

"Jesus Christ and if we did that they'd toss us both out of there for making it into our private play place because you were hired to go teach those people how to write their own writing and not stay in bed and screw your stupid head off 17 times a day."

And I moved on down and I began to lick at the stiff tip of her slippery clitoris as I said then Cindy could stay in Santa Barbara and I'd come see her every evening and Cindy was beginning to squirm her thighs around as I kept licking at her clitoris and she began to gasp out loud as she said:

"What the hell would I do in Santa Barbara all day all by myself while you were up there at your corny boring writers conference?"

And I kept licking at her clitoris as I looked up into her 2 ice blue tiny iris eyes that were looking down into my eyes and for an instant there it was eyes into eyes as we felt the fresh fruit juice loony foolishness that is all around us always and then I said there were a lot of things she could do in Santa Barbara all day all by herself because I said she could go feed the seals and talk to all the old people and visit the Franciscan Mission and then I moved up and I eased myself on into her once again and I began pumping and pumping and pumping away inside of her until I came again and this time my braincave came alive with blazing as I bathed myself in pools of flame and then I rolled over and I lay there like a lame meteor that had just fallen out of the sky and after a long moment I heard Cindy say:

11

"Listen Eliot why don't you just go off to your writers conference in California and I'll stay here in New York and play in my sick play and you can write me a nice long 17 page letter while you're out there."

And I said she had to be kidding because she knew perfectly well that I hadn't really written anything for the last 5 years because I get these weird dizzy spells and I also get these obscene phone calls from my crazy ex-wife and I also have to read through mountains of stupid student manuscripts so how the hell could I write anything like a 17 page letter to Cindy and when I said that she just snuggled in next to me and she said:

"Stop coming up with all sorts of sick excuses for why you're not really writing and just send me that letter while you're out there."

And I said okay that I would do that and then Cindy said:

"And you might also tell that bigtime lady agent of yours to send your first novel out to Central Studios in Los Angeles because I heard they're looking for material to make new feature film scripts."

And I said okay that I would do that also and then Cindy said:

"Tell me what the hell do they all do out there at that writers conference on Saturday night at San Marcos I mean do they all forget the fact that they're supposed to be a lot of hotshot writers and do they let themselves go apeshit on their last night out there or what?"

And I said I didn't know because I was always wiped out by the time Saturday night came around and Cindy said this year I ought to keep my eyes open to see what happens and I said okay that I would do that also and then I looked at my wristwatch and I saw it was 5:00 AM and I told Cindy she'd better get some sleep so she leaned over and she kissed me on the lips and then she rolled over and she went to sleep but I just lay there wide awake and I began to think about how I was a writing teacher who was not really writing and it felt like my whole life was a lie as if I had some sort of dehy-

dration of the heart or a polio of the soul or a cancer of the understanding and it felt as if my insides had been taken out and set aside
on dry ice because I thought ah god here I am 39 years old and I've
only published one lousy novel 7 years ago and it was called *A
Dream of Clarence* and it's about this kid named Clarence who is
unloading shells from a munitions truck when suddenly he sees this
one shell is beginning to slip through his fingers so he knows he is
about to be blown apart and in that instant he begins to eat the air
of everything he ever felt or thought or saw and he begins to taste
the acid sadness of his entire life and all the trouble in his bloodstream and the flood of all those bullshit lies that ever made him
believe that he could be at all lovable and that's what my lousy first
novel is all about and when it came out it got pretty mixed reviews
and there was one reader out in Nebraska who said I'd gotten close
to the problem of the novel in our time but most of the other reviewers didn't know what the hell to make of it and one phony
longwinded book reviewer even said I was such a fishy mishmosh of
paranoia that no one would want to keep reading the whole thing all
the way through to the end and after this novel had been out for
about a year I got an offer from this movie producer to make the
novel into a feature film script and that sounded okay until I met
the guy and he kept blowing cigar smoke in the air as he told me my
book would make a great major motion picture only we'd have to
cut certain parts like that scene where Clarence sees the shell is beginning to slip through his fingers so he knows he is about to be
blown apart and he begins to taste the acid sadness of his entire life
because the guy said that was nothing but a lot of arty farty stuff
and what he wanted to show was how this young kid had all sorts of
bad lays in the backseats of cars where they could use a lot of wide
angle shots of the kid getting laid on the backseat of a Chrysler and
a Mercedes-Benz and a Rolls-Royce and he said the high point of
the film would be this scene where the kid gets laid on the backseat
of a Volkswagen and it's so damn cramped in there the kid can't get
his cock out of the girl's crotch so the State Police have to come and

use a can opener to pry the two of them apart and this movie producer began to laugh so hard at that he started gagging on his cigar smoke and I was so pissed I told him what he could do with his filthy skin flick idea because if there's one thing I can't stand it's sticking in a lot of sick sex for its own sake and I know I just got through writing about how I made love to Cindy 4 times in a row tonight but that's different because that really happened and later on in this lousy novel I'm going to write another scene where I screw one of the students out there at the writers conference in California and that also really happened and so that's called character development and I'm not just sticking in a lot of sick sex for its own sake and then after that first novel had been out for a couple of years and it didn't seem to be really going anywhere then I sort of drifted into teaching and I taught a lot of student writers how to write their own writing and I ended up spending a lot of my own time reading through a lot of their manuscripts and then when summers would come around I'd always be so broke that I'd have to go teach at a lot of writers conferences so I could pick up a few hundred dollars extra and the first one I went to was the Denver Writers Conference where I met Clara and we had ourselves a whirlwind affair and a whirlwind marriage and a whirlwind divorce and then Clara had herself a whirlwind nervous breakdown that she never really got over and by that time I'd stopped writing completely so I was a writing teacher who was not really writing but that didn't seem to bother anyone else so long as I taught my writing classes and helped the students write their own writing then nobody gave a good god damn whether I was really writing or not but I gave a good god damn because I can tell you it's hell to be a writing teacher when you're not really writing anything yourself and these were some of the things I was thinking as I lay there next to Cindy Stevens and I looked at my wristwatch and I saw it was 6:00 AM and I thought why can't I just stay here in bed and make love to Cindy for the rest of this week instead of going out to that writers conference in California so I composed a telegram in the back of my head and this is what it said:

Ralph Perry/Director
San Marcos Writers Conference
San Marcos, California

Regret personal incapacity but unable to take part in this year's
writers conference so let Maureen Talbot take all my fiction
classes and all my individual manuscript conferences with my
apologies and best wishes

Eliot Morrison

But then I thought suppose I do send this telegram out there
and I stay in bed and make love to Cindy all week long and then
suppose we have one of our nightmare fights so I'm left here all
alone to space around in my apartment and I'll just wish I were out
there in all that bright California sunlight so I thought what the hell
I might as well go out there after all so I tore up the telegram in the
back of my head and I tossed the pieces out the sides of my eyes and
I began to drift off into a quiet twilight sleep for a couple of hours
and when I slowly rose to knowing where I was I saw Cindy was already up and she was throwing all her clothes on and I could tell
from the way she was pulling at her panty hose that she was pretty
pissed and when she saw I was awake she shouted out loud at me:

*"Listen you bastard now I'm going to be late for my rehearsal
and all because of you and your fucking infantile need to see me one
last time and this is going to stop right now because my analyst says
you may be a smart ass artist but you're also hell bent on making a
failure of all your affairs so why don't you just go off to your writers conference in California and when you come back to New York
just don't bother to get in touch with me not ever again because
I am through with you Eliot Morrison and this time I really
mean it!"*

And as Cindy was shouting out at me I got out of bed and I began to get dressed and when she paused to take a breath I told her I
was tired of listening to all her sick bitch quick switch mind life criticism and I said that went for her Ann Landers analyst also and by
this time Cindy was slamming things into her purse and she was
over at the door and she was trying to unlock the lock so I went over

and I began speaking very gently and very tenderly to her and I said I was sorry for what I had just said because I did love her very much but Cindy just kept standing there with her back to me so I reached out my hand and I put it on her shoulder and when she felt my hand on her shoulder she turned around and she shot a cold hard hate ray stare right through me and she said:

"You take your lousy fish hand off me you plainfaced creep because I don't like being touched by someone who's as homely and boring and stupid looking as you are!"

And when Cindy said this it came as such a cold shock blow to me that I slowly took my hand from off her shoulder and I began to back away from her all the while her words kept burning their way into my brain and the hot awful tears were beginning to stream on down my cheeks and Cindy was already out the door and she slammed it hard behind her right in my face so I stood there for a long moment frozen motionless and then I opened the door and I ran on down after her and she was already out on the street and heading down the subway stairs and she disappeared in the darkness there so I turned around and I walked back to my building and I opened my mailbox and I pulled out all my morning mail and I pushed it into my coat pocket and I went back out on the street again and I waved for a cab and I got in and I drove uptown to keep an appointment with Marcia Masters who has been my agent for the last 7 years and as I sat there in the cab I pulled out all my mail and I saw there were lots and lots of bills and lots of student manuscripts for me to read and there was also a brochure from the San Marcos Writers Conference that was about 3 weeks too late to get anyone to register and I stuffed everything back into my coat pocket and I looked out the window of the cab at all the people on the street and suddenly I had this flash image of a great aged elk that was trying to die in the shrubbery and underbrush and its milky eye was gazing out at autumn leaf and at the distant disinterested sky and I thought what the hell kind of crazy image is that because I could never put it in any novel I would ever write and just then the cab pulled up at the curb so I paid and I got out and I walked over to the building where Marcia Masters had her office and I rang at the buzzer downstairs and I went on in and I climbed one flight of stairs and there in a small office I saw Marcia Masters was standing behind her desk and she was leaning forward toward me to shake hands and I thought she was a gallant old gal who had been through all the wars and she had a warm heart for the underdog which was certainly what I was so I said hello and I sat down and I said listen I didn't think Marcia Masters had done enough with my first novel *A Dream of Clarence* because I was sure there was a good film to be made out of it and someone told me Central Studios was looking for material to make new feature film scripts and I said I thought Marcia Masters ought to send a copy of my book out there and when I said that Marcia Masters looked at me a long moment and then she sighed a long sigh and she said:

"Darling and I thought I knew all about writers and their crazy ways but this is beginning to get demented because here you haven't really written anything in the last 5 years yet you still wonder why that first novel of yours isn't getting any more mileage and you know the only reason I was able to locate a publisher for it was because Dussop was looking for a fast tax loss and your manuscript was the first thing that came across their desk and of course I'll be happy to send a copy of that book out to Central Studios because I know Hy Kantor out there only don't get angry if he sends it right back because it might not be what they're looking for."

And I sat there and I began to feel like a real hack as Marcia Masters kept right on going and she said:

"Incidentally darling I telephoned Dussop and I told them to send 25 copies of *A Dream of Clarence* out to that ridiculous writers conference in California although I wish you'd stop teaching all these writing classes and get back to trying to write your own writing."

And then Marcia Masters reached into her desk drawer and she pulled out a check and she passed it over to me and I looked at it and I saw it was for the book store sales of *A Dream of Clarence* over this past year and the amount was so small Marcia Masters hadn't even deducted her 10 percent commission from it and I asked her why she didn't just wipe me off her books because I was more trouble than I was worth and when I said that Marcia Masters looked at me and she smiled her handsome grandmother smile and she said:

"Darling you don't understand anything about this business at all do you because of course it's not worth my trouble carrying you for the pittance you've earned me over these past 7 years on that first novel of yours but I know someday you will write something that will make me very proud of you and then I shall earn back all the postage money I've spent on you so far."

And just then a buzzer sounded on her desk and a voice said there was a phone call for Marcia Masters from Los Angeles so she told me she'd better take the call because it was someone who had been trying to reach her all morning so I stood up and I shook her hand and as I left her office Marcia Masters called out after me:

"Darling don't you dare give my name to anyone out there at that ridiculous writers conference because I don't want this office piled high with mountains of stupid student manuscripts."

And I said I wouldn't give her name to anyone and then I left her office and I went downstairs and I got a cab back to my apartment and as I was sitting in the cab I pulled out the San Marcos Writers Conference brochure and I saw it was one of those foldout gloss stock jobs with a front cover photograph that showed a lonely old hotel that was perched on a cliff where the great waves came racing in to break against the slippery glistening rocks and off to one side there were some wooden stairs that led on down to a narrow strip of beach and in the photograph there were two young girls posed on the stairs and they were dressed in shorts and laughing their heads off and under the photograph it said:

THE SAN MARCOS WRITERS CONFERENCE
July 3–10

The picturesque San Marcos Hotel is situated on the scenic California coastline about 75 miles north of Santa Barbara off rustic Route One and the hotel itself has a spectacular view of the Pacific Ocean and it has its own elevator service and pay phone facilities and easy access to all nearby resort areas and on opening night there will be an outdoor barbecue on the private San Marcos beach and then all the daily meals will be served in the festive hotel dining room where there will be a gala farewell banquet on the last night.

Classes in fiction and nonfiction and poetry and marketing are taught by the distinguished San Marcos Writers Conference faculty which will also offer individual manuscript conferences with each registered student.

FEE FOR THE ONE WEEK: $425.00

And then on the inside of the foldout there was a photo of Ralph Perry the 80 year old Director and he was puffing away on a pipe and chuckling to himself as if the whole idea of a writers conference were some sort of silly joke and then there was a photo of his wife Laura Perry who was wearing a long black shawl and false eyelashes and she was gazing off in the distance as if she were looking for the lost soul of Robert Browning and then there was a photo of Ted Wylie who was the best selling author of *The Cardboard Carton* and *The Banana Factor* and he had a beady eagle eye and he was smiling a vicious cynical smile and then there was a photo of Gwendolyn Field who was the guest author of the popular sex novel *Safari* and she looked giggly and harried and breathless like a high school volleyball player and then there was a photo of Miriam Morse the poetry lady who had published 3 volumes of her own verse including *Held In His Hands* and *What Pain What Joy* and *Prism of Love* and she was wearing a large lavender bonnet and she looked like a bird that was just about to chirp and then there was a photo of me and I was the author of *A Dream of Clarence* and my photo showed my shaggy hair and my crumpled coat and the dislocated look in my eyes and then there was a photo of Maureen Talbot who was the Assistant Director and she looked like she'd screwed every writing teacher who had ever come to San Marcos and I folded the brochure and I shoved it back into my pocket and just then my cab pulled up in front of my building so I paid and I got out and as I stepped onto the sidewalk I felt one of my dizzy spells coming on so I stood there on the sidewalk and I thought:

here we go
into hee haw country

—a collapsing backwards and a dissolving of consciousness like a lozenge as I stood there waiting for the thing to pass through all its acid fizz state phases and then it began to go away and I was back standing on the sidewalk with bright sunlight all around me so I ran on up to my apartment to get my suitcase so I could go out to the airport but I heard the phone was ringing inside my apartment so I unlocked the door and I went in and I picked up the phone and I said hello and there was a pause and then I heard a voice on the other end and it said:

"Morrison?"

And it was a voice from out of the ice ages of my life and I said hello Clara and I asked her how she was feeling and she said:

"Listen shithead don't you go giving me any of that 'how is she feeling' crap because I know damn well you're about to go off to one of your ridiculous writers conferences because they sent me one of their phony foldout brochures in the mail this morning and there you are with your shaggy hair and your crumpled coat and the dislocated look in your eyes—"

And I said as a matter of fact I was just on my way out the door so I could catch a plane to fly out there to California this evening and Clara said:

"Yeah well listen shithead I just wanted to know how many of those cute little chickeepoos you'll be screwing out there because they'll all want to see how long your cock is because you're such a hotshot writing teacher who's not really writing anything and is that what you're going to be doing out there this year?"

And I said no I was just going to be trying to be the best writing teacher I can be and when I said that Clara said:

"Oh and will you listen to the shithead saying that he's just going to be trying to be the best writing teacher he can be and he was

saying that when I met him out at the Denver Writers Conference 6
years ago and let me see was that before or after he pulled down my
pants and screwed my ass off—"

And I told Clara if she was going to go getting gross on me I'd
just have to hang up on her and when I said that Clara said:

"Don't you hang up on me buddy because if you do I'll go
making big trouble on you and that's right I'll phone up the director
of that corny boring writers conference you're going to and that's
right I'll phone up old what's his name and where the fuck is it on
this phony foldout brochure oh yeah here it is and I'll phone up old
Ralph Perry and I'll tell him what a wretched letch you are so he'd
better lock up all his cute little chickeepoos and that should make
the old fart stop chuckling and sucking on his fucking pipe—"

And I told Clara if she called Ralph Perry and talked to him
that way she'd only show herself up as the full time mental case that
she was and when I said that Clara said:

"Don't you go giving me that old 'mental case' routine Morri-
son because you're the one that's the full time mental case the way
you keep going off to teach at all these writers conferences where
you can tell a lot of people how to write their own writing when you
haven't really written anything yourself for the last 5 years—"

And I didn't hear the rest of what she said because I hung up
the phone and I looked at my wristwatch and I saw it was getting
late so I grabbed my suitcase and went out and got a cab to go to
Kennedy airport and as I was riding out there I began to think
about something I had read once about an old German practice of
how they used to take someone who had been ripping the bark off a
standing tree and they would cut his navel out and nail it to the tree
and then they would make this person walk around the tree until all
his intestines were pulled out and wound around the tree and I
thought that's the way it feels to be a writing teacher who is not really writing and just then the cab arrived at Kennedy airport so I
paid and I got out and I took my suitcase on into the lobby and
I had my ticket checked and then I had a few minutes to kill so I
walked over to the paperback bookstore and I saw there was this

beautiful young woman standing there and wearing a soft sarape thing over a thin braless shirt and I saw her 2 tits were taut against the cloth and I began to have a subliminal flash thing about ripping all her clothes off and writing paragraphs of nonstop prose all over her belly and on up her ass cheeks and in under her thighs all the while I was balling her like crazy but just then the young woman turned toward me and she shot a cold hard hate ray stare right through me and then she stalked off to one of the other airline areas so I stood there and for a long moment I was frozen motionless and then I began to think ah god I'm in no shape to be going off to teach anyone anything and I just wish I were back at my own place and really writing something right now but just then out of the side of my eye I saw a garish red cover on a paperback book and there was this bright gold yellow banana on it and I looked and saw the book was *The Banana Factor* by Ted Wylie so I reached out and I picked it up and there on the back cover was the same photograph of Ted Wylie that was on the San Marcos Writers Conference brochure which showed his beady eagle eye and his vicious cynical smile and there were a lot of statements under the photograph saying what a best selling novelist Ted Wylie was and I thought what the hell and I'm going to share teaching a fiction class with this character so I may as well read his latest novel and find out where he's coming from so I bought the book and then I headed down to the waiting area for the plane that would take me out to the San Marcos Writers Conference in California.

This is the end of chapter one of this lousy novel and by this time you're probably wondering where the hell this whole thing is going to go because maybe you're not sure you want to keep reading the whole thing all the way through to the end and all I can tell you is I don't know where the whole thing is going to go any more than you do because the rest of this novel manuscript is not written yet and that means it is still up there in the air because that's where all real writing always is up there in the air because that's where all rare fair things always are up there in the bright areas of air and who knows when I do write down the rest of it you may end up liking the whole thing only just pay close attention to all these opening chapters because later on I'll be giving you a quiz to see how much you remember as you keep reading these lines that I am trying to write right now.

two/Saturday

And I got on the plane and I found an empty seat by a window and I sat down and I looked out at the ground crew that was busy loading bags into the side of the plane from a long toy truck that was piled high with suitcases and I began to think about how great it was making love to Cindy last night and I thought about how someday the 2 of us could go off to Vermont and live together in a small log cabin where I could write my own writing all day and Cindy could go walking in the woods and screw around with all the squirrels until it was time for us to stay up all night making love but as I sat there thinking all these things I suddenly thought how do I know Cindy isn't off fucking someone else backstage at her rehearsal right now like the electrician or the makeup man or the press agent and I began to get very angry because I thought how the hell am I supposed to be really writing anything when all I can ever think about is whether that hopelessly childish child is always off fucking someone else so then I thought when I get back to New York I just won't call her again so I won't ever see her anymore and just as I thought that thought a businessman sat down beside me on the aisle seat and I saw he was gray and tanned and vested and he looked like he was with some major corporation and he opened up his briefcase and he pulled out a lot of yellow legal pads and he began to write on one of them and I didn't much feel like talking to anyone on the flight so I looked out the window as the plane began to rev its jet engines and I felt the shudder of a sudden terrific roar forward as the plane began its headlong racing down the runway and then I could feel my whole body being buoyed upwards in the liftoff and then I could feel a yielding into empty air as the plane climbed slowly higher and higher skyward and then it began to glide through cloud banks and I could see a lot of thin smoke wisps begin to cut across the wing of the plane and I looked over at the businessman sitting next to me and I saw his head was lowered over his yellow legal pad and his ball-point pen kept scribbling across the faint green lines and he kept turning page after page over the back of the pad and I wondered what the hell was he writing so furiously and maybe it was some master plan to buy up all the small colleges in this country so they could be amalgamated into a huge university system that would then be administered by radar or else maybe it was a report on how one could have 10 times more orgasms by using a new kind of ox dung ointment or else maybe it was a proposal for a new way to grow instant oil wells on the other side of the moon and then I tried to spy out of the side of my eye so I could decipher some of the words he was writing but the whole thing was such an illegible scrawling to my sideways sight that I decided that I wasn't all that interested in it so I pulled out my paperback copy of *The Banana Factor* by Ted Wylie and I opened it up to the publisher blurbs on the flyleaf and they said this book was in its 17th printing and Ted Wylie's first novel *The Cardboard Carton* had already sold over 4 million copies and it was soon to open as a Broadway play and I turned to the first page of *The Banana Factor* and this is how it began:

It began with a simple surgical procedure that was performed on each newborn infant when the surgeon would make a slight incision at the base of the skull and slip a tiny electrode into the small slit and then he would seal it over again so the slit was not even noticeable and this insertion took less than 3 seconds but that tiny electrode would remain inside the infant's head for the rest of its life and as soon as the child grew older and became more of a feeling and thinking and seeing individual then the tiny electrode would begin to record every event that ever happened to him and then when the individual reached a certain age he would be required by law to go into a local read-out center 4 times a year where he would be strapped down on a table and these large vector circuits would be placed over the outside of his head and they would make a readout of the individual's entire life history impulse patterns and this readout would go into a master computer unit where it would be de-coded and analyzed to see if there were any dysfunctional response patterns and if there were any then the vector circuits would rescramble all the life history impulse patterns before they were relayed back into the individual's head and this entire process of readout and decoding and rescrambling took less than 3 seconds and then the individual would be unstrapped and he would be let up off the table and he would be given a little celluloid nameplate that would have his latest BF score printed on it and this BF score stood for the Brainard Factor that was named for Dr. Frank R. Brainard of New Hampshire who was the systems analyst who devised the complicated mathematical formulas for gauging the probability of someone's losing his sanity and after a while this BF score came to be known as the Banana Factor because the average man on the street knew that his BF score stood for the chances of his going completely bananas and 23 percent was considered a pretty fair BF score because 23 percent was what Dr. Frank R. Brainard figured were his own chances of going bananas so he used that as the norm for everyone else and under his new rating system 43 percent was the legal limit for holding public office or serving in the military or engaging in any form of professional practice and anyone with a BF score of over 72 percent was considered a pretty risky case so he was usually assigned to quiet jobs like sorting library cards or being a night watchman or tending remote control lighthouses and anyone with a BF score of over 85 percent was considered a social ward and he was told to stay home and only come out once a week to pick up his welfare check and anyone with a BF score of over 90 percent was considered a criminal or an anarchist or an intellectual and whenever one of these 90 percent plus BF scores turned up at a local readout center the vector circuit would immediately go to work and rescramble the individual's entire life history so that instead of coming from Brooklyn the individual would wake up thinking he came from some exotic tropical island and instead of having sick and twisted parents he would wake up remembering how selfless and loving his parents always were and instead of having had a lot of rotten love experiences he would wake up being grateful for having made love to some of the most beautiful women in the world and then this individual would be given a little celluloid nameplate with a new BF score of 30 percent across the board and after this BF score rating system had been going for some 17 years someone in Utah came up with a new method of computing BF scores for aggregate groups like industries and organizations and standing armies and these were called Corporate Banana Factors or CBFs and these scores were figured by taking the sum total of all the individual Banana Factors in any given group at any given time with special weighting on leadership and pretty soon the entire stock exchange began listing the CBF scores for every major business on Wall Street and this was a much more reliable guide to the ebb and flow of the economy than the old point system and the daily CBF listing looked like this on the financial pages:

GENERAL ENGINES	CBF 23% +
COLUMBIA METALS	CBF 47% +
PAN AUTOMOTIVE	CBF 72% −
UNITED CHEMICAL	CBS 16% +
HUDSON STEEL	CBF 31% −

And pretty soon there was a National Banana Factor or NBF and this was figured by taking the CBFs of 100 major corporations plus the CBF of the army and the navy and the air force and the coast guard and all the various State Police forces plus the Banana Factors of every congressman and each of the Supreme Court Justices and the President and the Vice-President and the resulting NBF was a fairly accurate reflection of the state of the nation at any given time and every morning the *Times* ran it in a small box on the upper righthand corner of the front page and this is how it looked:

WEATHER: Sunny today with 30% possibility of light showers by mid-afternoon. NBF: 62% but expected to rise after the President holds his press conference.

And pretty soon there was an International Banana Factor or

IBF and this was a statistical summary of the state of the whole world and every morning the Secretariat of the United Nations issued a newsletter with the IBF in big bold letters and any day that there was an IBF of over 87 percent all debate was suspended in the Security Council for the rest of the week.

And just then I slammed the book shut and I thought my god this is nothing but a lot of facile science fiction masquerading as a superficial study of fascism and I'm not sure I want to keep reading the whole thing all the way through to the end but then I looked over at the businessman sitting next to me and I saw he was still scribbling his indecipherable scrawl on those yellow legal pads and I thought that was even more depressing so I began to stare out the window of the plane at the starlight in the darkness and I thought here it is Saturday morning and the plane must be somewhere over Ohio and I began to wonder if Marcia Masters had sent a copy of *A Dream of Clarence* out to Central Studios so they could see if it would make a feature film script and then I began to wonder if Cindy was really off fucking someone else backstage at her rehearsal for *The Cardboard Carton* and then I began to wonder if Clara was phoning Ralph Perry right now long distance at the San Marcos Writers Conference to tell him what a wretched letch I was and how he ought to lock up all the cute little chickeepoos before I got out there and as I was thinking all these things suddenly the businessman stopped writing on his yellow legal pad and he looked over at me and he said:

"What's that you're reading there young man?"

And I told him it was a novel called *The Banana Factor* by Ted Wylie and the businessman said:

"Is it any good?"

And I said not really because I thought it was pretty sophomoric stuff and so the businessman said:

"If it's no good then why bother reading the whole thing all the way through to the end?"

And then he went back to scribbling on his yellow legal pad without waiting for an answer as if he had just been told a fast fact on the stock exchange and he had no need for any further information so I thought well to hell with you buddy and I went back to staring at the starlight in the darkness outside the plane window and suddenly I felt as empty as all that air that was out there between me and those millions and millions of stars that were in that great vacancy of space and I began to go into one of my desperation panic states and I had to do something to stay calm so I opened up *The Banana Factor* by Ted Wylie and I began to read the next chapter and this is what it said:

Once there was a man who lived in a small town in Kansas and he had a Banana Factor of 98 percent and that was a higher BF score than had ever been recorded before but this man had never had his real BF score printed on a little celluloid nameplate because every time he went into his local readout center and got strapped down on the table and had those large vector circuits placed over his head this man sent himself into an auto-hypnotic trance by fixing his inner eye on an instant of air and that way he could con the vector circuits into recording a fairly tame BF score of 41 percent and that was pretty decent for the small Kansas community where this man lived all his life so everyone at his local readout center always smiled and said what a pleasure it was knowing such a consistent BF score person and they would hand him his little celluloid nameplate with 41 percent printed on it and the man would walk out of the local readout center and he would go right back to his favorite pastime which was playing far out sex games with a lot of 10 year olds in his garage every day after school when the kids would come over and line up on either side of the garage and this man would tell all the girls to lift up their skirts and flash their small full tufts and then the man would tell all the boys to drop their pants and flash their lily white cocks and then the man would point to one of the girls and tell her to go over and kneel down on her knees in front of one of the boys and kiss the stub head of his crocus cock with her cute cupid lips until the cock got so throbbing hard that it was almost ready to come and then the man would tell the girl to lie down on the garage floor and he would tell the boy to kneel down and begin licking at the girl's nifty little slit until she was almost ready to come and then the man would tell the boy to slip his crocus cock on into the girl's petunia pink vagina and then they would begin to screw around on the garage floor and then the man would tell all the other boys and girls to line up in one long single file line and take turns sucking on his own grotesque erect banana cock and he would poke it in and out of their pouting mouths until it got so rock hard he could have pounded a nail into the wall with it and then just as the boy and girl were reaching their glorious little orgasm on the garage floor this man's grotesque erect banana cock began to shoot off great huge jets of gyzm that spurted up through the air and they landed with loud splats smack flat all over the garage floor and then the man made all the boys and girls get down on their hands and knees and lick up all the jiggly puddles of lukewarm creamy come—

And just then I slammed the book shut and I let it fall back on my lap as I thought ah god this is so gross and kinky and voyeuristic and it keeps going on and on heaping up all these run on sentences and endless paragraphs one on top of another until I was beginning to get giddy with dizziness and I looked over at the businessman sitting next to me and I saw he was still scribbling his indecipherable scrawl on all those yellow pads and that made me even more giddy with dizziness so I stared out the plane window at the stars that were out there in their own air and I tried to imagine what sort of person Ted Wylie was and I thought he was probably vicious and cynical and everlastingly clever because what other kind of man could get off on writing about a lot of far out sex games with a gang of 10 years olds and I knew he also got off on watching a lot of chipmunks kill a lot of guinea pigs inside a cardboard carton and I thought Ted Wylie must be hopelessly stuck between the floors of his own psyche because his own ego must be curled up in a small body ball and when I thought that thought I picked up the book again and I began to read through a lot more chapters that went into a lot more detail about the far out sex games this man played with his gang of 10 year olds and some of the games involved cats and dogs and clothesline rope and overhead mirrors and there was even one game with a long-eared donkey that the man borrowed from a nearby donkey farm and I began to feel a deep heartsick loathing for any culture that would reward all this illness and silliness by making such a book into a best selling novel but then I sighed a long sigh and I kept turning page after page of *The Banana Factor* until I got to the last chapter of the book and this is how it went:

After this man had been playing his far out sex games with all the 10 year old kids for half a year or so he began to get bored with the games that involved cats and dogs and clothesline rope and overhead mirrors and long-eared donkeys so he set out to undermine the entire Banana Factor rating system and he came up with his own completely new way to compute BF scores for each of the 10 year old kids and he did this by making all the boys line up on one side of the garage and he made all the girls line up on the other side and the man stood in the middle of the floor and he told all the boys and girls to start beating off on the count of 3 and to keep beating off until each kid came and as they were doing this the man held a stopwatch in one hand and a clipboard in the other hand and he began writing down the time it took each kid to come and then he began multiplying and dividing a lot of numbers on a pocket calculator until he came up with a new BF score for each kid based on how long it took each one to come and according to this new rating system 57 percent was a pretty fair Beat-Off Factor score but some kids got as high as 73 percent and one kid even hit 87 percent and when the man finished figuring out the new BF scores then he began to write them out on little celluloid nameplates and he made all the kids wear these new nameplates to school the next day where none of the teachers knew what these new BF scores were all about so naturally they assumed the kids had gotten them from their local readout center but a few teachers got concerned because these new scores were a lot higher than the old ones and it took a month or so before one of the parents finally got wise to what was going on at this man's garage every day after school and when this mother found out she phoned up the principal of the grade school and she started shouting out at him over the telephone:
"Listen and do you know what my Marylou has been doing every day after school for the past half year and I will tell you what my Marylou has been doing because she's been going over to an older man's garage and she's been playing a lot of far out sex games with a gang of other 10 year olds and she says they've been doing it with a lot of cats and dogs and

clothesline rope and overhead mirrors and once they even did it with a long-eared donkey and she says this older man's got all these 10 year old kids so organized they all line up in single file on either side of his garage and they do these sick and twisted things to each other and what the hell do you mean I should stop shouting because this is my Marylou who's been doing these things and she didn't know from nothing before this filthy pig of an older man got hold of her and I want to know what the fuck are you going to do about all this because you are Marylou's grade school principal and God knows how you couldn't have known that such weird sick things were going on right under your own nose and I am telling you if you don't do something about all this and fast then I will take you to court and hold you personally responsible for my Marylou!"

And then the mother slammed the telephone down so hard it almost broke the grade school principal's eardrum so he sat there for a moment and he was frozen motionless as he massaged his head with his hand and then he picked up the phone again and he dialed the State Police barracks and he told them everything this parent had just shouted out at him and after that all hell broke loose because the very next day 2 Kansas State Troopers drove up to the older man's garage and they got out of their State Police car and they sauntered over to the garage door where they saw the older man was lying inside stark naked on the garage floor and he was looking up at himself in an overhead mirror and he was lolling his enormous banana cock around in his hands as he waited for school to let out so all the kids would come over and play a new far out sex game he had just thought up involving a lot of dry cell batteries and just then the 2 Kansas State Troopers called out for the man to get up because he was under arrest for corrupting the morals of minors to say nothing of all the cats and dogs and long-eared donkeys so the man began to get up but just then one of the State Troopers kicked him in the head and then the other one began calling the man a weirdo faggot gross kinky voyeuristic Neanderthal and they kept this up for about 10 minutes until the man had been kicked stone cold unconscious and then they dragged him out of the garage and they shoved him into the backseat of their State Police car and they drove him down to the local readout center so they could get a BF score on him before they took him in and booked him as a criminal degenerate but because the man was stone cold unconscious he wasn't able to fix his inner eye on an instant of air and send himself into an auto-hypnotic trance and so he

32

couldn't con the vector circuits into recording a fairly tame BF score of 41 percent so when the readout came through it was an eyebrow raising 98 percent which was the highest BF score ever recorded at any readout center anywhere and when word of this got around there was a furious uproar in the small Kansas community and the editor of the town newspaper wrote a series of irate editorials in which he said these 10 year old kids had been defiled for life by this man's alleged satanic sex practices and he went on to say the real villain in this whole affair was Dr. Frank R. Brainard of New Hampshire with his complicated mathematical formulas for gauging the chances of someone's going bananas because here was some lunatic mutant in our midst who had managed to outwit the entire BF score rating system so now it was high time for modern science to admit how frail and fallible it was so we could all get back to the old eternal verities of the human heart and as soon as these editorials began to appear in the town newspaper in Kansas they were picked up by all the various wire services and then they were reprinted in all the big city newspapers and that was when a national newsmagazine decided to run a cover story on the man in Kansas who beat the BF score rating system so they sent a reporter to the small Kansas community to seek out some of those 10 year old kids and find out if they had really been defiled for life and the reporter got hold of one 10 year old girl who was busy blowing bubble gum and popping it in the air and he asked her whether she felt she had been defiled for life and she said:

"Nah not really because most of us kids were already into doing all that stuff on our own anyway so all this older man did was sort of organize us and I don't see why everyone is making such a big fuss out of all this because most of us kids thought it was a lot of fun."

And the 10 year old girl blew a big bubble and she popped it right in the reporter's face as he jotted down what she said and then he went off to seek out more of the 10 year old kids and most of them said pretty much the same thing except for one very nervous tall blond boy who said:

"Nah I don't feel like I was defiled for life or anything but I knew baseball season was coming up and I had to get the old arm into shape if I was going to pitch first string junior varsity so I was getting a little ticked that I had to keep going over to that guy's garage every day after school but that wasn't because I didn't like doing those things but it was just because I knew I should be working on my curve ball."

And when the national newsmagazine came out with its cover story on the man in Kansas who beat the BF score rating system and all these interviews with the 10 year old kids appeared in cold print there was a storm of protest all across the country and a Congressional Subcommittee began to hold a lot of televised hearings where a lot of Senators spent a lot of days in front of a lot of TV cameras deploring the cynicism in those interviews and they said that was all the evidence needed to prove those kids had already been defiled for life and some other Senators went on to wax indignant about the entire BF score rating system from the master computer units right on down to the vector circuits in the local readout centers because as one Senator from South Carolina put it:

"The American people can rest assured we will not let up on this inquiry until the whole banana has been peeled."

And meanwhile the man who had a 98 percent BF score was hustled off to the Institute for Psychosexual Reprogramming in Wyoming which was commonly known as the Banana Farm and this was a large reservation that had been set aside for individuals who had such dangerously high BF scores that they couldn't be safely reprogrammed so they were sent out there to the Banana Farm where they could vegetate the rest of their lives away and ordinarily no one in the outside world cared very much about the Banana Farm because it was such a dead end of identity but this man had created so much national attention that a major TV network news team decided to fly out there and do an in-depth interview with him so they set up their TV cameras on the long Wyoming lawns in front of the man as he sat behind a small iron table and the man was wearing a pair of white Banana Farm pajamas and he kept sipping at some black coffee in a plastic foam container and after a moment or so of a wide angle shot the TV news team interviewer came sauntering up to the small iron table and he sat down and he introduced himself to the nationwide television audience and then he turned to the man and he said hello and the man said hello and the interviewer asked the man how he was feeling and the man said he was feeling okay and then the interviewer asked the man what did he do out here all day all by himself and the man said he just sat behind this small iron table and he kept sipping at some black coffee in the plastic foam container and after a moment or so the man asked the interviewer if he knew any 10 year old kids and the interviewer said no he didn't and then the interviewer asked the man if he minded being interviewed in front of a nationwide television

audience and the man said why should he mind because it was
the TV network news team that was taking the real risk and the
interviewer asked what he meant by that and the man said
everyone here knew he was 98 percent and that means he was
only 2 points away from going bingo so of course there was a
bunch of armed guards hiding behind those azalea bushes with
a fishnet and a straitjacket and a lot of artillery so if the man
started sprouting bananas during the course of the interview
then those armed guards would all pounce down on everyone
there and sure enough when the TV cameras panned over behind the azalea bushes they saw there were 5 burly male guards
and one burly female nurse and they were all wearing gasmasks
and they were all crouching down in the shadows and 3 of the
male guards were holding an enormous fishnet and another of
the male guards was holding a canvas straitjacket and another
of the male guards had a lot of metal cannisters that looked
like nerve gas and the female nurse was holding a rifle with
telescopic sights and a lot of cartridges that looked like liquid
tranquilizer vials so they had enough equipment back there to
take care of a mad bull elephant and no one on the network TV
news team had been told anything about this and some of the
cameramen began muttering about what the hell if this man
started skidding on the banana skin of his own psyche during
the interview and why the hell should these TV news team people run the risk of being hit in the ass by a liquid tranquilizer
vial or being shrouded in a fog of nerve gas so the TV interviewer began to get edgy and he said "thank you very much"
to the man and then he switched the whole show back to New
York but then the interviewer began to stand up from the small
iron table and he knocked over the man's plastic foam container and the hot coffee went spilling all over the crotch of the
man's white Banana Farm pajamas and this man let out a loud
shout as he leaped up in the air and that was all the armed
guards needed to see and they came racing around from behind
the azalea bushes and three of them threw an enormous fishnet
all over everyone on the network TV news team and another
one grabbed the man and began strapping him up in the straitjacket and another one began shooting off all the metal cannisters until the entire area was shrouded in a fog of nerve gas and
the burly female nurse just stood there taking potshots at all
the squirming figures that were gagging and retching under the
enormous fishnet and after a while the figures stopped thrash-
ing around and everything became quite quiet so the armed
guards ran over to the man who was strapped up in the strait-

jacket and they saw that he was lying on his side and his eyes
were wide open and they were staring straight ahead in the air
and the man had a curious beatific smile on his face so the
female nurse reached down and she tried to take the man's
pulse but after a long moment she stood back up and she began
to shake her head very slowly and overhead the clouds were
accumulating in the high wide Wyoming sky and that was
the end of the man who outwitted the entire BF score rating
system.

And I read these last few lines of *The Banana Factor* by Ted
Wylie and then I slammed the book shut and I sat there on the
plane and I sighed a long sigh and I thought well now I know why
this book is a best seller because Ted Wylie found a way to indulge
the reading public's insatiable taste for sick smut while also pander-
ing to its intellectual pretensions for slick social satire and I thought
the whole book is nothing but a rotten tedious piece of nonwriting
but it's already in its 17th printing and it's probably going to be
made into a major motion picture and I wondered who they'd get to
play the part of the banana and as I was thinking these things I
stared out the plane window at the stars that were beginning to fade
into daylight and it began to dawn in all its early morning glory and
just then the businessman sitting next to me began to gather together all his yellow legal pads and he began to fold up his portable
writing desk and he tucked everything neatly away into his briefcase
and he stretched his long legs in a deep long yawn and then he sub-
sided into a comfortable slouch on his seat and he glanced over at
me and he asked acidly:
"If you didn't think that novel was any good then why did you
bother reading the whole thing all the way through to the end?"
And I knew damn well I'd finished reading the book because I
didn't feel like making small talk with the businessman and also because I was going to be teaching the same fiction class with Ted Wylie and I wanted to find out just how vicious and cynical the guy really was but I didn't think I should say any of these things to the
businessman so I just shrugged and I said I'd finished reading the
whole thing all the way through to the end for the same reason some

people stay watching a bad movie all the way through to the end because they've paid to get in and they want to find out how really bad a bad movie can be and when I said this the businessman began shaking his head and he said:

"You should always get up and walk out every time because life is too precious for you to go filling your head with a lot of swill and filth."

And I thought oh god he's going to start lecturing me and here I am trapped next to the window and I thought I'd better change the subject fast so I pointed to his briefcase and I asked him what it was he was writing and the businessman got a sober look on his face and he said:

"I'm finishing up the last chapter of a novel manuscript that I'm taking out to the San Marcos Writers Conference in California where I'm going to get some professional help on it so I can get it published."

And my heart sank and I prayed a fast prayer to whatever angels might be out there in the bright areas of air that I wouldn't get this man's novel manuscript to read because I didn't want to have to try and decipher all the scrawling on those yellow legal pads but then I wondered why this businessman hadn't picked up on Ted Wylie's name when I told him I was reading *The Banana Factor* by Ted Wylie but then I thought maybe he never got one of those foldout brochures that Ralph Perry put in the mails too late to get anyone to register and maybe this guy is just going out to the writers conference on blind faith that the faculty knows how to teach writers how to write their own writing and I looked at the man again out of the sides of my eyes and I decided there was something vaguely crazy about him but he kept right on going and he said:

"I tell you young man you ought to look into these writers conferences because they can take someone like you and make a real writer out of you in no time at all."

And I said I wasn't much for writers or writers conferences because my field was breeding radioactive blue worms for deep sea fishing and then I asked the businessman what his novel was about

37

and he looked around the plane to make sure no one else was listening in on us and he fixed me with a glassy stare and he pointed his finger upwards in the air and he said:

"Corruption in high places."

And since our plane was about 7 thousand feet high at the time I decided the corruption had to be in very high places indeed and just then the stewardess stood up in the front and she told us we were coming into Santa Barbara and would we please fasten our seat belts and the plane was already lowering lowering lowering and then it lowered some more until it looked as if it were going to skim the tops off the great waves of water with its wings and then there was the flat strip of earth rushing under us and the landing gear touched down and the plane bumped and screeched and it began to shudder as the jet engines raced backwards to brake the speed and then we were rolling along smoothly now at a steady ground speed past the brilliant runway lights and I stayed seated until the plane had nosed itself over to the airport depot and the jet engines had whined down to a complete stop and the businessman sitting next to me said:

"Which way are you going young man because I'm getting a cab to drive north to San Marcos and I'd be happy to give you a lift."

And I said thanks but no thanks and I wished him luck with his writers conference and I stayed in my seat as he got up and I watched him go down the passenger gangway and on into the airport and as I sat there on the empty plane I suddenly felt myself begin to go into a desperation panic state and I knew I had to phone Cindy in New York and ask her to fly out to California so I could meet her at the airport and go off to a motel with her where we could make love all night and then we could go around Santa Barbara tomorrow and we could feed the seals and talk to all the old people and visit the Franciscan Mission so I got off the plane and I went into the airport and I went over to the pay phones and I took out a dime and I dialed Cindy's number long distance collect in New York and I stood there as the phone rang about 10 or 11 times and then I thought Cindy was probably off fucking someone else right now because she was such a hopelessly childish child so I slammed the pay phone back on the receiver and I turned and I walked out into the open air of Santa Barbara.

_____

This is the end of chapter two of this lousy novel and by this time you should be wise to how I am trying to take all these words and strip them naked on the page so they will all lie there in their own air where they can stare up at you and make love to your wide open eyes and maybe then the sperm of these words will get inside and fertilize the egg of your head and then after you finish reading this lousy novel all the way through to the end then you may find that you are pregnant with my word sperms and who knows then maybe you may go off and give birth to a lousy baby novel of your very own and that's something for you to think about as you keep reading these lines that I am trying to write right now.

three/Sunday

And the waves of the Pacific made a brilliant spilling all along the
narrow strip of beach that stretched north from the San Marcos
Hotel and there was the crash of ocean as the great waves came in
and burst to surf and then they sent thin tongues of water all along
the beach as they withdrew back to the ceaseleₔs sea and in the wake
of all these waves the sand was littered with a wide spray of debris
and there were chips and bits of driftwood and occasional sea shells
and green and brown rubbery gelatin strands of seaweed with small
buds of air that pop when you squeeze them between your fingers
and the San Marcos Hotel was perched high above this narrow strip
of beach like a large bird that kept listening as the great waves came
in to break against the slippery glistening rocks and there were some
wooden stairs that went on up to the hotel and there was a gravel
driveway and a small kitchen enclosure that housed the garbage
pails that were always spilling over with soggy tea bags and empty
cans of tuna fish and the San Marcos Hotel itself was a composite
of all the lonely off-season tourist resorts from Maine to Florida or
from Oregon to Mexico only here it was the height of the tourist

season and the San Marcos Hotel was such a wreck and it had such a wretched reputation that all the hotel could do to keep itself going was book in a few seedy summer conferences and this was because the San Marcos Hotel had been built over 80 years ago by a Texas millionaire as a gift for his petite French wife and he had put in an elevator and an enormous kitchen area that was capable of creating the most exotic European cuisine and he had built a long wide porch so you could stand and see the spectacular view of the Pacific Ocean but his petite French wife spent one week in the oversized house and she said the floorboards creaked at night and the noise of the great waves breaking outside her window kept her awake all night and the sea breeze made the whole place sway in crazy ways so she finally left in a pique saying she never wanted to set foot in the place again and the Texas millionaire was so disheartened that he let the house stand unused for 40 years which only hastened its decay and then after his death the place passed through several owners until it was finally sold at public auction to Juan Alonzo Ruiz who was a short formal man who was always immaculately dressed in a pin-striped suit with cameo cuff links and Mr. Ruiz spent a large sum of money restoring the house so it could be used as a seaside resort hotel but the first season the tourist trade stayed away from the San Marcos Hotel the way dogs stay away from a maggoty bird corpse so during the second season Mr. Ruiz tried booking in week-long conferences from an agency in San Diego and the first conference that came to San Marcos was a convention of mail order houses that met to swap lists of customers who wanted sexually oriented materials and then there was a conference of hysterical clairvoyants who got together to forecast the end of the world and then there was a conference of terrorists that met to coordinate street gang riots in major American cities and the characters who came to these week-long conferences were the dregs of their profession and once or twice the San Marcos Hotel was almost burned to the ground and several times it was almost torn apart by fistfights and knifings and drunken brawls and shoot-outs and there were even a few drownings off the narrow strip of beach although no bodies were ever found so finally Mr. Ruiz complained to the San Diego booking agency that he wanted more high class week-long conferences at his hotel and he also insisted that every conference director post a $1000 bond at the beginning of the week and he also wrote out a list of house rules that he printed up and handed out to all the conference directors and he swore he would toss out any conference that broke any of these house rules:

1. *No shooting of guns or throwing of knives or breaking of furniture and no tossing of anyone out windows and no drowning in water and no fighting in rooms after 11:00 PM.*
2. *No lighting of fires in rooms at any time.*
3. *No doing of anything else to make trouble on the San Marcos Hotel.*

Juan Alonzo Ruiz
Manager
San Marcos Hotel

And once these house rules were handed out to all the conference directors things began to shape up a little but there was still a curious sense of seediness to all the week-long conferences that came to the San Marcos Hotel like the ones that came this year:

1. THE WORLD COUNCIL TO CHANGE TOURNAMENT CHESS RULES. This was a small group of rabid chess players led by its founder Major Winfield Scott Barnaby and it met once a year to discuss ways to outlaw the practice of castling during the opening 17 moves of all international chess matches and the group spent all its time signing petitions and sending them off to Congress and to the General Assembly of the United Nations.
2. COMPUTER DATING BUREAUS INC. This was an organization of dating bureaus that met annually to discuss standardizing the application forms that were used by all the different dating bureaus so then there would be billions of new matching possibilities opened up except the different dating bureaus could never decide what questions should go on the one standardized form so the members met once a year and argued about it.

3. WEST COAST INDEPENDENT INSURANCE COMPANIES. This was a group of companies devoted to thinking up new things to sell insurance on such as hiccups and polyps and blushing and amnesia and slips of the tongue and anything else that could go wrong with a person during the course of a normal lifetime.
4. THE EXECUTIVE COUNCIL OF CHURCHES INC. This was a group of P.R. people that was putting together a JESUS TRAIN that would travel around the country with a lot of authentic relics like splinters from the true cross and photographs of the Holy Land and there was also a woman who claimed to be descended from one of Jesus's sisters and she sang songs on a guitar about how it felt to have the same blood in her veins that Jesus had.
5. THE SAN MARCOS WRITERS CONFERENCE. Ralph Perry began this conference 7 years ago and conferees came from as far away as Los Angeles and San Francisco to have their manuscripts read and criticized by a staff of professional writers most of whom had never really written anything worth reading.
6. THE NORTH AMERICAN STUDY OF DEMOCRATIC INSTITUTIONS. This was a front organization for a Los Angeles syndicate that specialized in sneaking dirty money across the Mexican border and laundering it through a chain of Central American banks and then sending it back up to Miami Beach where it suddenly appeared as if from out of nowhere.

And Mr. Ruiz made all these conferences follow the same schedule of activities beginning with an opening night barbecue out on the narrow strip of beach on Sunday evening and then daily meals in the hotel dining room and all classes and meetings in the main hall and then there was a farewell banquet on the following Saturday evening and Mr. Ruiz employed 2 kitchen boys named Harry Holton and Sylvester Appleby who prepared all the meals which were mostly pasty mounds of tuna salad and endless gallons of insipid iced tea and Mr. Ruiz had a wife who lived upstairs on the fourth floor of the San Marcos Hotel and no one had ever seen Mrs. Ruiz because she never came downstairs and her meals were put on trays in the kitchen 3 times a day and then taken up on the ancient elevator and left outside her door and some of the conferees thought Mrs. Ruiz must be crazy but only Mr. Ruiz knew the truth about Mrs. Ruiz and Mr. Ruiz wasn't telling anyone anything because all he ever did was stand around in the lobby of the San Marcos Hotel looking immaculately dressed in his pin-striped suit with cameo cuff links and Mr. Ruiz thought most of the people who came to the week-long conferences were crazy and that was why he spent so much time standing around in the lobby because he was afraid someone might try to burn down his hotel and that was why he was in the hotel lobby on Sunday afternoon when I got off the bus from Santa Barbara and I walked into the lobby past 2 women who were both wearing plain blue business suits with silver JESUS TRAIN medallions on their breast pockets and these women stood and glared at me as I walked up to the reception desk where Jose the desk clerk was sitting and reading a paperback copy of *The Banana Factor* by Ted Wylie and this book was making Jose feel very dizzy indeed and that was a good thing because Jose had been the desk clerk at the San Marcos Hotel for the last 7 years and all he ever did was sit behind the reception desk and read paperback novels that made him feel dizzy and even though Jose was only on page 2 of *The Banana Factor* he could already feel his toes were beginning to tingle and his ears were beginning to ring and his head was beginning to spin around inside so Jose knew this was going to be a very good book indeed and so he did not even look up from his reading as I signed my name in the register and then I turned it around and I pushed it right under his nose so Jose had to stop his reading and stare down at my signature and he began to mouth my name over very slowly "Eliot Morrison" as if it were some sort of secret formula that would unlock a very mysterious riddle if he could only find the right way of saying it and suddenly a light lit up in his eyes as he said my name out loud and then he reached down and he got a large manila envelope that had my name written on it and he handed it over to me so I thanked him and I opened the envelope and I saw that inside there were a lot of student manuscripts and

also there was my room key and also there was a little celluloid
nameplate that said:

ELIOT MORRISON
FICTION

And there was a note that said:

Eliot:

Here are all the fiction manuscripts that have come in for
you so you can look them over before you schedule your individual manuscript conferences and do drop down to see me
when you get in.

Ralph Perry

And I stuffed everything back in the large manila envelope as I
started walking down to Ralph Perry's office and I began to think
about how Ralph Perry had spent so much of his life trying to write
and how he had so little to show for it because when he was a young
man he was a successful corporation lawyer in Philadelphia but always in the back of his mind he told himself that someday he would
devote the rest of his life to writing his own writing and what he had
in mind was a series of historical war novels and now here he was in
his early 80's and for the last 50 years he had been researching the
lives of all the famous sea captains who had ever served in the
United States Navy from the Revolutionary War right on up
through the two World Wars of the twentieth century and I had
read some of these novel manuscripts and they were the biggest col-
lages of trivia I had ever seen because they were so hopelessly clut-
tered with page after page of irrelevant detail such as what kind of
rope was used to tie what kind of knot during the Civil War and
what kind of button was worn on what kind of uniform during the
Spanish-American War and what kind of weather reports came
over the short-wave radios during the First World War and none of
these manuscripts had ever been published so they all stayed in their
black plastic bindings and Ralph Perry just kept working away at

45

them by inserting even more details about ropes and buttons the way a squirrel will keep poking more nuts in the hollows of a tall tree trunk and when Ralph Perry married his wife Laura Perry 50 years ago she was also filled with the romance of writing and she thought Ralph Perry's idea of writing a cycle of war novels was the most exciting thing she had ever heard but then when she began to read through a few of the manuscripts she got herself tied up in all those buttons and ropes and that was about the same time Laura Perry fell in love with the lost soul of Robert Browning and she also loved the lost souls of Alfred Lord Tennyson and Henry Wadsworth Longfellow and John Greenleaf Whittier but mostly she was in love with the lost soul of Robert Browning and she began to cultivate an air of lingering malaise so she always wore false eyelashes and a long shawl around her shoulders and when she sat down her fingers would lie open in her lap as if they were 2 broken birds that had just fallen out of the sky and it was Laura Perry who talked Ralph Perry into starting the San Marcos Writers Conference 7 years ago and she helped out at each and every conference in all sorts of selfless ways like passing out the little celluloid nameplates at registration and serving up a lot of crumby cookies and insipid iced tea during the class breaks and assisting Miriam Morse in reading through all the poetry manuscripts and then during the off season Laura Perry would go over to the San Marcos Hospital where she would read the poetry of Robert Browning to the patients there and she especially liked reciting the long narrative poems to the terminally ill patients and as for Ralph Perry his chief delight in doing these writers conferences was teaching the marketing course where he prided himself on covering all the important points on how to get a manuscript accepted by a major publisher and some of his important points were:

Always type your manuscript in double spaces
Always correct all your spelling mistakes
Always make carbon copies of your manuscript
Always staple your manuscript together
Always use the right size envelope

And this marketing course was full of a lot of other practical tips for writers and they were all delivered in a no-nonsense manner by Ralph Perry and the fact that he himself had never published anything anywhere didn't seem to bother any of the conferees because Ralph Perry was always so enthusiastic about how gosh darn easy it was to get something published if you just went about it in the right way and he always told all his classes that most of the major publishers today were making their real money by doing a lot of nonfiction self-help books like *How to Restore Hinges for Fun and Profit* and *How to Housebreak Your Dog so He Stays Housebroken* and *How to Teach Canaries to Fight Back* and he said this was the kind of book that any real writer ought to try to write and during the off season Ralph Perry kept on researching his war novels but he also kept busy bustling about and setting up schedules for the next year's writers conference yet no matter how hard he bustled every year the writers conference ran a deficit because Ralph Perry never seemed to be able to get the brochures out on time so at the end of each conference he had to pony up some money out of his own life savings to pay Mr. Ruiz for the hotel bill and even though Ralph Perry always groused about it he was still awful gosh darn proud to be Director of the San Marcos Writers Conference and as I came to the door of his office I saw he was sitting inside on his swivel chair and he was sucking on his pipe and when he saw me he waved me in and he said:

"Hi guy come on in and sit down and listen we're going to have a really swell conference this year because there are 47 people coming from Los Angeles and San Francisco and there's even a businessman who flew all the way in from New York and did I tell you Ted Wylie will be here with us this year?"

And I said yes I had seen it in the brochure that arrived just as I was leaving New York and Ralph Perry said:

"It was such a sudden stroke of good luck because I had gone down to hear Ted Wylie give a talk in Los Angeles and afterwards I went up to speak to him and I mentioned to him that I was the Director of the San Marcos Writers Conference and darned if he

47

didn't say right then and there that he'd like to come teach for us this year and wasn't that a swell break for us huh guy?''

And I said I wasn't so sure about that because I'd just finished reading *The Banana Factor* and I thought it was pretty sophomoric stuff and when I said that Ralph Perry pulled a long face and he said:

''Well yes you're probably right although I've never read either *The Cardboard Carton* or *The Banana Factor* but I must say when I listened to his talk in Los Angeles I couldn't understand how a grown man could get so excited about playing a lot of far out sex games with a gang of 10 year olds and my gosh what is this world coming to but then *The Banana Factor* is a best selling novel so it can't hurt our conference to have someone like Ted Wylie on our faculty and oh listen guy he's not arriving until Monday morning so I'd appreciate your taking the first fiction class tomorrow morning and would you do that for me huh guy?''

And I lied and said I'd be glad to do it and then Ralph Perry began to look very lost the way a courtroom lawyer will look very lost when he wants something really important from a jury and he said:

''You know guy I've been meaning to ask you for some time now that my last novel about World War Two is finally finished and that's the last of my cycle of historical war novels and I've been thinking about how all those manuscripts are just collecting dust over there in their black plastic covers because nobody seems to be much interested in publishing any of them and I wouldn't want this to get around the conference but I've decided to go ahead and have them printed privately and that will take quite a bite out of my life savings but I've decided it's the right thing for me to do so I was wondering if you'd be good enough to read through this last novel manuscript and maybe write out a small statement I could use on the dust jacket and I asked Ted Wylie to do it but he wasn't very civil about it and I guess he resents being asked to do that sort of thing so would you do this one small thing for me huh guy?''

And I lied and said I'd be glad to do it and Ralph Perry beamed and he said that was gosh darn swell of me and he handed me the novel manuscript in its black plastic cover and then he leaned back in his swivel chair and he looked out the window at the great waves that were coming in to break against the slippery glistening rocks and he said:

"Gosh you've got no idea how many of the conference people have been asking about you and they come up to me in the hall and they say is Eliot Morrison coming back here this year and when I tell them yes then you should see their faces light up because you know what a great favorite you are around here guy and of course you'll find time to write a lot of your own writing this week because this is such a great place to hold a writers conference because you can almost feel the creativity coming up from the floorboards and I always tell the conferees that if you can't write here then you can't write anywhere . . ."

And Ralph Perry's voice began to trail off and then he fell completely silent and he sat quite quiet in his swivel chair and it looked as if he might have slipped off on me so I stood up and I called Ralph Perry's name a few times but there was no response so I just shrugged and I picked up my large manila envelope and the black plastic manuscript of the war novel and I headed toward the door but just then I heard Ralph Perry's voice call out to me:

"Hey guy I almost forgot to tell you that I've got you down to introduce Gwendolyn Field on Wednesday night."

And I whirled around at the door and I said I'd be damned if I'd do any such thing because Gwendolyn Field was just a dumb cunt who wrote junk stuff and the only thing she'd ever done was one soppy pop novel about how she screwed her way across Africa and when I said that Ralph Perry pulled another of his long faces and he said:

"Well yes and I suppose you're right guy and I've never read *Safari* but I must say I've heard how it's filled with all sorts of filth and my gosh what is this world coming to but then she is one of our

foremost women writers and we do have to have someone to introduce her and I promised Ted Wylie I'd go easy on him over this
week and besides he's going to be giving the talk on Thursday evening on how he wrote *The Banana Factor* so it looks like you're the
only one who can introduce Gwendolyn Field and you're so gosh
darn good at this sort of thing so would you do this one small thing
for me huh guy?"

And Ralph Perry lowered his face and he looked up at me the
way a puppy looks at someone when it wants permission to go pee
on the carpet and I knew I was being conned but there was something so witless about Ralph Perry's whole approach to writers and
writing that I lied and said I'd be glad to do it and Ralph Perry
raised his face and he beamed and he said:

"Aw that's gosh darn swell of you guy so now you can go relax
and don't forget we have the outdoor barbecue tonight at 6:00 PM
down there on the beach and then there'll be a short staff meeting
up here at 8:30 PM and oh good gosh I almost forgot to tell you I
got a phone call from someone named Clara something and was she
an ex-student of yours?"

And I said Clara was an ex-wife of mine and I asked him what
the hell she had to say and Ralph Perry said:

"Well gosh darn guy that's the funny part because she just
kept shouting out something about how I should lock up all the cute
little chickeepoos whatever the heck that may mean and then she
hung up the phone."

And I told Ralph Perry to forget about it and I went out the
door and down the hall and just as I was coming to the hotel lobby I
saw Maureen Talbot was coming toward me and she had handsome
chestnut hair and 2 neatly pointed breasts that looked at you as you
were talking to her and when Maureen Talbot first came to the San
Marcos Writers Conference 7 years ago she was 21 years old and a
virgin and she went to all the writing classes and she listened to all
the lectures and she took endless notes and that first year the nonfiction teacher took her down to the narrow strip of beach and he
laid her there and then for the rest of the week he ignored her and

Maureen Talbot got so hysterical that she ran to Ralph Perry in tears and when Ralph Perry heard that someone on his own faculty had taken advantage of this innocent young woman he hit the ceiling but then after Ralph Perry went to bed with Maureen Talbot himself he calmed down and he offered her a permanent position as Assistant Director of the San Marcos Writers Conference so Maureen Talbot came back every year after that and she drifted from one writing teacher to another and over the past 7 years she had affairs with a poet and 3 novelists and 2 magazine writers and 5 literary agents and I had my own affair with her 5 years ago when I first came to San Marcos and the following year I was displaced by a writer of children's literature and Maureen Talbot would always type manuscripts for all the writers she was having affairs with and she would always listen to their life stories and then she would always write her own impression of each writer in her 5 large notebooks that she was going to publish someday as a novel that would tell everyone everything about writers and writing and during the rest of the year she would go looking for new writing teachers all over the West Coast and she would interview them and she would go to bed with them and 2 or 3 of them would occasionally take her up on her invitation to come teach at the San Marcos Writers Conference but the rest of them would just hop out of bed and go right back to writing their own writing and Maureen Talbot knew this was the way it was with writers so she never got bitter about how many of them just used her for a fast lay and as Maureen Talbot stood in front of me in the hall she began to say:

"I'm going to be assisting Ted Wylie in all his fiction classes and his individual manuscript conferences and I've already been seeing quite a bit of him down in Los Angeles and he's going to be a really great writing teacher."

And I asked Maureen Talbot if Ted Wylie's banana was as big as mine and she made a wry face and then she went on down to Ralph Perry's office and I kept on going into the lobby where Laura Perry was sitting behind the registration table and she was fishing around in a big bin there that was filled with things to give each of

the conferees like room keys and class schedules and a list of writing
DO'S and DON'T'S by Ralph Perry and Mr. Ruiz's house rules and
lots of little celluloid nameplates for the conferees to pin on their la-
pels and I saw the conferees were standing around the table munch-
ing on crumby cookies and sipping on insipid iced tea and they were
all saying things like:

. . . I kept at it a long time and a lot of important people
looked at it . . .

. . . well and will you look at television today because all those
writers just left because they couldn't take it anymore . . .

. . . oh I've just been fooling around with it to see what will
happen and that's why I need some really professional criticism at this point . . .

And I passed out through the lobby past a glass door where I
caught sight of myself and I saw my shaggy hair and my crumpled
coat and the dislocated look in my eyes and I thought ah god I must
look as unreal as I feel and I went on into the dining room where I
sat down at a corner table where I began to eat my tuna salad and
sip at my iced tea and I looked around and saw some other conferees were sitting at the other tables and just then Mildred Manson
got up and she came over to where I was sitting and she stood there
beaming a bright hello down at me so I beamed a bright hello back
up at her because Mildred Manson was a buxom dumpy matron
who had been coming to the San Marcos Writers Conference every
year for 5 years and she had been rewriting the same sickening saccharine sentimental short story every year and each time she re-
wrote it she made it even more sickening saccharine sentimental so
last year I told her she should either tear up the whole thing and toss
it out or else start from scratch and rewrite it all all over again and
now here she was standing beside my table and she was talking at
me about all the work she had put in on her short story over this
past year and how it was completely changed from the way it was
and as I sat there listening to her go on and on I began gazing

52

around the dining room at the other conferees and I saw there was this one young woman who was sitting off at a corner table all by herself and she was wearing a bright canary yellow dress and she had soft silk hair and she had large dark startled eyes that kept staring straight ahead in the air and she was eating the tuna salad on her plate although eating isn't exactly the right word for what it was she was doing to it because it was more like she was relating to it the way she would poke it around with her plastic fork and then she would arrange it into little mounds and then every so often she would lift a tiny bit of it to her lips and she would take a quick nibble at it and then she would put it back down and go poking it around some more with her plastic fork and just then I felt a sudden weight on my hand and I looked down and I saw Mildred Manson had slammed her hand down hard on top of my hand and she was saying:

"And you remember last year how you told me I should either tear the whole thing up and toss it out or else start from scratch and rewrite it all all over again and that's just what I did and I also wrote out all those long love letters the poor woman sends to her distant lover and they bring out the hidden heartache of what she's going through and if you've already looked at my manuscript then you know what I mean."

And I said I hadn't had a chance to look at her manuscript yet but I promised I would get to it this evening and Mildred Manson said she was so eager to hear what I thought about it and just then I saw the young woman in the bright canary yellow dress was getting up to leave the dining room so I took my hand from under Mildred Manson's hand and I picked up the large manila envelope and the black plastic manuscript of Ralph Perry's war novel and I said goodbye to Mildred Manson and I headed toward the door and when I got out into the lobby I saw the young woman in the bright canary yellow dress was standing over by the ancient elevator and she glanced at me with her large dark startled eyes and then she looked away so I went up to her and I asked if she had ever been to the San Marcos Writers Conference before and the young woman looked at me again and she said:

"No I've never been here before because last year at this time I was at the Des Moines Writers Conference and the year before that I was at the Houston Writers Conference and the year before that I was at the Laramie Writers Conference."

And I said it sounded like she went to a lot of writers conferences and she said yes she did and then she asked if I was one of the writing teachers here and I said yes my name was Eliot Morrison and she said:

"Then you must have a lot of my short stories because my name is Esther Martin but you don't have to read any of those things because they're not really worth anything so you can just chuck them all in the wastebasket."

And I looked at her to see if she was kidding or not but her large dark startled eyes kept staring straight ahead in the air and just then the ancient elevator arrived and its door opened with a creaky wheeze so we stepped on and the door closed and the ancient elevator began its jerky slow ascent and suddenly Esther Martin said:

"Oh you think you're such a good writer!"

And I wondered if she had said this to me or to herself but she was still staring straight ahead in the air as if she hadn't said anything at all and suddenly I had this subliminal flash thing that I was pulling her bright canary yellow dress up over her head and humping her right there on the ancient elevator and just as I thought that thought the ancient elevator lurched upwards and then it stalled between the lobby and the second floor and it began to emit a sick sweet acid scent and a thin blue wisp of smoke began to rise from the wiring overhead and then there was nothing but dead air as I began to pound on the button panel and I kicked at the door with my foot and finally the ancient elevator let out a weak wheeze like a senile dog and it began to lurch its way on upwards again and when it finally stopped at the second floor the door opened and Esther Martin got out and she was still staring straight ahead in the air as she went on down to her room and the door closed and the ancient elevator lurched on up to the third floor and I got off and I walked down to my room and I unlocked the door and I went in and I lay down on my bed and I tossed Ralph Perry's black plastic manuscript at the foot of the bed and I opened the large manila envelope and I pulled out all the student manuscripts and I began to leaf through them until I found 3 short stories by Esther Martin and I read through them and they were all about angels and the first one was about the angel Gabriel and the second one was about the angel Raphael and the third one was about the archangel Michael and these angels all came and talked to children or dogs or old people who were lonely and the angels had a lot of things to say about how to tie shoelaces and where to store cucumbers and the best way to buy bones but none of the stories seemed to have much of a point so I lay there on my bed and I began to wonder where Esther Martin was coming from and I thought maybe it might be fun to screw her if only she didn't keep staring straight ahead in the air and of course I had no way of knowing that Esther Martin was really coming from Hope Valley which was an intensive care unit outside Columbus in Ohio and when Esther Martin first went to Hope Valley she stayed there for 17 months and she mostly just sat around and stared straight ahead in the air and after a year or so she began blurting out things like:

"Oh you think you're so sick."

And Esther Martin's doctor was a kind man named Dr. Julian Nesbitt who didn't know what to do with Esther Martin because she didn't respond to any of his treatments and of course Dr. Nesbitt had no way of knowing that Esther Martin was simply suffering from an advanced case of Estherlessness or to put it another way Esther Martin had simply jumped headfirst into her own brainlake the way a frog plops headfirst into a pond only Esther Martin hadn't come up yet so after she had been at Hope Valley for 13 months she began writing words down on stray scraps of paper and these words were things like ANGEL and RADIANCE and RADISHES and when Dr. Nesbitt saw these words he told Esther Martin to keep writing down more words and pretty soon Esther Martin was writing dozens of short stories that were all about the angels Gabriel and Raphael and Michael and how these angels came and told people how to tie their shoelaces and where to store cucumbers and pretty soon Esther Martin had filled up 17 notebooks with her short stories but none of them gave any clue as to where Esther Martin was really coming from and actually Esther Martin came from the suburbs of Cleveland where her father was a junior partner in an oil company and her mother was a practising alcoholic and Esther Martin went to parochial school where she got good grades and a lot of scoldings from the nuns because Esther Martin was so unearthly and ethereal and the nuns thought she was precocious and assuming as if she were an apprentice for sainthood and the nuns were also plain jealous that Esther Martin had more of a mystical aura around her than they did the way she would always keep staring straight ahead in the air as if she were listening for the silent sigh of god and as soon as school was out Esther Martin would always race right home to see how her mother was doing and her mother would usually be sprawled all over the cellar stairs or else she would be lying fully clothed in the bathtub and Esther Martin would help her mother into the bedroom and make her lie down and then Esther Martin would race around downstairs straightening up and collecting all the empty bottles and glasses before father came home from the office and when father did appear tired and resigned at the front door Esther Martin would be there to greet him cheerfully and tell him that mother was not feeling well so father would sigh a long sigh and he would lay down his briefcase and kiss Esther Martin on the lips and just then mother would begin to make her slow descent down the stairs and she would be rubbing her forehead and complaining about a migraine headache and then they would all sit down to supper and Esther Martin would go racing in and out of the kitchen with cold tuna salad and iced tea and then after supper they would all go into the living room where father would read the evening newspaper and mother would look at television and Esther Martin would sit off in a corner doing her homework and about 9:00 PM mother would begin to complain of another migraine headache and she would go out into the kitchen and there would be the sound of a faucet running full force and dull clunks of ice in a glass and father would call out:

"Are you all right mother?"

And over the blast of running water mother would call out from the kitchen:

"I'm all right father I'm just getting dinner ready."

And then about 10:00 PM mother would go quietly blotto so Esther Martin would help her back upstairs and get her into bed and then Esther Martin would come downstairs again and her father would be sitting silently with his feet up and Esther Martin would sit off in a corner doing her homework and after a while father would sigh a long sigh and Esther Martin would smile a silent smile and this was all happening when Esther Martin was about 12 years old and later on it got much worse because mother would go ranting up and down the stairs about how there was something ungodly going on between father and daughter and glasses would crash and bottles would smash and ice cubes would go skidding in under the refrigerator but always when it was all over mother would go back upstairs and Esther Martin would sit downstairs with her father and they would sigh and smile at each other and later on Esther Martin went away to the College of the Sacred Heart in Ohio where she got good grades and a lot more scoldings from the nuns because she was even more unearthly and ethereal than before so the nuns managed to make life pretty difficult for Esther Martin in petty ways but Esther Martin always accepted this with grace and humility and that only irked the nuns even more and by the time Esther Martin graduated from Sacred Heart she was more otherworldly than ever although no one thought there was anything really wrong with her because she was just good old otherworldly Esther but that was about the same time that Esther Martin started having hallucinations where angels came and talked to her and they told her all about how it felt to go floating high up in the air where they could look down on all the towns and cities on the ground and anytime you saw anyone down there who was lonely or sad or unhappy you could weep for them and your tears would fall down down down through the air down to the ground and when your tears hit the person on the head then they would heal the person as if he had been touched by radiance and radishes and the more these angels told Esther Martin how it felt to float around in the air the less Esther Martin had to say to anyone else around her on the ground until pretty soon she stopped saying anything to anyone and that was when Esther Martin was sent away to Hope Valley where she sat and stared straight ahead in the air for 13 months and Dr. Nesbitt tried everything he could think of to get through to Esther Martin and he tried electric shock and experimental drugs and face to face therapy but nothing seemed to work until Esther Martin began writing words down on stray scraps of paper and then she went on to writing lots and lots of short stories about angels who came and told people to wear purple or to comb their hair backwards or to defrost their refrigerators and then sometimes wonderful things happened to the people and sometimes terrible things happened to the people and sometimes nothing at all happened to the people and there didn't seem to be much logic to any of it but then that didn't bother Dr. Nesbitt because he wasn't so sure there was all that much logic to anything so he told Esther Martin to keep writing her own writing and one day Esther Martin asked Dr. Nesbitt if he thought her short stories were any good and Dr. Nesbitt said he was no judge of literary merit so then Esther Martin asked him if she could go off to one of those writers conferences where you can get some really professional help with your writing and that seemed to make sense to Dr. Nesbitt so he arranged for Esther Martin to go to her first writers conference up in Vermont where the fiction teacher didn't know what the hell her short stories were about but he told Esther Martin they were exquisite and lyrical and she should keep writing more of them so Esther Martin kept writing and she kept going to more writers conferences and by this time she had 289 angel short stories that she carried around from one conference to another and most of the writing teachers said they were exquisite and lyrical although no one was really sure what they were all about but that was all right with Esther Martin because she wasn't so sure what anything was all about anyway and as I lay there on my bed I kept thinking it might be fun to screw Esther Martin if only she didn't keep staring straight ahead in the air and just then I looked at my wristwatch and I saw it was 6:15 PM and I was late for the outdoor barbecue so I got up and I threw on a clean shirt and I ran to the ancient elevator and I went downstairs and out onto the wooden stairs that led down to the narrow strip of beach where all the conferees were wandering around and I recognized some of the people who had been at San Marcos the year before like Roberta Heite who lived in Arabia for 2 months and she had written a novel about her experiences there with a camel named Fred and there was Joseph Baum who looked like a twinkly eyed little mouse and he had written a novel about how it felt to play on a major league baseball team and there was Lloyd Wainwright who had some sort of a criminal record and he tried to join the Wisconsin State Police but they busted him out before he had a chance to try on one of their sexy State Trooper uniforms and farther on down the narrow strip of beach Ralph Perry was standing by an iron barbecue that was smoldering charcoal smoke and there was a large tarpaulin spread over the sand with a lot of paper plates and napkins and plastic knives and forks and spoons and there were large open bowls of tuna salad and enormous gallon cannisters of iced tea and Ralph Perry was dressed in shorts and he kept bustling about and turning over tiny steak bits on the iron grill with a long-handled fork and from time to time he would call out that there was another batch of steak bits ready and everyone had better make tracks fast to get them while they were still hot and then there would be a general flurry of sand and paper plates as the conferees came running over to the barbecue to get their steak bits from the sizzling grill and after everyone had eaten all they wanted to eat then Ralph Perry stood up in front of the barbecue and he began banging with the end of his long-handled

59

fork on an empty gallon cannister of iced tea so everyone would quiet down and he said:

"Ladies and gentlemen in case you don't know who I am my name is Ralph Perry and I'm awful gosh darn proud to be the Director of the San Marcos Writers Conference and I just want to welcome each and every one of you to our 7th annual conference and I want to tell you that tomorrow morning the class schedules and the individual manuscript conference schedules will be posted on the main bulletin board so you can see when you will be meeting with the instructor of your choice and now let me go around and introduce the faculty and staff to you because Laura Perry is sitting right over here and next to her is Maureen Talbot our Assistant Director and Eliot Morrison is sitting over there and on my right is Miriam Morse our lovely poetry lady and Ted Wylie won't be arriving until tomorrow morning and then on Monday evening our guest speaker will be an editor from *Writers World* and on Tuesday evening all you conferees will be reading from your own work in the main hall and on Wednesday evening Eliot Morrison will be introducing our guest speaker Gwendolyn Field and on Thursday evening Ted Wylie will honor us with a talk about how he wrote *The Banana Factor* and on Friday evening Miriam Morse will give us a poetry reading from her latest volume of verse *Prism of Love* and on Saturday evening there will be the farewell banquet in the dining hall and I just want to say again that each and every one of you is welcome to the San Marcos Writers Conference."

And Ralph Perry began to sit back down again but he sat flat smack on a paper plate that had 3 or 4 uneaten steak bits on it so he stood back up again and he shouted out gosh darn as he began to feel around at the underside of his shorts that were smeared all over with steak grease and he said gosh darn again and just then the 2 kitchen boys Harry Holton and Sylvester Appleby began to circulate among the conferees and they began collecting all the paper plates and cups and napkins and the steak bits that were strewn all over the sand as one by one the conferees began to get up and go back up to the hotel and when the faculty and staff had gathered together in Ralph Perry's office for the meeting Ralph Perry was still fussing about the steak grease that was smeared all over the underside of his shorts and Laura Perry was trying to wipe them clean with some brown paper towels but it was no use so she sighed and she sat down and her long fingers lay open on her lap as if they were 2 broken birds that had just fallen out of the sky and Miriam Morse sat upright in her chair looking pert and nervous in her large lavender hat and Maureen Talbot sat holding an open notebook in her lap and when I came in I sat down in a broken rocking chair and Ralph Perry sat down in his swivel chair and he began discussing guidelines for the conference such as the individual manuscript conferences ("don't spend too much time with any one person because 30 minutes is all they've paid for") and the dining room ("do please try to sit around at the separate tables and mingle with all the conferees") and the evening programs ("it would be really swell if you could all come to each and every one of the evening talks because gosh knows it means so much to the guest speakers to have you all there") and then Ralph Perry said that Maureen Talbot would be running the book room and he said all the staff books were already on display and this included 75 paperback copies of *The Banana Factor* by Ted Wylie and 75 paperback copies of *The Cardboard Carton* by Ted Wylie and 25 paperback copies of *A Dream of Clarence* by Eliot Morrison and 25 paperback copies of *Sahara* by Gwendolyn Field and 25 hard cover copies of *Prism of Love* by Miriam Morse and then Ralph Perry said:

"Now I don't need to tell you anything about how to criticize their student manuscripts but I do want to warn you not to be so tough that you break their hearts because gosh knows there's nothing worse than seeing a lot of lost souls wandering around crying their eyes out because some writing teacher said something thoughtless about one of their manuscripts but on the other hand I don't think you should try to kid anyone either because after all they come to San Marcos to get good no-nonsense criticism and so I guess all I'm saying to you is that you should be as honest and as tactful as you can."

And then Miriam Morse raised her hand and she gave a nervous bird chirp as she reminded Ralph Perry about the Saturday morning staff meeting at the end of the week so the faculty could choose the San Marcos Writers Conference Awards and Ralph Perry said quite right and we should all be on the lookout for manuscripts we thought showed special merit in the fields of fiction and nonfiction and poetry and then Ralph Perry leaned back in his swivel chair and he gazed out the window at the great waves that came breaking in against the slippery glistening rocks and he said:

"This is such a great place to hold a writers conference because you can almost feel the creativity coming up from the floorboards and I always tell the conferees that if you can't write here then you can't write anywhere . . ."

And Ralph Perry's voice began to trail off and then he fell silent and he sat quite quiet in his swivel chair and it looked as if he might have slipped off on us and there was an embarassed silence in the office until Laura Perry began to motion to us that the meeting was over and we should all leave so one by one we all got up and we filed out of the office and I went upstairs to my room where I lay down on my bed and I began to look through all the student manuscripts and it didn't take me long to realize that most of them were pretty dreadful so I began to scribble a lot of notes in the margins and as I was doing this I thought ah god if they want to be writers then why don't they learn how to write but then I thought who the hell am I to be saying something like that when I haven't really written anything in 5 years and I should just keep my mind mouth shut and keep reading through these student manuscripts so I read one novel about a girl who kills her parents and runs away to Canada where she falls in love with a handsome pipe exporter and I read another novel about a young girl who has a camel named Fred and they live together in the middle of a desert with a band of friendly Arabs and I read another novel about a family that keeps sitting down to all sorts of full course roast beef dinners and I read another sickening saccharine sentimental short story about a high school English teacher who falls in love with a senior who graduates and goes off to the college of his choice and I read another short story about a suburban housewife who drops an enormous mahogany chest of drawers down a staircase on top of her husband and I read another short story about a young boy who wants to be a professional football player but instead he gets electrocuted in the bathtub and I kept on reading through the rest of the student manuscripts until my eyes began to blur and my head began to get heavy and I finally found one fairly good manuscript about a mountain climber who leaves a group of tourists on the wrong ledge of a sheer rock glacial gorge and when I had read through every last one of the student manuscripts I looked at my wristwatch and I saw it was 4:30 AM so I took out a sheet of paper and I wrote down a schedule for all my individual manuscript conferences and it looked like this:

TUESDAY	WEDNESDAY	THURSDAY	FRIDAY
1:00	1:00	1:00	1:00
Mary	Roberta	Mary Anne	Douglas
Wilde	Heite	Berre	Mercer
2:00	2:00	2:00	2:00
Mildred	Joseph	Susan	Dorothy
Manson	Baum	Restnor	Kingsley
3:00	3:00	3:00	3:00
Esther	Cleveland	Betsy	Marianne
Martin	Mason	Childs	Roseblatt

And then I got up off the bed and I stretched my arms as far as I could stretch them over my head and I felt all the blood begin to leave my braincave as I began to go off into one of my acid fizz state dizzy spells—

here we go
into hee haw country

—and I held one arm against the wall as I watched myself collapsing backwards into a lot of black holes that were eating the light alive inside my head and then after a moment I came back to myself so I walked down the hall to the ancient elevator and I rode down to the lobby where I posted the individual manuscript conference schedule on the main bulletin board and I saw Jose was still awake behind the reception desk and he was reading page 27 of *The Banana Factor* by Ted Wylie and he looked pretty dizzy when I walked past him and out onto the porch and down the stairs and onto the narrow strip of beach where I walked for a while and finally I lay down there and I gazed up at the California night sky starlight overhead and I could see the Milky Way was visible from one side of the horizon to the other and it was a high wide white that was made up of so many tiny lights and I thought there are over 100 billion stars up there in that one galaxy of light and there are over 100 billion galaxies like that one in our universe and who knows how many other universes there may be and who the hell am I to be lying down here looking up at all that light life because I knew that every one of those tiny pinpoints was sending out a living light line right down to my own eyes but here I was and I hadn't written one single living line of my own in the last 5 years and I thought my christ what would it take for me to get my life off its ass and write my own writing about the light that is alive inside my mind and would it mean I would have to go all the way through those fearful early years when I was so alone in my own orphan air until I came on that first fire that was far in the darkness of the heart and when I thought that thought I began to go into one of my desperation panic states and I had a sudden impulse to run back up to the hotel and phone Cindy long distance collect and ask her please to fly out here and I'd meet her in Santa Barbara airport tomorrow afternoon and we could make love all night and then next day we'd go feed the seals and talk to all the old people and visit the Franciscan Mission but then I sat up in the sand and I thought it's no good because Cindy is probably off fucking someone else right now as I am sitting right here on this narrow strip of beach and so I said to hell with her because she is such a hopelessly childish child and I may as well make up my mind that I will never call her again and I will never see her again and she can think I was eaten alive by a bunch of middle-aged teacher eaters out here and just then I felt a sudden shudder pass through me as I thought of facing the rest of my life alone and so I looked around at the sand on the beach and I saw that there was no one there and I looked out at the great waves in the open ocean and I saw that there was no solace in that wet metal sea and so I got up and I walked back up to the hotel and I went up to my room and I lay down on my bed and I fell asleep and I dreamed this dream:

An angel came to me and said his name was Virgil and I said Virgil who and he said just plain Virgil and he showed me his little celluloid nameplate and sure enough it said:

JUST PLAIN VIRGIL
GUIDED TOURS

And Virgil said he was going to lead me through the inferno of writers conferences so we began to walk along this narrow strip of beach where I saw all these writing students were racing in and out of the great waves and they were all waving their novel and short story and poem manuscripts over their heads and Virgil leaned over toward me and he began to whisper the secret life history of each of the student writers who were racing through the great waves and he told me how this one had poisoned her mother and how that one had stabbed his wife and how this one had blown up a State Police barracks and how that one had been unfaithful to her father and he said all these student writers were condemned to keep on writing their novel and short story and poem manuscripts through all eternity and I leaned over toward Virgil and I said that was all okay by me but why in hell was I condemned to keep reading all their manuscripts but as soon as I said that Virgil disappeared in a great wave of spray that came bursting in all over us and I was left there all alone in my own orphan air—

_____

This is the end of chapter three of this lousy novel and by this time you're probably thinking that all the characters in this lousy novel are as loony as fruit juice and if that's what you're thinking then you'd better take a good look around yourself right now because believe me things are much more loony out there where you are than they are in here because all I'm trying to do in this lousy novel is write down a tiny bit of the fresh fruit juice loony foolishness that is all around us always and so dear reader gentle reader shame on you for thinking you are any less loony than the characters in this lousy novel because the truth is you're such a fishy mishmosh of paranoia that you're as bad as I am and that's something for you to think about as you keep reading these lines that I am trying to write right now.

four/Monday

And when I got down to breakfast the next morning I sat at a corner table and I began to sip at my black coffee and at the table next to me there were a lot of conferees who were all joking about *The Banana Factor* by Ted Wylie because they had all read it and now they were busy assigning BF scores to everyone here at the San Marcos Writers Conference and every so often someone would say "so and so is a 93 percent" and the entire table would erupt in gales of wild laughter and it reminded me of junior high school days but then I said to myself come on now none of your damn loathing because these people are paying good money to make it possible for you to sit here and bitch at them so I leaned back and I lit a cigarette and I began to think about the fiction class I would be teaching later on in the morning and I wondered what the hell I would tell them about how to write their own writing and would they even listen to me if they knew that I haven't really written anything myself for the last 5 years and maybe I should just tell them what a failure I am and just then Douglas Mercer came over and he sat down next to me and he was the only black student here at the writers conference and he asked me if I had read his manuscript yet and I asked him which one was it and he said the one about the boy who wants to be a professional football player and I said oh yes the one where the boy gets electrocuted in the bathtub and Douglas Mercer said yeah that's the one and I said yes I did read it and I thought it was very interesting and just then the next table erupted in more gales of wild laughter as someone assigned another BF score to someone else and hands clapped and heads nodded knowingly and Douglas Mercer leaned forward toward me and he asked me what was with these writers conferences anyway and I said I didn't know but it would be pretty hard to imagine John Keats or Robert Burns or Emily Dickinson being caught dead at any of them and just then I looked across the dining room and I saw Esther Martin was sitting at a corner table between 2 other women and she was wearing a bright canary yellow dress and she was sipping at little spoonfuls of black coffee and the other 2 women were chattering away about what they thought Ralph Perry's BF score was and suddenly Esther Martin's left hand made a quick flick and it knocked over a salt shaker and that sent salt spilling all over the tablecloth and Esther Martin went right on sipping at little spoonfuls of black coffee as if nothing had happened but the other 2 women sat there with their mouths wide open and they were gazing at Esther Martin and wondering where she was coming from and meanwhile Harry Holton and Sylvester Appleby were busy clearing away the breakfast things from the tables and Harry Holton was also looking around at all these new conferees to see if there was anything sexy or interesting at this writers conference and he was about to shrug off all the women at this conference as a bunch of dumb cunts just like the ones at the JESUS TRAIN conference the week before but just then his eyes fell on Esther Martin who was sitting and sipping at little spoonfuls of black coffee and she looked like a lost angel with her bright canary yellow dress and her large dark startled eyes so Harry Holton motioned with his head for Sylvester Appleby to come over and take a good look at what was over there and Harry Holton narrowed his eyes significantly and he sucked in on his cheeks and he said:

"Interesting."

And Sylvester Appleby nodded his head so hard his hair fell all over his eyes and he also said:

"Yeah it's interesting."

And Harry Holton said:

"I'll bet she's wide open too."

And Harry Holton did a fast reading of all the secret sexual signals that Esther Martin was sending out and then he said:

"Yeah there's no doubt about it because that woman over there is definitely and unquestionably wide open."

And just then Esther Martin got up and she began to leave the dining room so I got up also and I went down to the main hall so I could listen to the end of Ralph Perry's marketing class in the main hall that was nothing but a large room with a dusty blackboard and an old oak desk that faced about 5 rows of chairs and when I went in I sat in the back row and Ralph Perry was just finishing up some pointers on how to get things published and he was saying:

> And for gosh sakes do be sure your cover letter tells the agent everything he'll want to know about what your manuscript is about so he can figure out how well he can sell it to the publisher because the publisher knows what the readership wants to read and after all publishing is selling and that's what writing is really all about.

And I thought that sounded pretty sad coming from someone who had never sold anything in his entire life but then I saw that everyone was busy taking notes on everything Ralph Perry was saying except for Esther Martin who was sitting across the room in the back row and she just kept leaning forward over her open notebook with her pen poised in mid-air as if she were suspended endlessly in space and when the marketing class was over Laura Perry wheeled in a little cart with lots of crumby cookies and insipid iced tea and she began serving everyone during the class break and I got up and I went over to the old oak desk and I sat down there and when the conferees had finished their crumby cookies and their insipid iced tea then they all got back to their seats and they opened up their notebooks and I looked out over the great vacancy of faces that were all waiting for me to begin talking to them and for an instant there I began to taste the empty space that was between me and all those students and I began to eat whole areas of air and for a long moment I was frozen motionless but then I started to talk about writers and writing and I said when you are really writing it is the easiest thing in the universe because it feels like you are listening to a distant brook that keeps on babbling to itself about itself or else it feels like the bright light of childhood when you were so alive with life or else it feels like an unseen inner energy that is spooky and delusional and it keeps on coming up with worlds that are more real than any words that you are trying to write in your notebook so all you have to do is write out everything you hear with your own inner ear and before you know it the page is a play place where you can create great shapes that are the images of all those ghosts that come and go far in the darkness of the heart and as I was saying these things I looked out over the class and I saw that all the students were writing down everything I was saying in their open notebooks and I thought my christ for someone who hasn't really written anything in the last 5 years I can give the best damn lecture on writing you've ever heard but then I thought ah god if these students could only see the conspicuous vacuity that is inside of me they'd all drop their notebooks and run for cover but I kept talking about how easy it is to write your own writing and when I finished giving the lecture I got up from the old oak desk and some of the conferees came rushing up and they started asking me how they could listen to their own brooks with their inner ears and I told them all they had to do was listen to the distance and they'd hear a babbling in the back of their heads and they looked as if they couldn't wait to try it because they were as eager as puppies at supper and I thought I wish I could be that frisky about getting back to writing my own writing and as I was standing there talking to them I was aware of a curious current that was coming at me from the back of the classroom and I knew that whoever was sending this curious current out at me was sitting and watching every move I made so I glanced over as casually as I could and I found myself gazing right into the same beady eagle eye that was on the back of my paperback copy of *The Banana Factor* by Ted Wylie and I saw that he was sitting there and smiling a vicious cynical smile as he kept staring at me and I thought who the hell does this Ted Wylie think he is anyway and of course I had no way of knowing this but at that exact same instant someone else was 3000 miles away and he was also thinking who the hell does this Ted Wylie think he is anyway and this person was standing on the corner of Madison Avenue and 53rd Street in New York City and he had just finished reading the last page of *The Banana Factor* by Ted Wylie and now he was tugging at his tiny white Viennese goatee and this person was Dr. Max Wittgenstein and he was thinking acid thoughts about Ted Wylie because Ted Wylie was the only patient who had ever walked out on Dr. Wittgenstein before his psychoanalysis was successfully completed and all Ted Wylie ever did during his psychoanalysis was lie there on the couch and tell endless anecdotes about all the pet animals he used to have as a child and these animals included: ants, rabbits, frogs, cats, gerbils, butterflies, dogs, guinea pigs, ducks, hamsters, snakes, canaries, toads, monkeys, parakeets, salamanders, goldfish, turtles, squirrels, pigeons, bats, eels, chipmunks, tadpoles, crabs, white mice, lobsters, spiders, snails, rats, parrots, chickens, scorpions, and wasps.

And Ted Wylie would lie there on the couch and he would tell Dr. Max Wittgenstein about how he had constructed a cardboard carton with a glass window in it so he could sit and watch all the curious disasters that took place when he put one species in with another species and he would tell endless anecdotes about what happened when he put lobsters in with canaries or mice in with spiders or frogs in with cats or chickens in with monkeys or eels in with goldfish or snakes in with crabs and sometimes he would put 3 or 4 different species in with one another to see what would happen and he had a regular colosseum going in that cardboard carton and his ultimate fantasy was to build an enormous astrodome where he could toss in every known species in the world and then slam the doors and watch what happened from an overhead helicopter and Ted Wylie said he estimated it would take about one week for all those species to annihilate one another and he had it figured that the only species that would survive would be lions and elephants and black widow spiders and while Ted Wylie kept telling all his endless anecdotes Dr. Max Wittgenstein would sit patiently and try to figure what extraordinary atrocities had happened to Ted Wylie's psyche in his fearful early years to make him into such a twisted witness of the sufferings of all these other species and once Dr. Wittgenstein leaned forward in his chair and he asked:

"How would you like it if zomeone lock you up in a kardboard karton zo you kouldn't get out?"

And Ted Wylie recoiled from that question as if he had been struck in the face because he couldn't stand the thought of being locked up with anything and in fact it was hard enough for him to spend 40 minutes in Dr. Wittgenstein's office with the door closed but he recovered from that question and he kept right on with more endless anecdotes and about halfway through the first year of his analysis Ted Wylie began telling a story about how he tossed a lot of wasps in with 6 pet mice and the wasps began stinging all the white mice to death but just then Dr. Wittgenstein leaned forward and he said:

"Zomezing happen ven you vas a zmall child makez you curl up in a zmall body ball inzide yourzelf iz vy you put deze animalz in un enclozure und unlez ve find out vat iz dat den you iz in big trouble."

But Ted Wylie wasn't all that interested in finding out what it was in his early childhood that made him so afraid of enclosures because he just wanted to get on with his endless anecdote about how the white mice got back at all those wasps before they died so Dr. Wittgenstein sat back and he kept listening as Ted Wylie told how the dying mice ate all the wasps and then Ted Wylie went right on to tell what happened when he tossed 17 pet canaries in with 13 pet garter snakes and that was more than Dr. Wittgenstein could take so he leaned forward again and he challenged Ted Wylie's use of that word "pet" because he said "pet" usually signified something one felt something for but as Ted Wylie seemed to be incapable of feeling anything for anything Dr. Wittgenstein said:

"Vy not ve juzt call dem 'zubchektz.' "

And that was all right with Ted Wylie because he didn't much care what you called something so long as he could get on with more of his endless anecdotes and he went on to describe what happened when he tossed 3 black bats in with a week-old kitten and that was when Dr. Wittgenstein leaned forward and he said in a sharp voice:

"Maybe zaves uz time if you chust write down deez tings."

And that seemed like a pretty dumb idea to Ted Wylie but when he left Dr. Wittgenstein's office that day he went to a stationery store and he bought a few looseleaf notebooks and a lot of reams of filler paper and then he went off to an Automat on 42nd Street where he sat at a corner table and he began to write page after page of endless anecdotes about all the curious disasters that took place when he tossed a lot of different species into the cardboard carton and these stories were antic and zany yet they were told with such a beady eagle eye for detail that when Ted Wylie shaped all the chaos and mayhem into something resembling a novel and he typed up the manuscript and he sent it off to an agent within one week it was sold to a major publisher who brought it out as *The Cardboard Carton* in hard cover and it was the oddity of the season because no one knew what to make of it except one book reviewer who said it was spellbinding in its weird and eerie sense of heartless cruelty and the book began to catch on with the reading public and Ted Wylie began to make piles and piles of money off the paperback sales and his agent sold the film rights to Hollywood and the screenwriters tried to rewrite the character of the zombie author who keeps peeking into the cardboard carton and they even gave him a kinky girlfriend to get a little love interest into the story line and when this movie version came out it won an Oscar for the actor who played the zombie author so then the producers began to plan a Broadway production and while all this was going on Ted Wylie just kept sitting in the 42nd Street Automat and he kept writing more endless anecdotes in his looseleaf notebooks only this time they were about a zombie banana man who lived in Kansas who played a lot of far out sex games with a gang of 10 year old kids and when Ted Wylie shaped all this chaos and mayhem into something resembling a novel and he typed up the manuscript and he sent it off to an agent within one week it was sold to another major publisher who bought it out as *The Banana Factor* in hard cover and paperback simultaneously and this was the novel that Dr. Max Wittgenstein had just finished reading as he stood there on the corner of Madison Avenue and 53rd Street and Dr. Wittgenstein had just slammed the book shut and he had just tugged at his tiny white Viennese goatee as he muttered to himself:

"Who de hell duz zis Ted Vylie tink he iz anyvay?"

And Dr. Wittgenstein shook his head in disgust because he thought the whole idea of having a Banana Factor rating system was foolish and futile and infantile and furthermore it offended his years of training as a psychoanalyst to think in such glib terms and what was worst of all was that Dr. Wittgenstein himself had been using his own MF score rating system for 35 years and that stood for a patient's Marbles Factor which was the chances of someone's going completely marbles and Dr. Wittgenstein used this same rating system whenever he interviewed a new patient because he would sit and listen to the person's life history and then he would tug at his tiny white Viennese goatee as he thought:

"Diz perzon haz un 83 perzent chanz of going marblz."

And so it was no wonder Dr. Wittgenstein was angry when he finished reading *The Banana Factor* by Ted Wylie because the book had unwittingly hit on the exact same rating system Dr. Wittgenstein had been using all his life as an analyst and now Dr. Wittgenstein was standing on the corner of Madison Avenue and 53rd Street and he was tugging at his tiny white Viennese goatee as he thought:

"Ted Vylie iz zo zick he haz un 95 perzent chanz uf going marblz."

And then Dr. Wittgenstein began scurrying along 53rd Street toward his Fifth Avenue office and at that exact same instant Ted Wylie was still sitting in the back of my classroom and he was smiling a vicious cynical smile as he fixed me with his beady eagle eye and I began to feel like an innocent chipmunk that had just been tossed into a cardboard carton with 5 killer monkeys so I turned and I walked out of the classroom and I headed on down to the dining room and Ted Wylie followed after me and I sat down at a corner table and I began to nibble away at my plate of tuna salad and Ted Wylie came right over and he sat down next to me so I turned and I asked him please to pass me the pitcher of iced tea and then I said he must be Ted Wylie because I recognized his photo on the back of his novel *The Banana Factor* that I had just finished reading and I lied and I told him I liked his book okay but Ted Wylie didn't show any sign of acknowledging my friendly remark because he just fixed me with his beady eagle eye and he said I must be Eliot Morrison because he recognized my photo on the back of my novel *A Dream of Clarence* that he had just finished reading and he didn't bother to lie about liking it because he said he thought it was nothing but a rotten tedious piece of nonwriting so I asked him if it was so bad then why did he bother reading it all the way through to the end and Ted Wylie just fixed me with his beady eagle eye and he said:

"That's my business."

And that sounded ominous so I changed the subject and I asked him why he had agreed to come teach at the San Marcos Writers Conference and Ted Wylie smiled his vicious cynical smile and he said:

"When old what's his name Ralph Perry came to Los Angeles a couple of months ago and asked me to teach at this asshole writers conference I was about to tell him to go fart off because *The Banana Factor* was being made into a major motion picture and *The Cardboard Carton* was in rehearsal for a Broadway opening so why the fuck did I want to play guru to a lot of student doodlers who couldn't write their way out of a wastebasket but then something made me change my mind."

And Ted Wylie paused and I could tell he was waiting for me to ask him what it was that made him change his mind but I didn't feel like playing into his game so I got up and I walked around him to get the pitcher of iced tea and I brought it back to my seat and I poured myself a glass of insipid iced tea and then I said I knew the actress who was playing the female lead in the Broadway version of *The Cardboard Carton* and I said this actress wanted to know what she was supposed to be playing in his play because she doesn't understand why she has to screw that zombie author right there onstage in front of an enormous mirror in the last act and when I said that Ted Wylie slapped his head with his hand and he said:

"My christ that girl is dumb and I don't care what she thinks she's supposed to be playing in my play so long as she just takes her clothes off and fucks that guy onstage in front of that enormous mirror so the audience can get to see them do it double."

And Ted Wylie had such a cool psychotic look on his face that he seemed to be from another planet but I went right on and I asked him if he thought Cindy Stevens was so dumb then why did he cast her in the first place and Ted Wylie said:

"The actress who played the part in the movie version told us we'd have to get someone who didn't have any brains at all to go along with what we wanted in the stage version so I told the director to go out and find me the dumbest actress in New York City and he said that was a pretty tall order because there were some really dumb ones out there and I said he could hold dumbdumb auditions for all I cared just so he came back with the dumbest of the dumb so he went out and he was gone for 3 weeks checking all the acting schools and the modeling agencies and the casting offices and he finally brought back this godforsaken gorgeous creature with bright gold hair and loose full breasts and 2 ice blue tiny iris eyes and I asked her what other shows she had ever done and she said she had been in a couple of Broadway plays and she told me once she had played Lady Macbeth out in Detroit so I asked her how she had played her and she said she had this idea about how Lady Macbeth didn't only wash her hands in the sleepwalking scene but she was washing her hands every time she was onstage she kept going scrub scrub scrub all the while she was talking to Macbeth or Duncan or Banquo and when she said that I knew she didn't have the brains of a brain-damaged rabbit so I said she was just the right actress to play in my play.''

And I was beginning to get angry as Ted Wylie kept going on about how dumb he thought Cindy was so I changed the subject and I asked him what made him change his mind about teaching at this writers conference and when I said that Ted Wylie smiled his vicious cynical smile and he said:

"You.''

And I choked on a sip of my iced tea and I asked:

"Me?''

And Ted Wylie fixed me with his beady eagle eye and he said:

"That's right Morrison it was you that made me change my mind about teaching at this asshole writers conference.''

And I said I didn't know what he meant by that so he leaned forward toward me and he said he had always wanted to write about a writer who wasn't really writing and he said what better place to find that kind of a tormented bird than on the staff of some asshole writers conference so when Ralph Perry asked him to come teach at San Marcos he agreed and then a few days later when Maureen Talbot came down to Los Angeles to get laid Ted Wylie made her start talking about all the writing teachers on the San Marcos faculty so she talked about Laura Perry and Miriam Morse and Gwendolyn Field and when she got to Eliot Morrison she said he was a writer who hadn't really written anything for the last 5 years and Ted Wylie knew he had his man so he ran out and he bought up everything Eliot Morrison had ever written which wasn't much because there was only one lousy novel about some idiot kid named Clarence who gets himself killed in a freak accident and it was nothing but a rotten tedious piece of nonwriting but that was okay because Ted Wylie said he was still going to write his new novel about me because I was a writer who was not really writing and as he said this I sat there aghast at everything he was saying but he went right on and he said:

"I've already done a lot of research on you Morrison because I've talked with your crazy ex-wife Clara and my god you really did a job on her because she'll never write another line for as long as she lives and I also talked with Marcia Masters your agent and she also shares my opinion of your lousy first novel although she's much too ladylike to say so to your face and I also talked with that businessman over there who sat next to you on your plane flight out of here from New York when you were reading my novel *The Banana Factor* and you were lying to me just now Morrison because you didn't like my last novel one bit and you even said it was pretty sophomoric stuff."

And I thought I have to stay calm because the only reason Ted Wylie is telling me all these things is because he's hoping I'll hop through a lot of hoops for him so then he can run off and write about me and I thought to hell with him and besides how do I know he isn't telling me a lot of bullshit lies about how he's already talked with Clara and with Marcia Masters and he didn't seem to pick up on it when I said I knew Cindy Stevens and maybe he doesn't even know I've been having an on again off again affair with her over this past year and I thought I'm going to call this bastard's bluff so I looked him right in his beady eagle eye and I asked him who that businessman was that I was sitting next to on the plane flight out here and Ted Wylie said:

"He says his name is Robert Ingersoll and he just gave me 17 yellow legal pads of the most incomprehensible ballpoint scrawling I've ever seen and I'm going to toss the whole thing at Maureen Talbot and let her do the manuscript conference with him because I don't want to waste any of my time on it."

And then I shifted back and I said I wanted to read whatever Ted Wylie wrote about me and he smiled his vicious cynical smile and he said:

"I'm afraid you have the wrong idea Morrison because I said I was going to be writing my new novel about you and not for you and so you'll just have to wait and buy the book when it comes out like everyone else."

And I said I wasn't sure I liked the idea of Ted Wylie's using me as the main character in his new novel and he said he didn't care a damn whether I liked the idea or not because we'd do our first interview tomorrow afternoon at 4:00 PM in his room and I said I wasn't sure I'd be there and he said he was sure I'd be there because I had too much at stake to stay away and just then Maureen Talbot came over to our table and she handed Ted Wylie a large manila envelope and he took it and he shook it open and the contents went spilling out all over the table and there were lots of student manuscripts and there was a room key and there was also a little celluloid nameplate that said:

TED WYLIE
FICTION

And Ted Wylie snorted a short snort of scorn and he tossed the nameplate over his shoulder and then he began leafing through the student manuscripts and he began muttering comments about how it looked like a lot of shit and Maureen Talbot said she'd be happy to read through the manuscripts and write out plot summaries so Ted Wylie wouldn't have to waste his time reading everything himself but he waved that idea away with his hand because he said he wanted to see with his own eyes just how bad these writers really were and besides he said he was a fast reader and he could get through the whole batch in less than an hour and he said he was going to be merciless in his criticism but he said Maureen Talbot could take those 17 yellow legal pads of ball-point scrawling by Robert Ingersoll and do that one herself and she nodded and she wrote a note to herself in her notebook and then she reminded Ted Wylie he was supposed to give the Thursday evening lecture about how he wrote *The Banana Factor* and Ted Wylie said:

"I'm not going to give any fucking lecture about how I wrote any fucking novel."

And Maureen Talbot said:

79

"But it's in the brochure and it says you'll also answer questions afterwards—"

And Ted Wylie slammed his hand down hard on the table and he said:

"I don't give a fuck what it says in the fucking brochure because I am not going to give any fucking talk about any fucking *Banana Factor* and the only reason I agreed to come to this asshole writers conference was so I could pick up some material for the new novel I'm writing right now and I told you all about all that when I was fucking you down in Los Angeles."

And Maureen Talbot straightened her back and she shot a fast glance at me and then she said she'd better go speak to Ralph Perry about the Thursday evening lecture and Ted Wylie said she could go speak to Jesus Christ about it for all he cared so Maureen Talbot turned and she left the dining room and Ted Wylie said:

"As for you Morrison I'll see you tomorrow afternoon at 4:00 PM in my room."

And Ted Wylie got up and he walked out of the dining room and I sat there for a long while sipping at my insipid iced tea and I was trying to sort out everything Ted Wylie had just said to me and I was wondering whether he was lying to me when he said he'd already talked to Clara and to Marcia Masters and I got up and I went out onto the porch and down the wooden stairs and out along the narrow strip of beach and I kept walking until I was far enough out so I could watch the great waves as they came in to break against the shore and as I was looking out at the open ocean there was someone standing at a window of the second floor of the hotel and looking down at me through a set of field binoculars and this person was watching every move I made and occasionally he would lay his binoculars aside and jot down a few fast notes in an open notebook and then he would look through his binoculars some more and this person was Ted Wylie and he had just finished making love to Maureen Talbot a few moments ago and it had been a swift cynical act in which Ted Wylie fixed his beady eagle eye on Maureen Talbot's face as he manipulated her sex with his left hand

and he made a lot of mental notes on how Maureen Talbot opened and closed her mouth as he kept tickling her clitoris and how her eyes went wide with surprise as he rammed his right hand on into her vagina and how she gasped out loud as he clenched his right hand into a fist and pulled it back and forth inside of her until she came and now Ted Wylie was standing over at the window looking down at me through his field binoculars and Maureen Talbot was lying on the bed watching Ted Wylie watching me and after a while Maureen Talbot said she talked with Ralph Perry and he said he would pay Ted Wylie an extra $250 if he would do the Thursday evening lecture and Ted Wylie snorted with scorn and he said:

"Tell him to make it an extra $500."

And Maureen Talbot said Ted Wylie ought to have a heart because Ralph Perry would have to take the $500 out of his life savings and Ted Wylie said he didn't have a heart and he wanted $500 so Maureen Talbot said:

"Okay so you'll get your $500 because Ralph Perry really wants you to do that Thursday evening lecture but I think you're being a pretty nasty bastard about it."

And Ted Wylie told Maureen Talbot to tell Ralph Perry to have the check ready right after the Thursday evening lecture and Maureen Talbot said okay and then she said:

"Do you think Eliot Morrison is a good writer?"

And Ted Wylie focused his binoculars down to where I was standing on the narrow strip of beach and he said:

"I don't think Eliot Morrison is a writer at all and that's exactly the kind of nonwriter I want to write about in my new novel."

And Maureen Talbot thought about that for a moment and then she sat up in bed and she opened the large manila envelope and she took out all the student manuscripts and she told Ted Wylie he'd better get started on reading them so Ted Wylie hung his field binoculars on the side of a chair and he sat down and he picked up the pile of student manuscripts and he began leafing through them and muttering about how it looked like a lot of shit and from time to time he would laugh a cruel laugh and read a few lines out loud to

Maureen Talbot before he tossed the entire manuscript over his shoulder so it landed smack flat on the floor and he would go on to the next one and just then I turned around and I began walking along the narrow strip of beach back up to the hotel and I went through the lobby and I got on the ancient elevator and I went up to my room where I lay down on my bed and my head was so heavy I drifted right off into a twilight sleep and this was the dream I dreamed:

I was standing outside a paperback bookstore where I saw Ted Wylie's new novel was on display and it had a garish black and blue cover with the title in big block letters across the bottom which said THE WRITER WHO WAS NOT REALLY WRITING and above the title there was a photo of me showing my shaggy hair and my crumpled coat and the dislocated look in my eyes so I went into the bookstore to buy a copy so I could see what bullshit lies Ted Wylie had written about me but just then I realized I had no money in my pockets so I decided I would have to try and shoplift a copy and just as I thought that thought a State Trooper came up behind me and he was aiming his service revolver at me and he began yelling out at me to freeze so I froze and he said I was under arrest for having thought that thought about shoplifting a copy of Ted Wylie's new novel about me and he said that was a very serious charge and the judge would probably throw the book at me and I said it was bad enough that Ted Wylie had written his rotten book about me but why did it have to be thrown at me also and when I said that the State Trooper snorted a short snort of scorn and he handcuffed my 2 ankles together so I had to hop my whole body up and down like a gigantic foot in order to jump on over to the State Police car and while I was hopping up and down the State Trooper began calling me a weirdo faggot gross kinky voyeuristic Neanderthal and he hit me with his service revolver and I fell down and he began kicking me in the head with his great black leather boot and all the bystanders outside the bookstore began applauding like crazy as I lay there stone cold unconscious on the sidewalk—

And I woke up from this dream to the sound of a lot of applause that was coming from downstairs and I looked at my wristwatch and I saw it was 9:40 PM and I realized I had missed dinner and whatever the Monday evening program was and then I remembered it was someone from *Writers World* who had just given a talk on how to make agents pay attention to you and as the applause died down I heard Ralph Perry's voice float out over the night air and he was saying gosh he'd never heard a better evening speaker in his entire life and then the conferees began coming out of the main hall and they were all talking about writing as if it were some kind of a trip they were planning to take to some foreign country as soon as they got all their travel clothes together and suddenly there was a knock on my door so I jumped out of bed and I opened the door and I saw Jose from the reception desk and he said there was a long distance phone call for me on the pay phone so I followed him on down in the ancient elevator and I went over to the phone booth and I picked up the receiver and I said hello and the voice on the other end said:

"Hello shitface and have you screwed any of your stupid students yet?"

And I said hello Clara and she said:

"Don't you hello Clara me because I asked you a question and I want to know if you've screwed any of your stupid students yet?"

And I said for gods sake Clara I just arrived and I taught my first fiction class this morning and she said:

"Oh so you taught your first fiction class this morning and what did you give them that old routine agout the distant brook that keeps on babbling to itself about itself?"

And I said as a matter of fact that was one of the things I was talking about this morning and Clara said:

"Well and I bet you had all those cute little chickeepoos sitting and creaming in their seats and now they're probably all lining up outside your door to get a good look at how big your own babbling brook is and tell me Morrison how big is it these days and is it still a good stiff 7 inches or has it begun to waste away since the last time I saw it?"

And I said it was doing just fine these days and I said incidentally I was wondering if Clara had been talking with anyone about me recently and Clara said:

"You bet your sweet ass I've been talking with someone about you recently because I was talking to old Ralph Perry yesterday about what a wretched letch you are and how he ought to fire your ass the hell out of there so you could get back to New York and begin trying to write your own writing."

And I said I knew all about all that but this was different because this was urgent because this was an emergency and I needed to know if Clara had been talking with anyone else about me recently because it could be very serious and when I said that Clara said:

"Oh yeah well so is what I'm talking about very serious."

And Clara hung up on me before I could find out whether or not she'd been talking with Ted Wylie so I stood there in the pay phone booth and I looked at my wristwatch and I saw it was 10:00 PM and that meant it was 1:00 AM in New York and I knew Marcia Masters was always up late so I pulled out a pocketful of change and I dialed her home phone number and I dropped a lot of change into the pay phone and after a few rings Marcia Masters answered and I said hello this is Eliot Morrison out at my ridiculous writers conference in California and I just wanted to know if she knew someone named Ted Wylie and had he been in touch with her recently and Marcia Masters said:

"Darling of course I know who Ted Wylie is because I met him several years ago when the film version of his first novel *The Cardboard Carton* opened in New York and I told him then I thought he was an absolutely brilliant writer but no darling he has not been in touch with me recently although I did happen to have lunch with his agent just last week."

And I said thanks a lot and I was sorry to bother her and then I hung up and I thought Ted Wylie was lying to me unless he got his agent to pump Marcia Masters for a lot of information about me but I thought that would have been a pretty weird luncheon with one writer's agent trying to get information out of another writer's

84

agent so the first writer could write a new novel about how the second writer wasn't really writing and I thought the whole thing was highly unlikely so I began to push at the door of the pay phone booth but it stuck so I had to press with my full body weight against it before it gave way and opened and I went bursting out into the hotel lobby past Jose at the reception desk who was sound asleep with his head resting sideways on page 49 of *The Banana Factor* by Ted Wylie and I got on the ancient elevator and I went back upstairs to my room and I knew I wasn't going to be able to sleep for a while so I placed a chair in front of the window and I sat there leaning my head out into the night air so I could look up at the stars that were up there in that great vacancy of space and the only other person who was still awake in the hotel then was Mrs. Ruiz on the fourth floor and she was slipping her long slender fingers between the curtains of her window so she could peer down at the narrow strip of beach and she began to remember all the nights when she used to have bullfights in her bedroom with Mr. Ruiz and she remembered how Mr. Ruiz used to like to strip naked and go snorting and cavorting around the room clapping his hands together in a rhythmic beat and shouting out OLÉ and then he would begin to paw at the dust with one hoof and he would lower his snout and he would flare out his nostrils in the air and his thick stiff Latin prick would stick out straight ahead as he went crashing into Mrs. Ruiz and he would go bumping her all around the room and try to mount her from the rear and Mrs. Ruiz remembered that was when she spit at Mr. Ruiz a quick bitter spit and then she threw him out of her room and she locked the door and she swore she never wanted to see him again and then she sat down at her desk and she began to write an epic novel about 17 generations of a noble Spanish family that went through blood duels and misty castles and exquisite senoritas and always overlooking everything there was the chaste gaze of the Latin Catholic Christ that was a fierce archangel sunlight blazing down on the white hot sandstone and now Mrs. Ruiz was on the last chapter of this epic novel and she was peering down at the narrow strip of beach and I was leaning my head out into the night air and I was wondering what it would be like to fuck Esther Martin in her bright canary yellow dress and I began to think of all the other things I could think of that were yellow and I thought of squash yellow and daffodil yellow and fresh lemon yellow and pear yellow and pineapple yellow and tired old lion eye yellow and buttered ear of corn yellow and autumn leaf yellow and mustard yellow and urine yellow and solo cello yellow and yellow pencil yellow and hayfields in bright daylight yellow and warm sand on narrow strip of beach yellow and mellow banana peel yellow and after I had thought all these thoughts I lay down on my bed and I fell asleep.

_____

This is the end of chapter four of this lousy novel and by this time you've probably figured out that I am out to get you so giddy with dizziness that your whole head will begin to feel awash in a conceptual stew and your toes will begin to tingle and your ears will begin to ring with a million long distance collect phone calls and there will be a hundred million live flies copulating inside your braincave as you keep reading this lousy novel all the way through to the end until you no longer believe your eyes that can see and your eyes that can smile and your eyes that can fill with madcap sadness and your eyes that can dilate with passion and your eyes that are alive with surprise and your eyes that can spy with sideways sight and your wide open eyes that are eating the air as you keep reading these lines that I am trying to write right now.

five/Tuesday

And Harry Holton and Sylvester Appleby the 2 kitchen boys were lounging around the small enclosure that housed the garbage pails outside the kitchen of the San Marcos Hotel and Harry Holton was talking about the waitress who worked at Betty's Diner off Route One and Sylvester Appleby was listening and agreeing with everything Harry Holton was saying as Harry Holton said:

"I'm telling you man that waitress is definitely and unquestionably wide open because you can see by all the secret sexual signals that she's sending out."

And Sylvester Appleby began nodding his head so hard that his hair fell all over his eyes because Sylvester Appleby was only 16 years old and he was a high school sophomore so what did he know about anything and he was also tall and sandy haired and he had a shy sideways smile and he was an awkward soul but he was enormously likable in his unassuming stupidity and he was working at the San Marcos Hotel over this summer so he could be close to his friend Harry Holton who was 19 years old and he had just finished his freshman year at Stanford University and he had told Sylvester

Appleby all sorts of stories about how great college was and how everyone was always going off to the foothill bars and getting laid and Harry Holton said he himself had gotten laid dozens of times over this past year and there was nothing to it because all you had to do was act as if you knew what you were doing but he said the real trick was to figure out whether a girl really wanted to get laid or not and he said he had learned a perfect way of doing this because he had mastered the Stanford secret sexual signal system which had been worked out on some computers by a couple of graduate students at the Stanford Research Center and he said once you knew this system really well then all you had to do was watch a girl very carefully and do a fast readout of the way she tilted her head and bent her elbow and twisted her wrist and then after you made a few fast computations in your head you could figure out whether she really wanted to get laid or not and Harry Holton said the theory behind this secret sexual signal system had been developed several years ago by a psychology major who wrote a 1717-page doctoral dissertation that was in the stacks of the Stanford library and this dissertation said there were trillions of tiny neutrinos that were racing through our bodies each instant of our inner lives and these neutrinos picked up all sorts of psychosexual messages that told everything there was to tell about everyone except one had to figure out how to read these neutrinos in the right way because as it said in the doctoral dissertation:

> These trillions of tiny neutrinos are curious currents that are continuously running through us and our consciousness cannot contain what they are saying but we can read their secret meaning if we will simply learn a few complicated mathematical formulas and that way we can figure out whether or not someone really wants to get laid.[17]

And this was pretty heavy stuff and the footnote didn't help that much because it referred the reader to another doctoral dissertation that was in the stacks of the Berkeley Public Library at the University of California and Harry Holton checked that out and he also read through all 1717 pages of the doctoral dissertation in the Stanford Library and this was the only serious reading Harry Holton did during his whole freshman year of college but he made up his mind he was going to master the secret sexual signal system so he began memorizing all the complicated mathematical formulas and then he began going off to all the foothill bars where he would sit alone at one end of a bar sipping at a Tom Collins and he would pick out a girl at the other end of the bar and he would begin to study her very closely and he would do a fast readout on how she tilted her head and bent her elbow and twisted her wrist and then he would feed all this data into his braincave computer and he would let it all slosh around awhile until it sent back the answer as to whether or not this particular girl really wanted to get laid and usually by the time Harry Holton had gone through this readout and computation in his head the girl would have left the bar and she would probably be screwing her ass off in the backseat of someone else's car but that didn't bother Harry Holton because he was more interested in learning how to work the secret sexual signal system and now Harry Holton was telling Sylvester Appleby all about how foolproof the system was and how you just had to work hard to get the whole thing right but Harry Holton said he would teach the system to Sylvester Appleby if he promised to take it very seriously and spend a lot of time working at it on his own and Sylvester Appleby promised he would do these things if Harry Holton would teach him the system and just to show how serious Sylvester Appleby was about it he began writing down all the things Harry Holton ever told him in a small pocket notebook and these are some of the things Sylvester Appleby wrote down:

> Harry Holton says if a girl twists her wrists clockwise while she is talking to you then that means she really wants to get laid unless she is also bending her elbow in against her waist and that means you better stay away from her.

> Harry Holton says if a girl tilts her head sideways while she is talking to you then that means she really wants to get laid but if

you don't do it fast then she will hate you for the rest of her life.

Harry Holton says if a girl tells you she doesn't really want to get laid then that means she does really want to get laid but if she tells you she does really want to get laid then that is a sure sign that she doesn't really want to get laid.

And when Sylvester Appleby was off by himself he would take out his small pocket notebook and he would read over all these things and he would try to learn them all by heart so when the time came for him to get laid with a girl he would know all about how to do it the way it ought to be done and Sylvester Appleby was working this summer at the San Marcos Hotel so he could save up enough money and go down to Mexico City with Harry Holton at the end of the summer and Harry Holton promised to take Sylvester Appleby to a real Mexican whorehouse if Sylvester Appleby would pay for all their food and gas and also pay for the whorehouse bill as well and Sylvester Appleby had agreed although he wasn't sure why they had to go all the way down to Mexico City and spend a lot of money to go to a real Mexican whorehouse when the secret sexual signal system was supposed to tell them all they needed to know about when a girl really wanted to get laid but then what did Sylvester Appleby know about all this and he was just glad he had a friend like Harry Holton who would take the time to teach him everything he needed to know like he was doing right now in the small enclosure that housed the garbage pail outside the kitchen because Harry Holton was saying:

"I'm telling you man she is definitely and unquestionably wide open and it would be really easy to get into her pants."

But Sylvester Appleby hadn't been paying close attention so he asked:

"Into whose pants?"

And Harry Holton frowned a frown of disgust and he said:

"The waitress that works at Betty's Diner off Route One dummy and listen if you're not going to pay close attention to what

I'm telling you then I just won't bother teaching you any more of the secret sexual signal system."

And Sylvester Appleby felt his heart begin to beat in rapid panic beats and he said:

"I'm sorry Harry honest I am and I swear I'll pay really close attention to everything you say from now on."

And there was a long pause and Harry Holton frowned another frown of disgust and then he said:

"Listen did you write that letter I told you to write so you could slip it to the waitress when we both go up to Betty's Diner on Thursday evening after work?"

And Sylvester Appleby gulped a big gulp and he said yeah he'd written the letter and he went groping around for it in his coat pocket and when he found it he pulled it out and he handed it over for Harry Holton to read and this is what it said:

Dear Waitress at Betty's Diner:

Hi there I'm the guy that comes in with my friend Harry Holton and Harry Holton's the one who knows all about the secret sexual signal system and we've both been noticing the way you twist your wrist and bend your elbow and tilt your head sideways and Harry Holton says that's always a sure sign you really want to get laid so if it's okay with you then we'll both be over there on Thursday evening and all 3 of us can go out and get laid in the back of our pickup truck and everything will go okay because Harry Holton knows all there is to know about these things.

Very truly yours,
Sylvester Appleby

And Harry Holton read the letter over and he narrowed his eyes significantly and he sucked in on his cheeks and he began to shake his head and he said:

"No good."

And Sylvester Appleby said:

"Is it no good because it isn't written okay?"

And Harry Holton said:

"No dummy because it's written okay except you blow the whole thing when you come right out and tell her we both know she really wants to get laid because if you tell her that then she'll say she doesn't really want to get laid because that's the way the secret sexual signal system works so you have to pretend you think she doesn't really want to get laid."

And Sylvester Appleby began nodding his head until his hair fell all over his eyes and he gulped a big gulp and he crumpled up the letter and he tossed it over into an open garbage pail and Harry Holton said:

"We'll just have to go up to Betty's Diner on Thursday evening and play the whole thing by ear."

And Sylvester Appleby kept nodding his head because he was hoping Harry Holton would forget about that dumb letter where he almost blew the whole thing by telling the waitress something you're not supposed to tell her and Sylvester Appleby knew that was just one more example of how dumb he was and it was a lucky thing for him he had a good friend like Harry Holton to keep teaching him all the things he needed to know and as he was thinking all these things I sat down in the back of Ted Wylie's fiction class and I began watching Ted Wylie smile his vicious cynical smile as he began attacking a lot of student manuscripts in front of the whole class and he would pick up a short story and he would read a short section like the following:

Elmer wanted MaryLou but he also wanted to write about MaryLou so he never knew whether he wanted MaryLou or whether he wanted to write about MaryLou so he just sat around and he sighed a lot.

And Ted Wylie snorted a short snort of scorn and he said:

"This is the kind of mindlessness that goes on in all your writing because if this idiot Elmer doesn't know what he wants then how the hell is the reader supposed to know what he wants and I'd say the best thing for this author to do would be to give up writing entirely and go in for tombstone rubbing or animal husbandry or child beating or something really useful.''

And Ted Wylie would fix his beady eagle eye out on the class and challenge anyone to say anything against what he had just said and no one said anything so he smiled his vicious cynical smile and he crumpled up the student manuscript and he tossed it over his shoulder and he went on to attack another student manuscript and as I sat there watching all this I thought Ted Wylie is the most destructive teacher I've ever seen and when the class was over I slipped out the back door and I made my way down to the dining room where I sat alone at a corner table nibbling at some tuna salad and sipped at some insipid iced tea and I saw Harry Holton was standing over by the kitchen door and he was watching Esther Martin in her bright canary yellow dress as she sat on the other side of the dining room and she was poking around at her tuna salad with a plastic fork and Harry Holton did a quick readout of her head tilt and her elbow bend and her wrist twist and he fed all these things into his braincave computer and he let it all slosh around a while until it sent him back an answer that he had hit bingo with Esther Martin because according to the secret sexual signal system Esther Martin was more wide open than any woman he had ever put through his braincave computer so Harry Holton stood there by the kitchen door smirking a dirty smirk as he filed this information away for future reference and then he ducked through the double doors into the kitchen and I sat there at my own table smoking a cigarette and getting ready for my first individual manuscript conference and I remembered Ralph Perry had said we should give each student only half an hour but I knew I couldn't do any decent criticism in less than one hour so I knew I was in for some long afternoons and by the end of the week I would be completely exhausted but I figured what the hell I wasn't doing anything else with my life right now so I took one last long drag on my cigarette and I put it out and I got up and I headed out of the dining room and through the hotel lobby past Jose at the reception desk who was reading page 86 of *The Banana Factor* by Ted Wylie and I kept on going to the reading room where I saw Mary Wilde was already waiting for me so I sat down and I took out her novel manuscript that was titled *Odyssey to Freedom* and this is what it was about:

A young girl hates her parents because they won't let her go out with any of the boys she wants to date so she rigs up a dioxide bomb inside the engine of her father's car and the next day when her father goes into the garage and starts the car there is a terrific sudden dull thud explosion that blows the father straight through the roof of the garage and lands him in the yard next door stone dead and when the mother hears the explosion she lets out a loud shout and she runs over to the telephone to call up the police but when she lifts the receiver it triggers a tiny electronic mechanism hidden inside and a great wave of electricity goes racing through her body so her eyeballs begin to bulge out of her head and her hair begins to stand out straight and she falls down stone dead on the floor so then the young girl packs up all her bags and she runs out of the house and she gets on a train that takes her all the way up to Canada clickety clickety clickety and as she sits there on the train she stares out the window at the passing farmlands and she thinks maybe she shouldn't have killed her parents but then she sighs a long sigh and she says to herself well it's done and it can't be undone and all that really matters now is the new life I'll make for myself in Canada and when the train arrives in Montreal the young girl gets off and she walks down a street and she goes into a coffeehouse and she sits down and she sees there is this handsome young pipe exporter sitting at the next table and he says hello and she says hello and they talk for a few minutes and they both fall in love so they get married and one morning about a month later the young girl is lying in bed next to her handsome young pipe exporter husband and she wonders whether she ought to tell him what she did to her parents and then she just blurts it all out about the dioxide bomb and the tiny electronic mechanism inside the telephone and how both parents fell down stone dead and after she tells all this to her husband she looks him in the eyes and she asks him if it makes him think any less of her for doing what she did and after a long moment her handsome young pipe exporter husband puts his arm around her and he draws her warm tender young body in close to his own body and he whispers in her ear that it only makes him love her more.

And I thought this had to be the most twisted tale of homicide and ersatz romance I had ever read but after listening to the way Ted Wylie attacked all those student manuscripts this morning I was going to try to be as kind and constructive as I could be with Mary Wilde so I told her the one thing I couldn't figure out was whether she was putting me on or not and Mary Wilde looked at me and she said:

"Do you mean is it a spoof and I should say not because I wrote the whole thing out of my heart and the only problem I'm having with it is the ending because I can't decide what to do with this young husband and wife after they pledge their undying love for each other."

And I said she could always have them make a suicide pact and drive their car off the top of Mount Royal and plunge down to their deaths because that way the girl would get punished for what she did to her parents but they would stay close together right up to the end and when I said that Mary Wilde began shaking her head in disagreement and she said:

"But why would these young people want to commit suicide now that they've finally found each other?"

And I thought it was odd that Mary Wilde had no sense of the girl's having done anything wrong by killing off both her parents but I said if you don't want to punish the girl then why not have her tell her handsome young pipe exporter husband that she's pregnant and when I said that Mary Wilde began shaking her head again in disagreement and she said:

"But they've been married for only one month so how could the young girl be pregnant unless you're trying to suggest that she's done something immoral?"

And I thought my god this Mary Wilde is some sort of moral zombie and just then I had a subliminal flash thing that I was standing on the table and peeing all over her novel manuscript but I told myself to stay straight and I said well the young girl could wait for 9 months before she told her handsome young pipe exporter husband about how she knocked off both her parents and then she could also tell him she was pregnant and when I said that Mary Wilde began shaking her head again in disagreement and she said:

"But then they wouldn't be newlyweds anymore and I'd lose all that fresh honeymoon love they have for each other."

And I said listen just do it the way I say and this young girl can give birth to a child that will grow up and kill off both its parents and you can go on like that and before you know it you'll have a whole epic cycle of killer kids killing their parents and falling in love with each other and giving birth to more killer kids and when I said that Mary Wilde sat and stared at me and then she began to pencil a few notes in her open notebook and she began to gather up her novel manuscript and she said:

"I do believe you might have something there Mr. Morrison so I'm going to go off and think about making an epic cycle out of this."

And Mary Wilde looked radiant as she left the reading room and I looked at my wristwatch and I saw it was 2:00 PM and Mildred Manson came in and she sat down and I took out her short story manuscript entitled *Forsaken Heart* but before I had a chance to say anything about it Mildred Manson began talking a torrent of talk and she said:

"I never told you this before Mr. Morrison but my husband Mr. Manson does not approve of my writing and he forbids me to mention it in his presence so I have to fib to him and every year at this time I tell him I'm going up to San Francisco to look at some art shows because if I told him I was writing at a writers conference he'd have a fit because I once wrote a short story about a trip we took to Colorado and Mr. Manson got into a terrible argument with a State Trooper and he made such a fool of himself and when I wrote about it in a short story and I showed it to him his face began to get as red as a beet and he began to wave my short story manuscript around in the air and he shouted out at me about how this was all the thanks he got for taking me to Colorado because I made him out to be such a fool in my short story and ever since then he has forbidden me to mention my writing in his presence and I think he must be jealous of my ability to express my inner creative nature in my writing.''

And I said that's what it sounded like and then I began leafing through *Forsaken Heart* and this is what it was about:

> A high school English teacher falls in love with one of her students who is repeating his senior year so he can score well on his Scholastic Achievement Tests and go off to the college of his choice and every day after school the English teacher meets the senior down by a bridge that overlooks a rushing waterfall and they go walking into the woods where they make love and afterwards the English teacher helps the senior with his studies and when he takes his Scholastic Achievement Tests he scores in the upper 90th percentile so he can go off to the college of his choice and the high school English teacher writes him long letters every day about how her heart is yearning for him but the student never answers any of her letters so at the end of the story the high school English teacher goes and throws herself over the bridge that overlooks the rushing waterfall.

And I had read this short story many times before and I still thought it was a sickening saccharine sentimental manuscript but before I had a chance to say so Mildred Manson leaned forward toward me and she said:

"You remember last year you told me to write out some of those letters that the high school English teacher writes to her student so I wrote out every single one of them."

And Mildred Manson produced a large wad of papers from her purse and she handed them over to me and I glanced at the first page and I saw it was a letter that the English teacher writes to her student and this is how it went:

Dearest Joe:

Remember that first time I called on you in Senior English class and I asked you to read aloud from *The Scarlet Letter* and oh how beautifully you read about the dreadful guilt that Mr. Dimmesdale was feeling toward Hester Prynne and Joe I miss you so much and I wish you would write to me and tell me how do you like the college of your choice and yesterday I went down to the bridge that overlooks the rushing waterfall and do you remember how we used to walk into the woods and make love there and then afterwards I would help you with your studies and you know Joe if I don't hear from you soon then I may just go and throw myself into that rushing waterfall and good luck with your freshman composition class.

Lucy Twitchell

And as I was reading through this letter Mildred Manson leaned forward toward me and she slammed her hand down hard on top of my hand and she said:

"Did you get that reference to *The Scarlet Letter* because that's supposed to bring out all the dreadful guilt that Lucy Twitchell is feeling about having had an illicit relationship with one of her very own Senior English students."

And I said yeah I got it but then I asked Mildred Manson why she didn't develop Lucy Twitchell's death in more detail because I said that must be a pretty spectacular way to go by throwing yourself headfirst into a rushing waterfall but when I said that Mildred Manson took her hand off my hand and she shrank back in her chair and her hand fluttered over her heart and she said:

"I don't want to upset the poor reader with how Lucy Twitchell gets all torn apart on those hard sharp rocks because after all the whole thing is really a metaphor for how her yearning heart is being torn apart each and every day that goes by without any letter from her dearest Joe."

And I said I thought it was still a pretty sickening saccharine sentimental short story and I said it was no wonder Joe never answered any of those sappy love letters and I said the best thing for Mildred Manson to do right now would be to rewrite the whole story one more time and to put in a lot more straightforward specific detail about how they made love and what sort of questions they worked on for the Scholastic Achievement Test and how Lucy Twitchell got torn apart when she went over the rushing waterfall and when I said that Mildred Manson let out a long low wail and she said:

"Are you telling me to rewrite this whole short story all over again because I've already rewritten the thing 3 times and I had to do it secretly late at night after Mr. Manson had gone to sleep because I told you how he hates the idea that I can express my inner creative nature in my writing and I've never told you this before Mr. Morrison but my husband and I have not been living together as man and wife for the past 17 years if you know what I mean."

And Mildred Manson's voice trailed off in the air and she began to dab at here eyes with a tiny handkerchief she took out of her purse so I said listen Mrs. Manson all I'm asking you to do is rewrite this short story one more time so it will be a little less sickening saccharine sentimental and when I said that Mildred Manson snuffled in her tiny handkerchief and then she began to collect her short story manuscript and she got up and she left the reading room and I looked at my wristwatch and I saw it was 3:00 PM and Esther Martin was standing outside in the hotel lobby and she was wearing a bright canary yellow dress and she looked as if she were not quite sure whether she should come in or not so I motioned to her and she walked in cautiously and she sat down and she began staring straight ahead in the air with her large dark startled eyes and I took out her short stories and this is what the first story was about:

Once upon a time there was a young girl named Stevenson who was out walking across a green field under a high wide sky and for as far as she could see there was a living river and the distant hills were rising silent on the horizon and suddenly the angel Gabriel appeared to Stevenson and he shone as if he were alive with light and he began to point over to the East where there was a tall church steeple that seemed to reach right up to the top of the sky and the angel Gabriel told Stevenson to go climb that church steeple and she would see to the very ends of the earth so Stevenson went to the church steeple and she began to climb on up to the top of the tall church steeple and sure enough when she got up there she could see to the very ends of the earth but suddenly she lost her grip and she began to fall down down down all the way down through the air down to the ground where she broke her head wide open and her blood went spilling out all over the green field and when that happened the angel Gabriel disappeared.

And I said the story was exquisite and lyrical but I didn't see the point of it because why did the angel Gabriel tell Stevenson to climb to the top of that tall church steeple if she was only going to fall down and break her head wide open and when I said that Esther Martin just sat there staring straight ahead in the air with her large dark startled eyes and after a long pause she said:

"The angel Gabriel didn't mean for Stevenson to fall."

But I said the angel Gabriel must have known it was dangerous for anyone to climb to the top of that tall church steeple and was Esther Martin trying to say that you shouldn't trust angels in green fields and Esther Martin didn't say anything to that and she just sat there frozen motionless in her chair and I noticed that her eyes were beginning to glaze over as if she had just gone off into an ice age all her own so I reached over and I touched her on the arm but there was no response so I called out Esther Martin in her ear but there was still no response until all of a sudden she blurted out to no one in particular:

"Oh you're always trying to defend yourself!"

And I looked around to see who Esther Martin was talking to but there was no one else there and when I looked back I saw Esther Martin had gathered up her short story manuscripts and she had run out of the reading room in a blur of bright canary yellow dress so I sat there feeling as if I had just had a casual chat with someone from outer space and I looked at my wristwatch and I saw it was 4:00 PM and I thought this is the time I'm supposed to be upstairs in Ted Wylie's room for that interview he wants to do with me but to hell with it because I'm not going to go along with his idea of writing a novel about how I am a writer who is not really writing and besides I'm tired right now and I need to go lie down for a while but for some odd reason I got up and I went out through the hotel lobby past the reception desk where Jose was reading page 89 of *The Banana Factor* by Ted Wylie and I got on the ancient elevator and I pushed the button for the second floor and I went down to Ted Wylie's room and I stood outside his door for a long moment and I thought what the hell am I doing here and just then I heard Ted Wylie's voice call out for me to come in before I had even knocked so I opened the door and I went in and I saw Ted Wylie was sitting in a chair by the window and he had an open notebook in his lap and there was a set of field binoculars hanging from a strap on the back of his chair and Ted Wylie was fixing me with his beady eagle eye as he said:

"Sit down Morrison and tell me who was the greatest influence on your writing."

And I sat down and I said Mozart was the greatest influence on my writing and Ted Wylie smiled a vicious cynical smile and he said:

"How the fuck could a musician like Mozart have any influence on your writing and never mind don't bother answering that because I'm after more important stuff like here you are 39 years old and you haven't really written anything for the last 5 years and yet you set yourself up at this asshole writers conference as a professional writing teacher so I want to know what bullshit lies you tell yourself about why you're not really writing and don't give me any of that bat crap about how you get these weird dizzy spells and a lot of obscene phone calls from your crazy ex-wife and how you have to read your way through mountains of stupid student manuscripts because I don't want to hear a lot of sick excuses for why you're not really writing."

And I said I had no intention of answering any of his questions about why I wasn't really writing and I said the only reason I was up there in his room this afternoon was to tell him to forget about using me as one of the characters in his new novel but Ted Wylie interrupted me and he said:

"No no Morrison you're not going to be just one of the characters in my new novel because you are going to be the single central character in it."

And I said all the more reason for him to forget about it because I said if he did go ahead and publish anything about me I'd sue him for every last cent he had and when I said that Ted Wylie snorted a short snort of scorn and he said:

"Not a chance Morrison because I'll change the names around so you'll be Morris Eliot and there'll be all the usual disclaimers in front of the book about how this is entirely a work of fiction so its characters and events and story lines are wholly imaginary and any similarity or resemblance or likeness to any past or present or future characters or events or story lines is entirely coincidental and that way you won't have a legal leg to stand on and if you do stir up a fuss you'll just be helping to boost my book sales."

And then Ted Wylie reached down and he picked up a paperback copy of my lousy first novel *A Dream of Clarence* and he began rifling through the pages to find something so I sat there staring at the back of my book where there was this photo staring right back at me showing my shaggy hair and my crumpled coat and the dislocated look in my eyes and when Ted Wylie found the page he was looking for he began to read the following passage out loud:

And when Clarence felt the shell begin to slip through his fingers on its way down to the ground then suddenly he began to eat the air of everything he ever felt or thought or saw and he began to taste the acid sadness of his whole life and all the trouble in his bloodstream and the flood of all those bullshit lies that ever made him believe that he could be at all lovable—

And Ted Wylie slammed the book shut and he tossed it over his shoulder so it landed smack flat on the floor behind him and he said:

"That's really nothing but a rotten tedious piece of nonwriting Morrison because what the hell do you mean this character Clarence began to eat the air of everything he ever felt or thought or saw

102

because that's like talking about how many angels can balance on the head of a pin."

And I said it was an idea I had about how everything is always telescoped together in one single instant of air and I said I've experienced time like that a lot of times and I said someone out in Nebraska agreed with me and he thought I was getting pretty close to the problem of the novel in our time and when I said that Ted Wylie began to smile a popelike smile and he said:

"I wouldn't let that silly twiddle go to your head Morrison because the truth is this Clarence character of yours is nothing but an incompetent sap who's so clumsy he goes and blows himself up so I don't know why I should give a flying fuck about him because I'm after more important stuff so why don't you tell me something about your personal life like why did you marry that mad basket case Clara and there must have been something in you that was as loony as fruit juice to let yourself get hooked up with all her fresh fruit juice loony foolishness."

And I said my marriage with Clara was none of his damn business and Ted Wylie scribbled something down in his open notebook and then he said:

"Well then suppose you tell me about that meaningless affair you had with Maureen Talbot when you came to San Marcos 5 years ago and you can begin by describing what the 2 of you liked to do in bed."

And I said my affair with Maureen Talbot was none of his damn business either and Ted Wylie scribbled something else down in his open notebook and then he said:

"Okay Morrison and if you're going to be that way about it then I guess I'll just have to take Maureen Talbot's word for what a tacky lay you are but that seems to be pretty silly especially as you're going to be teaching here all week because you could just as easily go out and get me some fresh material by screwing one of your stupid students and then you could come back up here and tell me all about it and you might begin by trying to screw that Esther Martin who always wears those pissy yellow dresses and I've got a few ideas about some kinky things you could do to her.''

But I was already halfway out of the room and I slammed the door behind me hard and I got in the ancient elevator and I went down to the lobby where I walked onto the porch and I stood there for a long moment staring out at the red and orange sunset and just at that instant Maureen Talbot walked into Ted Wylie's room and she took off all her clothes and she sat down on the bed and she spread her legs apart but Ted Wylie was so busy scribbling in his open notebook about the interview he'd just had with me that he didn't even notice until suddenly he looked up at Maureen Talbot and he said:

"I'm not getting anywhere with Morrison so it's going to be up to you to tell me what the two of you liked to do in bed.''

And Maureen Talbot clamped her legs together and she said:

"Oh come on I can't go telling you all sorts of personal things like that.''

And Ted Wylie snorted a short snort of scorn and he said:

"Of course you can and so stop being such a tight ass and tell me what did he like for you to do?''

And Maureen Talbot thought for a long moment and then she said:

"Well he liked for me to lick at his stiff prick so it would stand up thick and rigid and my god you're not going to put that in your new novel are you?''

And Ted Wylie was scribbling away in his open notebook so Maureen Talbot kept going and she said:

"And he also liked for me to suck on his nuts and slosh them around inside my cheeks and Jesus you're not going to put that in your new novel are you?''

And Ted Wylie was scribbling away in his open notebook so Maureen Talbot kept going and she said:

"And then when he did get his hot cock inside of me he liked to pin both my arms up over my head so I'd be lying there like a piece of meat beneath him and christ you're not going to put that in your new novel are you?''

And Ted Wylie was scribbling away in his open notebook so Maureen Talbot let out a wretched little whimper and she said:

"How can you know when it's okay to tell the truth about someone else?"

And just at that instant I was still standing downstairs on the porch and staring out at the red and orange sunset and after a while I turned around and I went back upstairs to my room and I lay down on my bed and I fell asleep and I dreamed this dream:

I was on a nationwide television talk show that Ted Wylie was moderating and he was saying how much he wanted to be kind and constructive about my lousy first novel *A Dream of Clarence* and he began by holding up a copy for the TV cameras to see and he said: *"This first novel of yours is very well printed and the publishers did an excellent job of putting the numbers on the right pages so one page comes right after another page just the way it is in the novels of Tolstoy and Dostoevski and Dickens and Hemingway and Faulkner so as far as the pagination is concerned you're right up there with all the old masters—however—"* —and here Ted Wylie fixed his beady eagle eye right into the TV camera lens as he went on: *"—however that is as far as I am able to go in recommending your book to our nationwide television talk show audience because as far as the rest of your book is concerned—"* —and here Ted Wylie began ripping pages out of the book and tossing them over his shoulder so they landed smack flat on the studio floor behind him— *"—as far as the rest of your book is concerned it is nothing but a lot of rotten tedious nonwriting and if this television talk show audience will forgive my saying so the rest of your book is nothing but a lot of bullshit!!"* —and at that the studio audience exploded in wild spontaneous applause at what Ted Wylie was saying about my book and I just sat there in my chair staring straight ahead in the air as 3 TV cameras came dollying in to get a close-up look at my shaggy hair and my crumpled coat and the dislocated look in my eyes—

This is the end of chapter five of this lousy novel so that means we're halfway through the whole thing so why don't you take a break and go outside and get a little clean air so you can clear your head of all the fresh fruit juice loony foolishness you've just been reading about only be sure you get back here before too long or else you'll never find out what happens to Esther Martin or Sylvester Appleby or Jose at the reception desk and you'll never know whether Ted Wylie keeps on writing his new novel about how I am a writer who is not really writing and the only way you'll ever find out any of these things is if you keep reading these lines that I am trying to write right now.

six/Wednesday

And Jose stayed awake all night at the reception desk reading *The Banana Factor* by Ted Wylie and now he was on page 127 and he was beginning to get giddy with dizziness and his whole body was beginning to rock backwards and forwards to the rhythm of the writing and anyone watching him would wonder who was Jose this nervous mouse of a man because he had no friends at all and he had no love life at all and all he ever had were these cheap paperback novels he kept reading behind the reception desk and most of the time he didn't have any idea what any of the books were about because all he really knew for sure was whether they made him feel dizzy or not because this was the same kind of dizziness Jose got when he closed his eyes and recited his full name which was Jose Pancho Villa Jimenez Francisco Miguel Pedro Moya Don Carlos Manuel Garcia Humphrey Bogart Mendez Jesus Rodriguez and every time he said this full name over to himself Jose felt very dizzy indeed and Jose could also get the same kind of dizziness every time he thought about his childhood in a tiny village named San Luis Moya which was a little north of Mexico City where Jose learned to read at a very early age because his 17 older brothers and sisters told him it was his job to read in the English language newspaper and find out what time the next scenic tour bus came through San Luis Moya so the Rodriguez children could all go out and form a great long chain line across the dusty dirt road to stop the bus so then they could all climb on board and go running up and down the aisles selling all their various wares to the American tourists and these wares were a lot of wax candles of the beatific madonna and also a lot of wax candles of grotesque erect penises and the Rodriguez children made these candles from some master molds they stole from a traveling salesman and there were also a lot of crudely embalmed bull testicles that the Rodriguez children stole from where the dead bulls were stacked up outside one of the bull rings in Mexico City and they boiled these big bull balls in a weird brew of alcohol and resin until they looked like so many pale brussels sprouts and there were also a lot of handprinted lists of all the whorehouses in Mexico City and what the going rates were and these were the wares the Rodriguez children sold to the American tourists who were on the scenic tour buses and usually they sold a lot of the embalmed bull testicles and a lot of the whorehouse lists and sometimes they sold a few of the grotesque erect penis candles and occasionally they even sold one or two of the beatific madonna candles and then the Rodriguez children got off the bus and they divided up the money among themselves and then they would wait for the small child Jose to read in the English language newspaper and tell them when the next scenic tour bus would come along so they could form another great long chain line across the dusty dirt road and Jose did not like this life at all because he thought those American tourists could go find their own whorehouses and they did not really need the grotesque erect penis candles or the beatific madonna candles and as for the embalmed bull testicles they belonged to the bulls so in between the scenic tour buses Jose would sneak down to a nearby dump where he would sit on top of a great mountain of steaming garbage and he could read much more than just bus schedules there because there were also a lot of old phone books

and torn racing forms and outdated bullfight posters and labels on
empty tomato cans and Jose could even read some beat-up parts of
paperback books and he didn't always understand whatever it was
he was reading but as long as he could sit up there on top of that
great mountain of steaming garbage he could read things over very
slowly and he could taste the sound of each word in his mouth and
then sometimes Jose would begin to feel a real tingling in his feet
and a ringing in his ears as if a tiny mosquito were trying to telephone him long distance collect inside his braincave and then sometimes Jose would begin to get giddy with dizziness as if a lot of flies
were flying in and out of his brainwaves and when this happened
then Jose would know that whatever it was he was reading was very
good indeed and as he grew older Jose would begin to hitch rides on
the scenic tour buses as they came back from wherever they went
with those American tourists and Jose would flag the buses down at
a turn of the dusty dirt road and he would give the bus drivers a few
of the embalmed bull testicles so they would drive him all the way
into Mexico City and Jose would head straight for the men's room
outside one of the big bull rings and this men's room was always pu-
trid with the stench of all the backed-up toilets and the stink of the
place was like the stink of the stalls where the great bulls stomped
around with their heavy hoofs in their own bullshit until it made a
sweet stink in the air and Jose would stand in the middle of this
men's room and he would look at all the scrawlings on the walls that
were there and they were a great mosaic of world writing because
there were more words there than Jose had ever seen before and he
saw there were scrawlings in pencil and scrawlings in ink and scrawlings in crayon and scrawlings in chalk and scrawlings in lipstick and
he saw there were scrawlings in Spanish and English and German
and French and there were some scrawlings in Chinese and Japa-
nese ideograms and there were even a few early Egyptian hiero-
glyphs and Jose didn't care where the scrawlings came from or how
they were made so long as he could stand there in the middle of the
men's room and read them over very slowly and taste the sound of
each word in his mouth and then Jose would try to make up a pic-

ture to go along with each word so he would remember it and sometimes he would stand there for long hours and he would read the names of men with short statements after their names saying what these men were and he would read the names of women with short statements after their names saying what these women did and he would read the phone numbers you could call if you wanted someone to do something to you and he would read the names of places you could go if you wanted to do something to someone else and Jose would stand there and he would read these things over to himself and he would taste each word in his mouth and he would never take his eyes off any of the scrawlings until he had made up a picture to go along with each word so he could remember it and then he would move his eyes over to the next scrawling and one day Jose read a scrawling that was written next to the very last toilet stall and it was in pencil and it was written in the shaky hand of a retired Texas Baptist minister who had visited Mexico City the year before and the words were printed in large block letters and this is what they said:

REPENT AND BE SAVED FOR THE WORLD IS DOMED

And of course the retired Texas Baptist minister meant to write that the world was doomed but his eyesight was getting a little blurry and domed was what he wrote and domed was what Jose read as he stood there in the middle of the men's room and Jose frowned a curious frown as he tried to make up a picture of the world with a large glass dome around it like those glass domes that covered over the wax flowers in the Church of the Immaculate Conception in the tiny village of San Luis Moya and when Jose pictured that picture in his mind he shrugged and he left the men's room and he began to walk back home along the dusty dirt road and that was a long time ago but if anyone were to come up to Jose at the reception desk of the San Marcos Hotel and ask him what the world looked like Jose would pick up a pencil and he would draw a picture of the world with a large glass dome around it because that was how deeply Jose believed everything he ever read and you might say Jose was the ideal reader because reading was the only thing he really enjoyed doing although he didn't understand very much of what he was reading but he always knew when a book took a sudden turn of some sort because his head would begin to spin and dip in an instant of dizziness like when you sit too long in the afternoon sun and pretty soon your whole head feels awash in a conceptual stew and during this past week Jose had been reading *The Banana Factor* by Ted Wylie and he had no idea what the book was about with all its talk of BF scores and the far out sex games with a gang of 10 year old kids but the more Jose kept reading in the book the more he began to get giddy with dizziness and he had stayed awake all last night and now he was on page 127 and he was so giddy with dizziness he didn't even raise his eyes at 11:11 AM on Wednesday morning when I came racing out of the ancient elevator because I had overslept and I was late for my fiction class and I ran on down the hall to the classroom where I went in and over to the old oak desk and I sat down and I looked out over the great vacancy of faces that were all waiting for me to begin talking to them and for an instant there I began to taste the empty space between me and all those students and I began to eat whole areas of air and for a long time I was frozen motionless but then I began to talk about writers and writing and I said all fiction is a skillful distillation of reality and unreality and everyone began to write that line down in their open notebooks and I kept talking about how to write your own writing out of what was real and what was unreal and all the while I kept talking I was aware that there was another voice that was also talking in the back of my braincave and this other voice was saying:

Why do I always bleed when I teach and why is it always such a brilliant spilling as I lacerate my ass in front of a class because it always feels as if I am a football player who fades so far back he loses sight of all possible pass receivers so he stands there in an instant of air as he waits for the crush of muscle that will send him collapsing backwards on himself as he still holds on to that damn ball or else it always feels as if I am a soldier who falls forward over a lot of barbed wire so his buddies can use his body to make a breakthrough and bleeding is needed so he's bloodied or else it always feels as if I am a lay analyst who keeps receiving all these projections from his patients who are working their way through their own undertow so they see him as their father mother brother sister husband wife son daughter lover or whatever else happens to be lacking in their lives or else it always feels as if I am an orphan who is eating his own air and he keeps on wandering around wondering what will become of him or else it always feels as if I am some godforsaken priest who has fallen out of all grace so he keeps tasting the wafer of displacement and these are some of the things it always feels like as I lacerate my ass in front of a class—

And this other voice kept talking in the back of my braincave as I kept telling the class how to write their own writing out of what was real and what was unreal and the students kept writing it all down in their open notebooks except for Betsy Childs who was sitting in the front row and I saw she was doodling a lot of stick figures in her open notebook and these stick figures were all fucking each other in all sorts of oddball positions and when I looked up at Betsy Childs I saw her blouse was unbuttoned 3 buttons down and one breast was hanging loose and juicy like a ripe fruit that was about to fall from a tree branch and Betsy Childs looked up and she saw my eye was eyeing her breast so she smiled a mischievous smile at me and she turned the page of her open notebook and she kept doodling a few more stick figures that were fucking in all sorts of oddball positions and I finished teaching the class by saying all fiction is a skillful distillation of reality and unreality and then I got up from the old oak desk and I ducked out the door and I walked down the hall to the dining room and I went to a corner table where I sat down and I began to sip at some insipid iced tea as the rest of the conferees began to come into the dining room and I saw Harry Holton was standing over by the kitchen door and he was watching for Esther Martin in her bright canary yellow dress so he could point her out to Sylvester Appleby but Esther Martin didn't come into the dining room and she hadn't been in the fiction class either and I began to wonder where she was as I lit a cigarette and I blew the beautiful blue fumes in the air and then I looked at my wrist-watch and I saw it was 1:00 PM so I put the cigarette out and I got up and I walked out of the dining room and down to the reading room where Roberta Heite was already waiting for me and she was tall and thin and she had fierce gray eyes and I sat down and I pulled out her novel manuscript and this is what it was about:

An American girl from East Norwalk in Connecticut goes to the Middle East and she becomes a bedouin and she has her own camel named Fred and she camps out in the desert every night where she sleeps under Fred the camel and there is a small band of friendly Arabs that wanders by and they wake her up so she sings them a lot of songs on her kuishi which is an Arabian guitar that has 17 strings on it and one of the songs she sings is:

here on the sand
I hold your hand
the stars above
will see our love

And the Arabs like the song okay so they ask her to be their chief priestess and she says okay so she gets to settle all their arguments and she performs all their weddings and funerals and a few days later an English airplane flies overhead and it crashes in the desert sand and all the crew is killed except for one copilot who is a handsome young R.A.F. officer and the American girl from East Norwalk nurses the young officer back to life and she asks him will he stay there in the desert with her and with Fred the camel and the R.A.F. officer says okay so the girl sings a funeral service on her kuishi for all the other crew members who got killed and then she buries the airplane in the sand so no one will know a plane crashed there and then she sings a wedding service on her kuishi for the R.A.F. officer and herself and then they both climb on top of Fred the camel and the 3 of them disappear over the dunes.

And I said the plot was pretty dopey and there were also some factual errors about the Middle East because I said for one thing I doubted if there was any such instrument as the kuishi with 17

strings on it but Roberta Heite began shaking her head and she
started explaining how the kuishi was an authentic instrument that
had been invented 23 centuries ago by a bedouin tentmaker out of a
lot of old tent lines and she began to demonstrate what trick finger-
ing it took to play all 17 strings at the same time and her 2 hands
began going lickety split all over her knees and they looked like 2
spider crabs that were racing their way through a mad mating dance
and I asked her why the girl from East Norwalk and the R.A.F. officer had no names because the only character in the whole novel who
had a name was Fred the camel but Roberta Heite wasn't listening
to me because now she was busy sketching a picture of a kuishi in
her open notebook so I thought to hell with it and I leaned back and
I had a subliminal flash thing of spreading Roberta Heite's legs and
letting Fred the camel have a go at her and I wondered how large a
camel's sex could get and I wondered how Roberta Heite would feel
if she were walking around with a lot of camel sap in her vagina but
I snapped myself back and I looked at my wristwatch and I saw it
was 2:00 PM so Roberta Heite closed her notebook and she picked
up her novel manuscript and she left the reading room and Joseph
Baum came bouncing in and he was a small bald-headed man in his
early 60's who looked like a twinkly eyed little mouse and he had a
madcap habit of leaping in and out of his seat and I took out his
novel manuscript and this is what it was about:

> A man inherits 17 million dollars so he buys a major league
> baseball team and he travels around the country with it but the
> team keeps losing games until one day the first baseman gets
> hit in the eye by a line drive and he has to be sidelined so the
> millionaire owner goes in to play first base and when he comes
> up to bat he hits a pitch out of the park for a home run and the
> next time he hits another home run and the next time he hits
> another and this goes on for the rest of the season with the
> millionaire owner hitting home runs out of every park they
> play in so of course the team goes on to win the pennant and
> the world series and by this time the millionaire owner has hit
> more home runs than any baseball player in the history of the
> game.

And I thought this had to be one of the most thinly disguised wish fantasies I'd ever seen and I asked Joseph Baum if he ever played baseball himself and his face fell into one of the saddiest landscapes imaginable and he said:

"No time play baseball because alla time work business."

And I said that's okay only tell me how old is this millionaire owner who keeps hitting all these home runs and Joseph Buam thought for a moment and then he said:

"Lemme see is around 63—yah—is 63 years old."

And I said I didn't see how a 63 year old man could hit a home run out of the park every time he came up to bat and when I said that Joseph Baum leaped to his feet and he shouted out:

"Is easy!!"

And he began to swing both his arms around and he went crashing into the table and he spilled the pages of his novel manuscript all over the floor as he landed flat smack on his back and he lay there with his little feet racing around in the air as if he were running an upside down base path and I helped Joseph Baum get right side up again and I sat him back in his chair and I said listen it's a great story and forgive me for doubting that a 63 year old man could hit all those home runs so why don't you just work the whole thing over a little bit and then send it somewhere like *Sports World* and Joseph Baum's twinkly little mouse eyes glistened with delight as he said:

"Yah?"

And I said yah so Joseph Baum leaped to his feet and he began pumping my hand in thanks and then he scooped up the pages of his novel manuscript from off the floor and he bounced out of the room and I sat there thinking what harm is there in telling that little man he'd written a great story and just then I looked over to the door and I saw Cleveland Mason was waiting there so I motioned him and I began looking for his manuscript but I couldn't find anything and Cleveland Mason said:

"I didn't give you anything."

And I said did he have anything for me to look at now and Cleveland Mason said:

"No because I haven't really written anything yet."

And I asked him what he was doing at a writers conference if he hadn't written anything and Cleveland Mason said:

"It may sound foolish but I wanted to know if you thought I could write anything."

And I looked at Cleveland Mason and I wondered whether this quiet guy was on the level or not and I said well he might as well try writing his own writing and I said I'd be happy to look at anything he wrote before the end of the week and when I said that I saw Cleveland Mason's face begin to tense up and he said:

"That's very kind of you but I'm not sure I can write anything."

And I said he'd never know unless he gave it a try and Cleveland Mason said yes he guessed that was so and so he stood up and he shook my hand and he thanked me and he left the reading room and I sat there wondering where the hell I got the balls to go telling anyone he ought to try writing his own writing when I hadn't been really writing anything for the last 5 years and suddenly I felt very tired so I got up and I walked out through the lobby and I got on the ancient elevator and I rode up to my room and I lay down on my bed and I drifted off into a twlight sleep and I dreamed this dream:

I was standing on a narrow strip of beach and I was holding the final manuscript of this lousy novel that I am trying to write right now and suddenly I felt it was beginning to slip through my fingers and all the pages began to go spilling all over the sand where they would be blown out into the open ocean and I knew they would be lost forever in the sweet peace of the deep sea and in that instant I began to eat the air of everything I ever felt or thought or saw and I began to taste the acid sadness of my entire life and all the trouble in my bloodstream and the flood of all those bullshit lies that ever made me believe that I could be at all lovable—

And just then I heard a distant knocking sound and it grew louder and louder and then I heard a sobbing sound and it was coming from outside my door so I opened my eyes and I got up off my bed and I went over to the door and I opened it and there was Mildred Manson standing in the hall and she let out a long low wail and she said:

"Excuse me Mr. Morrison but may I please come in and speak with you because something terrible has just happened—"

And I told Mildred Manson to come in and she wept her way over to sit on the edge of my bed and she began to dab at her eyes with a tiny handkerchief and I stayed leaning up against the wall as I asked her what was the terrible thing that had just happened and she held out her short story manuscript *Forsaken Heart* for me to see and she said:

"I know what you told me yesterday that I should rewrite my whole story one more time so it would be a little less sickening saccharine sentimental and oh how I wish I had listened to your wise advice but no I had to be a stubborn fool because I wanted to prove that I knew more about writers and writing than you did and now just look at what's happened to my poor short story."

And Mildred Manson turned her manuscript over and I saw Ted Wylie's handwriting was scrawled all over the back page and this is what it said:

This is an idiotic short story and if you want my advice I think you should give up writing entirely and go in for bloodletting or masturbation or blowing up airplanes or something really useful—

And I asked Mildred Manson why the hell she took her short story to that vicious cynical sadist and Mildred Manson let out another long low wail and she said:

"But you were so harsh and negative and you said my story needed so much work and I had already rewritten it 3 times and I had to do it secretly late at night after Mr. Manson had gone to sleep because he hates the idea that I can express my inner creative nature in my writing and we have not been living together as man and wife for the past 17 years so when you told me to keep working on my story I thought maybe I ought to go get a second opinion on it so I took it to Ted Wylie and I asked him to look at it and—and . . ."

And Mildred Manson's voice trailed off in a weak wail and her hands began to flail the air as if they were 2 fish that had just been taken out of the water and then she burst into tears so I told her to stop all her bawling because I said Ted Wylie was a horse's ass who didn't know how to teach anyone anything and when I said that Mildred Manson narrowed her wet red eyes into fine tiny slits and she said:

"How do I know all you writing teachers aren't secretly working together against all us poor writing students and maybe you all get together at the end of every day and you all laugh at us behind our backs because you're just like my husband and you don't really want me to express my inner creative nature in my writing!"

And Mildred Manson was on her feet now and she was coming toward me with a fierce fire in her wet red eyes and she shot a cold hard hate ray stare right through me as she said:

"Yes that's it you don't really want me to go on trying to write my own writing!"

And I said that was nonsense because I was trying to be the best writing teacher I could be and when I said that Mildred Manson began to nod her head very slowly up and down as if she were about to give me one last chance to prove that I really and truly did care about her writing and she said:

"Is Marcia Masters your agent in New York?"

And I said yes she was and then Mildred Manson said:

"I think what I need now is a very professional opinion on my short story so if you really and truly do care about my writing then you'll send this manuscript to Marcia Masters and ask her what she thinks about it."

And suddenly I had a flash image of Marcia Masters as she was reading through Mildred Manson's short story and I saw her face looked as if she were being force-fed enormous doses of tabasco sauce and just as I had that flash image I felt myself beginning to go into one of my blackouts—

here we go
into hee haw country

—and I put my arm behind me to brace myself against the wall as I felt myself collapsing backwards in a lot of acid fizz state phases and when I began to come back to myself I saw Mildred Manson was still standing in front of me and she was still staring at me through her wet red eyes so I said Mrs. Manson I'm sorry for what Ted Wylie wrote on the back of your short story manuscript but right now why don't you go back to your room and try to get some rest and when I said that Mildred Manson began to hiss at me through her teeth and she said:

"You're just like all the others because you don't really care about my writing."

And Mildred Manson shook her short story manuscript in my face and then she turned and she stalked out of the room and she slammed the door behind her and I lay back on my bed and I put my hand over my forehead to feel how much sweat there was there and I felt there was a lot and at that exact same instant Ted Wylie was sitting all alone in his room on the second floor and he was reading through Maureen Talbot's 5 large notebooks so he could get some background information on me for the new novel he was writing about how I was a writer who was not really writing but it didn't take Ted Wylie very long to find out that Maureen Talbot's 5 large notebooks were a hopeless jumble of junk because they were stuffed full of pictures and post cards and love letters and autographed dust jackets and programs of readings and a lot of lecture notes and a lot of diary entries that read like a secret history of the sex life of the San Marcos Writers Conference and some of these diary entries went like this:

—Made love to Ralph Perry last night and afterwards he told me gosh it was swell but he didn't even finish so I asked him was there anything wrong but his voice began to trail off and then he fell silent and he lay there quite quiet in bed and it looked as if he might have slipped off on me but then I figured he was probably thinking about one of those sea battles that he's always writing about—

—Spent last night with Eliot Morrison and I asked him did he like oral sex and he said not if that meant talking about it and he can be a terrific lover when he wants to be but most of the time he's just collapsing backwards on himself and going off into hee haw country—

—Mr. Ruiz likes to strip naked and go snorting and cavorting around the room clapping his hands together in a rhythmic beat and shouting out OLÉ and then he begins to paw at the dust with one hoof and he lowers his snout and he flares out his nostrils in the air and his thick stiff Latin prick sticks out straight ahead as he goes crashing into me and he goes bumping me all around the room and tries to mount me from the rear but I told him this was certainly a very interesting aspect of Latin culture but it wasn't really my style—

—Poor little Jose that nervous mouse of a man and it's no wonder he hides behind the reception desk all day reading his paperback novels because I've never seen such a teenie peewee in all my life and while he was lying beside me in bed he pointed at my boobs and he said they were both domed whatever the hell that means—

—Met Ted Wylie last night in Los Angeles and he jerked me off with his hand while he kept watching the expression on my face and when I asked him would he come teach at the San Marcos Writers Conference this summer he said yes he would if I'd put out for him while he was there and I said that was a really gross thing for him to say and then I told him okay so long as he made love to me instead of just jerking me off with his hand and he snorted a short snort of scorn and then he asked me to tell him all the things I used to do with Eliot Morrison in bed and I said I wasn't sure I'd tell him because after all some things are personal—

And Ted Wylie kept turning page after page of Maureen Talbot's 5 large notebooks until he finished skimming through all of them and he decided it was a disaster of writing because it was the biggest collage of trivia he had ever seen and he dropped them on the floor and he kicked them over toward the wall with his foot and then he got up and he left his room to go downstairs to the porch and get some fresh air and at that exact same instant I got up off my bed and I left my room to go downstairs to the porch and get some fresh air and I saw Ted Wylie was already out there and I thought oh my god I hope he doesn't see me but he turned around and he fixed his beady eagle eye on me so I asked him how he liked teaching at the writers conference and Ted Wylie smiled a vicious cynical smile and he said:

"It's about as maniacal and demented as I thought it would be but then I don't give a flying fuck whether Suzie Twoshoes or Harriet Hemorrhoid can shit a hatful of short stories because they're all such a pathetic bunch of losers they couldn't write their way out of a wastebasket."

And I began to go back into the hotel but Ted Wylie said:

"Incidentally Morrison I won't need to do any more interviews with you because I just got a lot of hot material on you from reading through Maureen Talbot's notebooks."

And I said that must have been fun reading because Maureen Talbot likes to think she's screwed everyone who's ever come to the San Marcos Writes Conference all the way from Ralph Perry and Mr. Ruiz all the way down to Jose at the reception desk and I said it would take a trained analyst to figure out which affairs did take place and which ones were only in her own mind and I wished Ted Wylie luck in sorting out all the assorted distortions and when I said that there was a long pause and then Ted Wylie said:

"Are you trying to tell me Maureen Talbot's notebooks are nothing but a lot of bullshit lies?"

And I said that was a pretty fair approximation of what I was trying to tell him so Ted Wylie thought about that for a while and then he said:

"Okay Morrison I won't use any of that material I got out of Maureen Talbot's notebooks if you'll get me some fresh material and you can begin by screwing Esther Martin out on that narrow strip of beach at 10:00 PM tomorrow night so I can watch the 2 of you through my field binoculars and is that a deal?''

And I said it was no deal because Esther Martin had enough problems without Ted Wylie's leering at her in the mirror on the ceiling of the whorehouse of his mind and when I said that Ted Wylie said:

"I'm not only going to be leering at her Morrison because after you make it with her down there on that narrow strip of beach then you're going to come up to my room and you're going to give me a full report on what kind of body she has underneath those pissy yellow dresses and does she have cute boobies you can chew on and do the nipples come to fine tiny tips and what does her little clit taste like and is her vagina loose and juicy around your throbbing cock and these are some of the things you're going to tell me all about so I can write them in my new novel.''

And I felt like I was having an extended conversation with an open sewer so I turned around and I walked off the porch and through the lobby and I had a sudden impulse to call Clara and find out whether Ted Wylie had ever really talked with her so I walked past Jose who was sound asleep at the reception desk and I went over to the pay phone and I closed the door and I groped around in my pocket and I pulled out about 4 dollars in change and I told the operator to put through a person to person call to Clara Morrison in New Haven in Connecticut and I heard the phone begin to ring 5 times and 6 times and 7 times and I wondered whether Clara was lying dead of an overdose of her own madness when I heard her pick up the phone and she said:

"Huh.''

And she sounded dim and distant the way she always was before she got her hate rays heated up and the operator asked if she was Clara Morrison and she said huh so the operator told me to deposit 3 dollars and 55 cents and so I did and then I said hello and Clara said:

"Huh.''

And I said this was Eliot Morrison and Clara said:

"Huh."

And I said I had to ask her a question and there was a long pause and then suddenly Clara shouted out into the phone:

"Hello shitface and have you been screwing any of your stupid students out there and now you want to tell me all about it?"

And I said no that wasn't why I called because I had something important to ask her and Clara said:

"Oh when I call you it's not important but when you call me then I'm supposed to pay attention because it's important and is that it buddy?"

And I asked Clara if she had ever heard of someone named Ted Wylie and there was another long pause and then Clara said:

"Well and suppose I have heard of him buddy and just suppose I have and what the hell do you want to make out of it?"

And I said I didn't want to make anything out of it but I had to know whether this Ted Wylie ever got in touch with her because he was writing a sick novel about how I was a writer who was not really writing and he told me he had talked with her and that she had given him a lot of background information about me and I just wanted to know if that was true or not and then there was another long pause and then Clara began to talk again but this time her voice was soft and low the way it was ice ages ago when she was a gentle tender soul who cared very much about me and she said:

"Eliot you know damn well I would never give anyone any information about you to put in a sick novel and the only reason I phoned Ralph Perry was so you'd get your ass kicked out of there and then you'd have to get back to trying to write your own writing because that's what you have to do baby and you know it as well as I do so if this Ted Wylie character wants to write a sick novel about you then he can come kiss the piss off my pussy because I swear I'd never tell anyone anything about you and that's a promise you can count on."

And I said thanks Clara because that means Ted Wylie has

been lying to me all along and when I said that Clara shouted out into the phone:

"Now shitface you get your ass the fuck out of there and back to New York so you can write your own writing!!"

And I said in a few more days I might do just that and then I got off the phone and the fistful of change dropped down into the belly of the pay phone and I began to push at the door of the phone booth but it was stuck so I began to kick against it but nothing happened so I began to rock the whole pay phone booth back and forth until its wooden thighs began to grate against the floor and Jose woke up at the reception desk to see the pay phone booth was swaying back and forth in the hotel lobby and Jose thought it had come to life like a jumping bean only he didn't know I was the helpless worm that was trapped inside it so Jose began clapping his hands together in beat to the rhythmic swaying of the pay phone booth but just then I broke the door open and I came bursting out into the hotel lobby and Jose stopped clapping his hands together and his mouth dropped open as I raced over to the ancient elevator but just then I ran right into Gwendolyn Field who had arrived to give the evening lecture and she looked giggly and harried and breathless like a high school volleyball player and she said:

"Hi there Eliot and I understand you're going to be introducing me tonight and is that right?"

And I thought oh my god I'd completely forgotten about that but Gwendolyn Field kept right on talking and she said:

"I just hope this writers conference isn't like the last one I was at because everyone there kept asking me so many dumb questions about how it felt to be a woman writer and I think that's so patronizing and demeaning and dumb and I just wish people would stop calling me that."

And I took Gwendolyn Field on into the dining room and I sat her down next to Ralph Perry who said he was awful gosh darn proud to have her give the evening lecture and I sat down and I began to wonder what I was going to say about her soppy pop novel

Safari and Gwendolyn Field kept right on babbling about how much she hated to be called a woman writer and when we finished dinner we all got up and we went down to the main hall and I stood up at the podium to face the evening audience and before I knew what I was saying I said we were all pleased to have Gwendolyn Field with us here this evening and she was going to tell us all about how it felt to be a woman writer and I turned and went back to my seat as Gwendolyn Field shot me a look that would have withered a pine tree as she went up to the podium and she said:

I think introductions like that are such cheap shots and they're really nothing but a lot of shit bitchiness when they introduce me as a woman writer because I think that's so patronizing and demeaning and dumb and I just wish people would stop calling me that—

And then Gwendolyn Field went on to read a few chapters from her best selling novel *Safari* that told all about how it felt to be a woman writer and after she'd finished reading she said she'd be happy to answer any questions from the audience and Maureen Talbot was on her feet right away and she asked:

"How can you know when it's okay to tell the truth about someone else?"

And Gwendolyn Field gobbled up the question the way a goldfish gobbles up a piece of goldfish food and she said:

"It's always okay to tell the truth about anyone else because that's all we ever have to write about."

And I thought dear god that's all Maureen Talbot needs to be told because now she'll be off at her typewriter typing up her 5 large notebooks and telling everything about everyone she's ever screwed and just then Ralph Perry was on his feet and he was pointing to his wristwatch and he said:

"I hate to be the one to break off this wonderful program Miss Field because gosh knows we've all read your wonderful novel *Safari* that tells all about how it feels to be a woman writer and we're so darn proud to have you here with us this evening but I see it's getting late so perhaps we'd better call it a day."

And the audience applauded and some of the conferees came up to ask Gwendolyn Field how it felt to be a woman writer and I slipped out the back door and I began to wonder where Esther Martin was because I hadn't seen her all day but just then I felt a tug at my elbow and I saw it was Ralph Perry and he had an anxious puppy expression on his face as he said:

"Did you get a chance to read through my World War Two novel manuscript yet huh guy?"

And I said no I hadn't had a chance to look at it yet but I would get to it before the end of the week and I'd write a statement he could use on the dust jacket of his book and Ralph Perry said:

"Aw thanks guy."

And I got on the ancient elevator and I rode on up to the second floor and I got off and went down to Esther Martin's room and I stood there outside her door for a moment and then I knocked and there was a long pause and then the door opened and Esther Martin stood there in a bright canary yellow dress and her large dark startled eyes were wide open and I said hello and I noticed that she hadn't been at any of the classes today or at any of the meals or at the evening lecture and I was just wondering if there was anything wrong and there was a long moment of silence as Esther Martin stood there in her own air and then she stepped backwards and she said:

"Thank you very much but I've been writing more of my short stories."

And I asked her if I could come in for a few minutes and she didn't say anything so I went into her room and I sat down and Esther Martin walked over to her desk and she sat down and I asked her if I had upset her by what I'd said about her angel Gabriel story and she said:

"Oh no because you were quite right to say that story was pointless because it was pointless and I know that is a fault and a weakness but I always write all my stories the way my angel voices tell me to write them because I've been writing them that way for the last 5 years and I wouldn't know how to write them any other way."

And I sat there and I thought that sounded like a pretty nutty view of art but then I thought who the hell was I to be saying anything was nutty because at least Esther Martin has been writing her own writing for the last 5 years which is more than I've been doing for the last 5 years and just then Esther Martin picked up a letter that was on her desk and she handed it over for me to read and this is what it said:

Dear Dr. Nesbitt:

Here I am at the San Marcos Writers Conference in California this week and there is a fiction teacher named Eliot Morrison and he said my angel Gabriel story was exquisite and lyrical but it should have more of a point and of course he is right and he is a kind man who says my name in my ear when I am not here and I will miss him next week when I go on to the Arizona Writers Conference and then on to the Santa Fe Writers Conference and then the following week I will be coming back to see you at Hope Valley.

Sincerely,
Esther Martin

And I passed the letter back to Esther Martin and I asked her what Hope Valley was and she said:

"It's a place for people like me who are crazy."

And suddenly Esther Martin's left hand shot out and it sent the letter skimming off her desk and sailing through the air until it dropped down plop in the wastebasket and Esther Martin sat there staring straight ahead in the air as if nothing had happened and then after another long moment she suddenly blurted out to no one in particular:

"Oh you're so ashamed to let him see you like him."

And I said if Esther Martin got all her short stories together and sent them on to me in New York I'd be happy to show them to my agent Marcia Masters and she could try to find a publisher for them and I pulled out a pen and I wrote my name and address on a piece of paper and I put it on her desk and there was another long pause and then Esther Martin said:

"Thank you very much but I don't think my angel voices want to have their stories brought out in book form because if they did they would have told me so."

And that sounded just as nutty as her nutty view of art but then I thought she hasn't eaten anything at all today so I asked her if she wanted to walk on up to the diner that was off Route One and get a tuna fish sandwich and some iced tea and Esther Martin said:

"Thank you very much but I'm not hungry."

And I thought I'd better leave her alone with her angel voices so I got up and I went over and I kissed her right on the lips a quick passionless benediction kiss and then I said good night and I turned and I walked out of her room and I took the ancient elevator up to my room on the third floor and I was feeling pretty good about myself as I went in and I was so free and easy in all my body parts and just then I remembered I had promised to write Cindy a letter while I was out here and even though I hadn't really written anything for the last 5 years I thought what the hell I might as well give it a try so I went over to the desk and I picked up a pen and a piece of paper and this is what I wrote:

Dear Cindy:

Here I am at the San Marcos Writers Conference in California and I asked Ted Wylie why you have to fuck that guy onstage in front of an enormous mirror and he said so the audience can get to see you do it double and that's not much of an action to play in his sick play but then that's how sick and twisted Ted Wylie is and right now he's trying to write a new novel about how I am a writer who is not really writing but here I am really writing this letter to you right now so that means Ted Wylie's novel about me is already hopelessly outdated and kaput and listen I miss you and I kiss your bright gold hair and your loose full breasts and your 2 ice blue tiny iris eyes and I'll call you as soon as I get back to New York.

Eliot

P.S. It's lucky you didn't come out here with me because this writers conference is the pits.

And I folded the letter and I stuffed it into an envelope and I tossed it over by the door so I'd be sure to mail it in the morning and then I lay down on my bed and I thought my god here I am really writing again and how odd it all is how very very odd and my god I am such an oddball among oddballs.

This is the end of chapter six of this lousy novel and by this time you've probably figured out that I am trying to write about a lot of things that all take place in a single instant of air because it's this idea I have about how everything is always telescoped together in one single instant of air and I've experienced time like that a lot of times and that's why so much of this lousy novel takes place in the air because all real writing is always up there in the air there where all rare fair things always are up there in the bright areas of air and that's something for you to think about as you keep reading these lines that I am trying to write right now.

seven/Thursday

And I woke up feeling so free and easy in all my body parts and then I remembered that I had dreamed this dream:

I was in the middle of a large henhouse and I was collecting a lot of eggs from all the different hens that were sitting around on their roosts and as I went from hen to hen I would pick up each egg and I would look at it and then I would begin talking to the hen that laid it and I would tell her whether I thought her egg was any good and I would tell her what I thought she should do to lay a much better egg next time and then I would move on to the next hen and I kept this up until I came to one hen that had laid the biggest egg I had ever seen in my entire life and I picked the egg up in my hands and I felt how round and huge and smooth it was but just as I was about to put it down again I felt it was beginning to slip through my fingers and suddenly it exploded right there in the air and there were chips and bits of eggshell that went flying all over my hands and I could feel the warm ooze of egg yolk was leaking liquid all over me—

And I lay there in bed remembering this dream and suddenly I felt my hands were really wet with a warm ooze and I realized I had had a wet dream and shot off all over both my hands and I thought well and no wonder I feel so free and easy in all my body parts because now I am finally relaxing out of the reach of this corny boring writers conference so I can begin to feel the flow of my own juices again and I got up and I wiped the wet from off my hands and I got dressed and I picked up the letter I had written to Cindy and I went downstairs and I dropped the letter in the mailbox next to the reception desk and then I went through the dining room and out into the kitchen to get myself some coffee and Sylvester Appleby was hanging around by the large kitchen sink and he poured me a cup of coffee and I asked him what he wanted to be and he shrugged his shoulders and he said he didn't know except he knew he was going to go to a real Mexican whorehouse with his friend Harry Holton at the end of the summer and he made a shy guffaw so that his hair fell all over his eyes and I thought Sylvester Appleby is enormously likable in his unassuming stupidity and I thanked him for the coffee and I went back into the dining room and I sat down at a corner table and I began to sip at my coffee and just then I felt a sudden weight on my hand and I looked up and I saw Mildred Manson was standing next to me and her hand was pressing down hard on my hand and she said:

"I just wanted to say that I am sorry for what happened yesterday afternoon in your room because I certainly wasn't trying to make such a fool of myself."

And I took my hand from under her hand and I sipped at my coffee and I tried to imagine what kind of a fool Mildred Manson could make of herself if she really set her mind to it but she kept right on and she said:

"I could just slap myself for ever doubting your wise advice and as for that Mr. Ted Wylie he can go stuff his sick twisted opinions up his you know what and I am not the only writing student here that feels that way because this entire conference looks like the aftermath of a battlefield with all the poor victims of his individual manuscript conferences that he's tried to cripple with his vicious cynical criticisms and even my husband wouldn't be so cruel and brutal with other people's feelings."

And I said Ted Wylie had some very serious problems of his own and just then I saw Harry Holton was standing over by the kitchen door and he was whispering to Sylvester Appleby about Maureen Talbot who was sitting at another table and Harry Holton was saying that according to the secret sexual signal system Maureen Talbot was such a cold broad that she'd probably never had a single sexual experience in her entire life and Sylvester Appleby was nodding his head in agreement to that and then Harry Holton began whispering about Esther Martin who was sitting off at another table and he said that according to the secret sexual signal system Esther Martin was definitely and unquestionably wide open and she would be ready to ball both Harry Holton and Sylvester Appleby on Friday night and Sylvester Appleby began nodding his head in agreement to that and then Harry Holton whispered:

"As for tonight man we're going to do that waitress up at Betty's Diner so be sure you clear all these creeps out of the dining hall tonight as fast as you can."

And Sylvester Appleby nodded is head in agreement to that as I turned and I told Mildred Manson to rewrite her whole story one more time so it will be a little less sickening saccharine sentimental and then I got up and I walked out of the dining room and through the hotel lobby where Jose was sitting at the reception desk reading page 139 of *The Banana Factor* by Ted Wylie and I went out to the porch and down the wooden stairs and onto the narrow strip of beach where I walked along a long way until I finally sat down on the sand and I lay back and I stared up at the high wide sky overhead and I tried to imagine where all those millions of tiny stars in the night sky were right now that everything was blue and beautiful in the bright daylight and then I closed my eyes and I began to doze off in a sweet twilight sleep under that blazing day star and it felt as if I were up there in the air there where all rare fair things always are up there in the bright areas of air and then suddenly I woke up and I sat up and I looked at my wristwatch and I saw it was 1:00 PM so I got up and I ran back up to the hotel and through the lobby and on into the reading room where Mary Anne Berre was already waiting for me and she was a tall austere European woman with a stone cold stoic face that gave the impression of having lived through god knows what of suffering and devastation in her lifetime yet she was not about to discuss any of it with anyone so I took out her novel manuscript and I began flipping through it and this is what it was about:

A European family sits down to all sorts of full course roast beef dinners and everyone makes polite meaningless conversation as the novel goes from chapter to chapter with elaborate descriptions of all the thick rich slabs of blood red roast beef that are heaped up steaming hot on plates and there are also lots of string beans and turnips and cucumbers and radishes and cole slaw and small brown roast potatoes and there are even oven fresh rolls that are smothered over with a lot of melting homemade butter but mostly there are the thick rich slabs of blood red roast beef.

And this was all very mouth-watering but not very mind-filling so I told Mary Anne Berre that she wrote a pretty good roast beef dinner but she should also probe into her characters a little more to see where they were all coming from but when I said that Mary Anne Berre turned her stone cold stoic face aside and she said:

"I do not want any what you call probing because in my lifetime is enough of probing so I only write roast beef and if to you is interesting then to me is enough."

And she spoke with such quiet courage and dignity that I didn't have the heart to press the point any further but still I couldn't help wondering what ghastly past was hidden away in all those thick rich slabs of blood red roast beef and I knew that she would probably keep on heaping up steaming hot servings out of her unconscious for the rest of her life and she would drip word gravy all over each page plate but I knew that nothing I said would make any difference so after I pointed out some places where she

133

might add a few more small brown roast potatoes then Mary Ann Berre began to gather her novel manuscript together and she got up to leave the reading room and I looked at my wristwatch and I saw it was 2:00 PM and Susan Restnor came in and she sat down and she was in her early 30's and she had an attractive body and a full round face that was punctuated by delicious red lipstick and I took out her short story manuscript and this is what it was about:

A suburban housewife is helping her husband move some furniture around in their house and they are halfway up the stairs with a great huge mahogany cabinet when suddenly the husband trips and slips and he falls down backwards and the enormous heavy mahogany cabinet comes crashing down on top of him so his rib cage is crushed to mush and his guts begin to gush out pus and custard as he lies there at the foot of the stairs and the suburban housewife just stands there at the top of the stairs as she stares down at the broken body of her dead husband.

And this story was pretty ghoulish stuff but it didn't quite make clear whether the poor husband trips and slips accidentally or whether the housewife drops the great mahogany cabinet down on top of him on purpose so I asked Susan Restnor which it was and she just looked at me in wide-eyed wonder and she said:

"Well and does it make any difference because the husband is dead and that's all that really matters isn't it?"

And I had a hunch that Susan Restnor was into a pretty strong homicidal fantasy but I also had a hunch that I'd better handle the whole thing very tactfully so I suggested she might try writing out both possibilities and I said first she could write about how that great huge mahogany cabinet drops down on top of the husband by accident and I said then she could write about how the housewife drops it down on top of her husband on purpose and I said that way she could see which way she really wanted the story to go but when I said that Susan Restnor just sat there staring at me and she said:

"Do you mean I should have that poor woman drop that great

huge mahogany cabinet down on top of her husband accidentally and then I should have her lug that enormous thing all the way back upstairs and drop it down on top of him again on purpose and I couldn't do that because the damn thing weighs half a ton and I could never get it back upright and then lug it all the way back upstairs by myself and drop it down again—''

And suddenly Susan Restnor realized she had lapsed into the first person so she clapped her hand over her mouth and she began to blush beet red like the delicious red of her lipstick and just at that same instant I had a subliminal flash thing of grabbing her hand from off her mouth and ramming my rock hard cock on in between those full round lips but Susan Restnor was still staring at me in cold shock astonishment that she had been writing her own homicidal fantasy so I leaned forward toward her and I tried to calm her down and I said why not try rewriting the entire short story in the first person so then you can see whether you want to kill your husband accidentally or whether you want to kill him on purpose and when I said that Susan Restnor looked at me in disbelief and she said:

"You mean you're not shocked that anyone would really and truly want to do such a thing?"

And I said I wasn't shocked but I just wanted to know what was going on in the short story and when I said that Susan Restnor began to nod her head very slowly as if she were now living in a new moral universe where anyone could do anything to anyone so long as it was clear what was going on and suddenly her face had an eerie calm like the calm that came over Ivan Karamazov when he said "everything is permitted" and Susan Restnor reached out and she gathered up her short story manuscript and she got up with all the cool aplomb of someone who has just been admitted into Murder Incorporated and she left the reading room as if she were heading off on her first hit job and I looked at my wristwatch and I saw it was 3:00 PM and Betsy Childs came bouncing into the room and she was short and pert and sexy in a mischievous way and I took out her novel manuscript and this is what it was about:

A young girl is a woman cadet at West Point and during her first year there she gets laid in all sorts of different ways like in a tank and on top of a helicopter and inside a missile silo and under a pup tent and on horseback and on mess line and during a free fall parachute drop and underneath an armored car and down in a foxhole and right in the middle of the ranks of the Army marching band.

And as I looked through this manuscript Betsy Childs moved her chair up closer to mine and she smiled mischievously and she said:

"Listen don't take that thing too seriously because I just wrote it for a laugh."

And I said it was a lot of fun but there wasn't much depth to it and when I said that Betsy Childs slumped back in her chair and she said:

"You mean it's nothing but a lot of porn writing huh?"

And I said not exactly but I thought Betsy Childs should explore why this young girl acts out all her erotic capers in a military setting in the middle of all those rigid rules and regulations because it would be interesting to know why she screws as easily as she salutes and when I said that Betsy Childs said:

"You mean maybe all that military stuff reminds her of some early authority figure like her father and maybe all her screwing around now is really her way of fucking her old man and if I put in more stuff about her childhood and all then maybe she'd be a more believable character and hey yeah I see what you mean I think you've really got something there."

And Betsy Childs reached out and she patted me a playful pat on my knee that went right through me like a sudden bolt of bright blue steel and I began to get so aroused I wanted to bounce Betsy Childs right off to bed like the mischievous little sex kitten that she was and just as I thought that thought Betsy Childs winked a wicked wink at me and she jumped up off her chair and she scooped up her manuscript and she headed over toward the door and I felt myself get right up and follow after her through the door and out into the hotel lobby and over to the ancient elevator where we both stood waiting for it to open its door and we got on and Betsy Childs looked over at the buttons and she said:

"Your floor or mine?"

And I said either one was okay by me so she pressed the second floor button and we rode on up and got off and we walked down to her room and she unlocked the door and we went in and Betsy Childs slipped her blouse off and she tossed it over on to one of the piles of clothes that were strewn all over the floor and then she turned around and she faced me and I looked down at her round full breasts that were hanging loose and juicy like 2 ripe fruits that were about to fall from a tree branch and she said:

"Cute aren't they?"

And she reached out and she undid the buckle on my belt and then she unzipped my fly so my pants fell down to the floor and she looked down at my throbbing cock and she began to stroke on it with her hand as her mouth came up to mine and her tongue flicked in between my lips and then all of a sudden she was bouncing over onto the bed and she threw off the rest of her clothes and she sent her panties skimming out through the air and they dropped down plop in the wastebasket and by that time I had my own clothes off and I was lying down beside her on the bed and I had my hand on her wet sex and the next instant I was lying over her and sliding easily in and out and Betsy Childs lay there underneath me and she was smiling up at me as I began to thrust away at her neat small mound that met me at each thrust and I kept pumping and pumping and pumping away inside of her until suddenly I felt myself beginning to let go and that was when I thrust as hard as I could thrust on in and up and ah god I was gone in an explosion of composure and it was like an ocean flowing over me and then I felt myself collapsing backwards in a blackout as I rolled over on my side beside her and Betsy Childs snuggled up against me and she whispered in my ear:

"I knew I could do it for you baby."

And I went swimming in an underwater duck pond where there are these centuries of sand and large dark shapes that keep darting in and out in their slow motion going and for a long moment I was floating all alone down there in the sweet peace of sleep and then when I came back up for air I saw Betsy Childs was lying on her side beside me and she was smiling at me and she said:

"I knew the moment you walked in to teach our fiction class on Monday morning that I was going to fuck you."

And I asked if she had seen that particular event on the main bulletin board and Betsy Childs made a wry face and then she leaned her head back on the pillow and she said:

"You needn't worry about my following you around this place like some lost puppy because I already have my main man here."

And I tried to guess who her main man was and I asked if it was Ralph Perry or Ted Wylie or Cleveland Mason or Robert Ingersoll or Harry Holton or Sylvester Appleby or Jose at the reception desk and Betsy Childs just shook her head and she let out a little giggle and she said:

"It's sweet Douglas Mercer who knows how to take care of me just fine and we made it Sunday evening when we both got here and we've been screwing 3 or 4 times a day ever since then and it's made this corny boring writers conference almost bearable because if he weren't here I'd probably be going up and down the halls doing all the doorknobs out of utter desperation but thank god Douglas Mercer knows how to take care of me just fine."

And Betsy Childs smiled the smile of a woman who knows who her main man is all the while her left hand was casually caressing my limp cock and I asked her if she thought there was much sex going on here at the writers conference besides what she had going with Douglas Mercer and Betsy Childs scrunched up her face in disgust and she said:

"I've seen more sex in a supermarket and I only hope these people put all their juices into their writing because they sure as hell haven't put any of it into their lives except for that dear Mr. Baum the bald little baseball man with the twinkly mouse eyes because he's always running up and down the halls with his fly wide open and his cute little cock is sticking right out there in the air and he keeps knocking on all the doors and asking if anyone wants to watch him hit a home run and all the dear man really wants is for someone to watch him swing his little bat around but as for the rest of these people they're nothing but a lot of lost zombies and tell me what the hell do they all do on Saturday night at San Marcos I mean do they all forget the fact that they're supposed to be a lot of hotshot writers and do they let themselves go apeshit on their last night out here or what?"

And I said I didn't know because I was always so wiped out by the time Saturday night came around so Betsy Childs would have to keep her own eyes open and see for herself what happens on Saturday night at San Marcos and then I told her to take good care of Douglas Mercer and not tell him that she'd made it with me and she said of course not and then she kissed me on the lips and she was up off the bed and picking up her clothes from the piles that were strewn all over the floor and so I got up and I put my own clothes on and we went over to the door and Betsy Childs looked up at me and she winked a wicked wink and she said:

"See you in class!"

And we went downstairs in the ancient elevator and I left her in the lobby and I walked past the reception desk where Jose was reading page 141 of *The Banana Factor* by Ted Wylie and that reminded me that Ted Wylie was giving the evening lecture tonight and it would begin in a few minutes but I'd already missed both lunch and dinner and I didn't feel like listening to all his cynicism on an empty stomach so I went out onto the porch to watch the great waves as they came in to break against the slippery glistening rocks and just then Maureen Talbot came out on the porch and she came over and told me that she had just finished a really ghastly manuscript conference with Robert Ingersoll and I asked her what he had written and she said:

"God knows because it's all on 17 yellow legal pads and it's such an indecipherable scrawling that I can't read any of it so I just have to take his word for what it's all about and he says it's about corruption in high places."

And I asked Maureen Talbot what kind of high places Robert Ingersoll says he's writing about and she said:

"He claims he's a plainclothes Jesuit and he's written an exposé of the College of Cardinals and he says he has the inside story on every papal election that's taken place in the last 50 years and most of the book is about this one pope he refuses to identify but he swears this pope never wore any underwear beneath his robes and instead he had this handmade Italian contraption that he strapped around his waist and I can't go into the details but the whole point is that this pope was trying to reach orgasm at the exact same instant that he raised a wafer up over his head and there's this famous photograph of this pope holding a wafer in the air and he has the most sublime beatific expression on his face and I told Mr. Ingersoll I thought the whole thing was pretty gross but he swears it's the truth."

And I asked Maureen Talbot if she thought this Robert Ingersoll was on the level or not and she said:

"How the hell should I know because like I told you I couldn't read one word of his manuscript because it's such an illegible mess so I have to take his word for everything he says is there and for all I know he could be the pope himself in disguise."

And I said I'd been having some pretty bizarre individual manuscript conferences myself and then there was a long pause so I said I'd made up my mind I was going to tell Ralph Perry that I wouldn't be coming back to San Marcos again next year and when I said that Maureen Talbot drew herself up straight and she said:

"Don't you dare say anything to hurt that old man because this writers conference is all he has left in the world so if you shake his faith and break his heart I swear to god I'll never speak to you again."

And I thought my christ here's Maureen Talbot who's screwed every writing teacher who's ever come to this corny boring writers conference but when the chips are down her heart still belongs to old Ralph Perry and I thought that was sort of touching so I said of course I wouldn't do anything to hurt Ralph Perry and then Maureen Talbot took me by the elbow and she said we'd better get into the main hall or else we'd miss Ted Wylie's evening lecture and I knew I couldn't say no so I went along with her through the hotel lobby and just then Cleveland Mason came up to me and he said:

"Excuse me Mr. Morrison I just wanted to tell you I'll have something to give you by the end of the conference."

And I said that was fine and he shook my hand and I kept going into the main hall where I sat down in the back row next to Robert Ingersoll and he turned his tanned face to me and he said:

"I've just had a really ghastly manuscript conference with some smart aleck young woman who couldn't even read my novel manuscript and Jesus Christ I'd like to know what the fuck's wrong with my writing my god damn novel in my own handwriting on 17 yellow legal pads and I think what that sick bitch needs is a good swift kick in the crotch."

And I thought this guy doesn't sound very much like a plain-clothes Jesuit and just then Ralph Perry got up at the podium and he began saying how gosh darn proud he was to have Ted Wylie here this year and we had all read *The Banana Factor* and we all knew what a really wonderful best selling novel it was and now Ted Wylie was going to tell us all about how he wrote it and everyone in the audience applauded as Ted Wylie got up and he went over to the podium and he fixed his beady eagle eye out over the audience and after a long pause said he had absolutely no intention of saying anything about how he wrote *The Banana Factor* because he said it was no one's fucking business how he wrote anything and then he said:

These asshole writers conferences are nothing but a lot of chickenshit and the only reason you're all here is because you're hoping some of my success will rub off on you but you're such a bunch of rotten tedious nonwriters that the only thing that could ever rub off on any of you would be more of your own chickenshit.

And everyone in the audience thought this was just another example of Ted Wylie's famous genius for satire so there were a lot of self-conscious chuckles all over the main hall as Ted Wylie went on to attack everything else in sight including the ancient elevator and the pukey tuna salad and the pissy iced tea and the creepy cretin people at the San Marcos Hotel like that little illiterate who sits behind the reception desk and then after about 10 minutes of this he said that was all he felt like saying and he was about to leave the podium when Laura Perry raised her hand and she stood up in the audience and she began by saying how much she had always admired Mr. Ted Wylie's work and she had always wanted to ask him whether he thought art had a civilizing influence on humanity and after she asked this question there was a long pause as Ted Wylie fixed his beady eagle eye on Laura Perry and then he said she was welcome to come up to the podium and try to civilize his ass because he said art never civilized anything and the only people who ever thought so were a lot of phony poets like Robert Browning and Alfred Lord Tennyson and Henry Wadsworth Longfellow and John Greenleaf Whittier and he said these poets were nothing but a lot of impotent pansies who couldn't make a good crap in a hat and when he said that Laura Perry began to sink backwards into her chair and one of her false eyelashes fell off and she sat there gasping for air and tugging her long shawl around her shoulders as Ted Wylie said art was a pain in the ass and then he walked out of the main hall into the hotel lobby so Ralph Perry jumped up to the podium and he said gosh what a swell treat it was to hear Ted Wylie tell us all about how he had written *The Banana Factor* and then Ralph Perry ran on out to the hotel lobby where Ted Wylie was waiting for his $500 check and Ralph Perry handed it to him and he stuffed it into his pocket and then he walked over to the ancient elevator and he went up to his room and just then all the conferees came out of the main hall and they were all standing around holding their copies of *The Banana Factor* and they were hoping that Ted Wylie would come back and autograph their books so they could take them home and show them to their friends and I was still sitting in the back row of the main hall and I noticed Esther Martin was also sitting there and she was staring straight ahead in the air so I got up and I went over to her and I asked her how she liked Ted Wylie's talk but Esther Martin just sat there frozen motionless in her chair and I saw her large dark startled eyes were glazed over as if she were in an ice age all her own so I reached over and I touched her on the arm and there was no response so I called out Esther Martin softly in her ear but she was silent for a long moment and then all of a sudden she blurted out:

"My angel voices aren't talking to me anymore so that means I'll never write again for the rest of my life."

And I said I was sorry to hear her angel voices weren't talking to her anymore but I said she could still go on writing out of her own voice but when I said that Esther Martin kept staring straight ahead in the air and after a long pause she said:

"I can't write anything out of my own voice because I don't have a voice of my own and that's why I'll never write again for the rest of my life."

And I asked Esther Martin why her angel voices weren't talking to her anymore and after another long pause Esther Martin said:

"My angel voices stopped talking to me because you came to my room last night and you kissed me on the lips."

And suddenly Esther Martin disappeared in a blur of bright canary yellow out of the main hall and I lost sight of her among all the other conferees who were still milling around hoping Ted Wylie would come back and autograph their books so I sat down again in the back of the main hall and I thought what an oddball world it was because here I was really writing again after 5 long years of not writing and now Esther Martin had stopped really writing after 5 long years of writing and I wondered if there was some sort of weird calculus in the universe that made one person stop writing as soon as another person started writing and as I was sitting there thinking these things Maureen Talbot was sitting upstairs on the edge of Ted Wylie's bed and she was asking Ted Wylie what he thought about her 5 large notebooks that he had read over last night and Ted Wylie was sitting in his chair by the window and he was trying to focus his field binoculars down on the narrow strip of beach because I was supposed to be seducing Esther Martin down there at 10:00 PM tonight and Maureen Talbot kept asking Ted Wylie what he thought about her notebooks and she said:

"Come on now you can tell me the truth because I want to know what you really think of my writing."

And Ted Wylie mumbled something about how the 5 large notebooks gave him a little bit of background material for his new novel about how I was a writer who was not really writing but Maureen Talbot kept pressing him and she said:

"No no I know you were using them to get background material for your new novel about Eliot Morrison and that's okay but I want to know beyond all that because what do you think of my writing and do you think those 5 large notebooks are ready to be published?"

And this was more than Ted Wylie could take so he whirled around in his chair and he shouted out:

"Published?? My Christ in heaven overhead and you've got to be out of your idiot mind because those notebooks are no more ready to be published than the lunatic doodlings on some men's room wall in Mexico City are ready to be published because all you've got there in those 5 large notebooks are a lot of adolescent babbling so the only thing those notebooks are ready for is a great raging bonfire!!"

And Maureen Talbot swallowed hard but she knew she had to press on and ask the really big question so she said:

"Listen I don't much care what you think of those notebooks the way they are right now because I know they probably need a lot more work here and there and my god it's not as if I were asking you to help me get them published or anything like that but what I was wondering was if I did manage to locate a publisher for them then would you maybe write out some sort of a statement that I could use on the dust jacket of the book?"

And Ted Wylie shot a fierce razor stare right through Maureen Talbot and he shouted out:

"A statement?? How dare you ask me to write out a statement for those half-assed records of your whoring after every writer you could wrap your grubby legs around and the only men you haven't screwed here at San Marcos are those 2 idiot kitchen kids and that's only because they're too stupid and retarded to figure out how wide open you really are!!"

And Maureen Talbot swallowed hard again and she said whatever Ted Wylie thought about her life style was okay with her but he could still write out a statement for her book and when she said that Ted Wylie shouted out:

"A statement?? I'd rather write a statement about pigslop or diarrhea or venereal disease because those notebooks of yours are a thousand times worse than all these things and so the only statement I can make about them is that they should be taken out behind the San Marcos Hotel and they should have kerosene poured all over them and then they should have a match lighted to them so they will all go up in the purifying flames!!"

And by this time Maureen Talbot was beginning to get the idea that Ted Wylie didn't think so highly of her writing so she jumped up off the bed and she grabbed her 5 large notebooks and she ran over to the door where she turned around and she shouted out at Ted Wylie:

"Ted Wylie you're such a cold son of a bitch and this whole writers conference is wise to you and your popelike pose of knowing all there is to know about writers and writing and the truth is you're in big trouble because you don't know who you are as writer or as a human being because all you can get off on is watching a lot of animals kill each other inside a cardboard carton and playing a lot of far out sex games with a gang of 10 year old kids and fist-fucking me so you can watch the ecstasy expression on my face and all I can say to you is you'd better get your ass to a psychiatrist and fast before you lose your mindless mind!!"

And Maureen Talbot went slamming out of the room so Ted Wylie opened up his notebook and he began writing down all the things she had just shouted out at him and just then there was a loud

145

sound outside the window and it sounded like the slamming of a car door and it was followed a moment later by the sound of an engine starting up and this was Harry Holton and Sylvester Appleby driving out of the gravel driveway in the San Marcos pickup truck because they were on their way up to Betty's Diner off Route One so they could make it with the waitress there and Harry Holton was saying to Sylvester Appleby:

"I'm telling you man from all the secret signals she's sending out this is one hell of a wide open waitress."

And Sylvester Appleby was nodding his head so hard his hair fell all over his eyes because he was thinking how lucky he was to have a good friend like Harry Holton who took the time to explain things like the secret sexual signal system and he only hoped he didn't do anything stupid to goof things up tonight and when Harry Holton pulled off Route One into the parking lot beside Betty's Diner they both jumped out and they tried to look as cool as they could as they walked through the door of the diner and there were a couple of truck drivers sitting at the counter and the short order chef was standing behind the little kitchen window and he was scrambling up some eggs on the sizzling griddle and the waitress was sitting on the other end of the counter and she was wearing a black nylon uniform and she had dark hair and dark eyes and she wore a bored expression on her face as if she'd give anything to be anywhere else right now and Harry Holton and Sylvester Appleby went over and sat down at one of the corner booths so the waitress got up and she came over to them and she flopped 2 menus down on the table and then she stood there waiting to take their orders and she began to balance first on one foot and then on the other foot and then she began to run her hand along the back of her hair as Harry Holton studied the menu and then he looked up and he said he'd have a tuna salad sandwich and a glass of iced tea and Sylvester Appleby said yeah he'd have the same so the waitress tilted her head sideways as she wrote their orders down on her pad and then she scooped up the menus and she went behind the counter and she slapped the order slip down on the kitchen window shelf where the chef was handing up 2 plates of scrambled eggs for the 2 truck drivers and Harry Holton leaned forward toward Sylvester Appleby and he said:

"Hey man and didya see the way she was tilting her head sideways when she took our orders?"

And Sylvester Appleby nodded his head and he said:

"Yeah."

And actually Sylvester Appleby had seen no such thing but what the hell he knew how dumb he was and if Harry Holton said the waitress was tilting her head sideways then that's what she must have been doing and just then Harry Holton sucked in on his cheeks and he leaned his head back in the booth and he narrowed his eyes wisely and he said:

"That means she is definitely and unquestionably wide open so we can make our move tonight."

And Sylvester Appleby gulped a big gulp because suddenly he wanted to have more time so he could pull out his small pocket notebook and read over all the things he'd ever written there about how to make it with a woman but he couldn't do that now because Harry Holton would think he was more dumb than he really was so Sylvester Appleby just sat there and the palms of his hands began to get sweaty so he put them in his pants pockets and he started staring at the ketchup bottle that was standing by the napkin dispenser but then his heart began to go in rapid panic beats so he gave up on the ketchup bottle and he started staring at the salt shaker and he began to pray a silent prayer to whatever gods were up there in the California night sky that he would do whatever he was supposed to do when it came time for him to make it with the waitress and as if in answer to his silent prayer just then 2 California State Troopers walked in through the door of the diner and they were wearing blue and gray uniforms and they wore wide-rimmed hats and black leather boots and black holsters and black straps that went up over their shoulders and their names were State Trooper Emerson Quaid and State Trooper Paul R. Stevens and Emerson Quaid was the only black State Trooper in the county and everyone on the force was in awe of him but no one was more in awe of him than his partner Paul R. Stevens and these 2 State Troopers went over and they sat down in a booth on the other side of the diner and when the waitress came over to where they were sitting State Trooper Paul R. Stevens ordered coffee and a mustard donut and State Trooper Emerson Quaid corrected him and he said:

"You mean custard."

And State Trooper Stevens said yeah he meant custard and State Trooper Quaid ordered coffee and a donut filled with something other than custard so the waitress shifted her weight from one foot to the other foot and she said:

"Lemme go see if we got one a them what's filled with coconut cream."

And the waitress went around the counter to check out the other donuts and as she went by one of the truckdrivers he winked at her and he said:

"How ya doing there cutie?"

And the waitress shot a cold hard hate ray stare right through the truck driver so he just shrugged and the 2 of them got up and they paid for their scrambled eggs and then they went out of the diner door and they climbed into their double rig and they went roaring off into the night air on their run from Los Angeles to Seattle and just then the waitress came back around the counter and she was carrying 2 cups of coffee and a custard donut and a donut filled with coconut cream for the 2 state troopers and then she went back to the little kitchen window where she picked up the 2 tuna salad sandwiches and 2 glasses of iced tea and she took these over to Harry Holton and Sylvester Appleby in the corner booth and then she stood there writing out their check and while she was doing this Harry Holton began to edge his right elbow on into her left thigh but the waitress was so spaced out she didn't even notice what he was doing but Sylvester Appleby noticed and he started gagging on a large swallow of iced tea and he went into such a mad spasm of gagging that he upset his glass of iced tea and it went spilling all over the waitress and she let out a quick yelp as she jumped back from the booth and looked down at her black nylon uniform to see the iced tea had left a wide wet stain on her and Sylvester Appleby was still gagging so badly his face began getting beet red and just then State Trooper Emerson Quaid got up and he came running down the diner to see what the hell was going on and he saw Sylvester Appleby's face was beginning to go from beet red to cucumber green so Trooper Quaid started to slap Sylvester Appleby on the back a lot of hard sharp slaps and that made Sylvester Appleby gulp in a lot of huge lungfuls of fresh air and that stopped the gagging so Sylvester Appleby sat there panting like a dog that has just been rescued from drowning and State Trooper Emerson Quaid looked down at the 2 kitchen boys and he said:

"What are you a couple of college kids or something?"

And Harry Holton said yeah that's what they were and they were working over at the San Marcos Hotel for the summer and Sylvester Appleby said yeah that's what they were and he was all set to go on and say they were going to go to a real Mexican whorehouse at the end of the summer but Harry Holton kicked at Sylvester Appleby under the table and State Trooper Quaid said:

"Listen you kids stay outa trouble yhear?"

And Trooper Quaid walked on back to his booth at the other end of the diner where State Trooper Stevens was sitting and admiring the way Emerson Quaid had handled the situation and the waitress went whimpering around the counter on her way to the kitchen where she began wiping at her black nylon uniform with some brown paper towels and just then Harry Holton leaned forward toward Sylvester Appleby and he said they'd better cool it with the waitress tonight because those State Police were on the scene and Sylvester Appleby gulped a big gulp of relief but then he tried to look disappointed and he said:

"Yeah gosh darn the luck and that means we'll just have to do her on some other night."

And then they both got up and they took their check on over to the counter and the chef came out through the swinging doors and he rang up their check on the cash register and then they waved good night to the State Troopers as they walked out of the diner and they got into the pickup truck and Harry Holton began to drive out of the parking lot and onto Route One but he was so pissed at Sylvester Appleby that he didn't say anything for a few minutes and then he finally said:

"Boy did you ever screw that up and just as I was beginning to get somewhere with that waitress because I had my god damn right elbow in her left thigh and you could tell she really liked it by the look on her face so I was getting all set to start humping her in the crotch when you had to begin that goofy stupid gagging so that nosy State Trooper came over and broke everything up."

And Sylvester Appleby knew that Harry Holton was right in what he was saying but still Sylvester Appleby wasn't exactly sure of what had happened so he said:

"Hey Harry how do you know for sure that waitress wasn't so spaced out she didn't even notice that you had your right elbow in her left thigh?"

And that was more than Harry Holton could take so he just kept driving along Route One but he was thinking:

Okay for you you stupid asshole and if you don't believe me about the secret sexual signal system then that's your own dumb fault and I never should have bothered trying to teach the whole thing to you in the first place and this is what I get for wasting my time on some moron high school sophomore for god's sake so just don't expect me to talk to you anymore and you can forget all about my taking you down to a real Mexican whorehouse now that I know you're nothing but a stupid asshole—

And Sylvester Appleby picked up on all these thoughts that Harry Holton was thinking and his heart began to beat in rapid panic beats and he started talking very fast and he said:

"Aw hey come on Harry and I know I'm nothing but a moron

high school sophomore and a stupid asshole to boot but if you keep teaching me the secret sexual signal system then maybe someday I may be able to do it as well as you do.''

And there was a long pause as Harry Holton kept driving along the state highway and finally he said:

''You know it took a lot of guys a lot of time and it took a lot of patience and faith to work out this secret sexual signal system and it took me a lot of time to try to teach the whole thing to you but I can tell you right now you're not going to get anywhere with it unless you start breaking your ass right now.''

And Sylvester Appleby began nodding his head so hard his hair fell all over his eyes because he wanted Harry Holton to know he was going to start breaking his ass right now and Harry Holton thought what the hell and if this kid is willing to pay both our ways down to Mexico City at the end of the summer then I may as well keep teaching him so he said:

''Okay then listen carefully because I'm going to teach you one of the most useful things you'll ever learn about how to make a girl really want to get laid and that's when a woman turns her back on you and you come up behind her and you put your hand on her shoulder while her back is turned to you then that really makes her want to get laid and have you got that?''

And Sylvester Appleby nodded his head that he got that and he could hardly wait to get back to the San Marcos Hotel so he could write it down in his small pocket notebook and then Harry Holton said:

''So we didn't make it with that waitress tonight but we'll go back and do her on Saturday night after the farewell banquet is over and meanwhile there's always that Esther Martin at the writers conference and you can take my word for it she is definitely and un-questionably open so we'll do her tomorrow night.''

And Sylvester Appleby nodded his head that they'd do Esther Martin tomorrow night and just then Harry Holton turned the pickup truck into the gravel driveway of the San Marcos Hotel and the headlights went glaring across the windows of the hotel lobby where Jose was sitting at the reception desk reading page 160 of *The Banana Factor* by Ted Wylie and Jose looked up to see who was driving in at this hour but when he heard Harry Holton and Sylvester Appleby slamming the doors of the pickup truck Jose just shrugged and yawned and he went back to reading page 161 of *The Banana Factor* and at the exact same instant in the uppermost window of the San Marcos Hotel a pair of slender hands reached out to part the curtains and a pair of fierce dark eyes peered down at the 2 kitchen boys as they made their way across the gravel driveway and these hands and eyes belonged to Mrs. Ruiz who was just about to finish writing the last page of the last chapter of her epic novel about 17 generations of a noble Spanish family that went through blood duels and misty castles and exquisite senoritas with the chaste gaze of the Latin Catholic Christ that was a fierce archangel sunlight blazing down on the white hot sandstone and at that exact same instant I was still sitting in the back of the main hall trying to figure out why I was really writing after 5 long years of not writing and why Esther Martin was not really writing after 5 long years of writing and finally I got up and I walked out to the porch and I went down the steps to the narrow strip of beach where I walked along a long way until finally I stopped and I stood there for a long moment watching the great waves as they made their way on in to burst into surf and suddenly I saw a bright canary yellow blur go flying by me in the night and this bright blur was heading out into those great waves and I saw that it was Esther Martin and she was on her way out to drown herself in the open ocean and the next instant I was running after her down the wet sand and into the bursting surf and when I caught up with her I grabbed at her arm and I began to yell her name in her ear ESTHER MARTIN and I asked her what the hell she thought she was doing but Esther Martin just stood there in the bursting surf and she kept staring straight ahead in the air and finally she blurted out to no one in particular:

"Oh so now you're going to let him see the freak show."

And I began to lead her on back through the bursting surf and all the way up to the dry sand where I tried to make her sit down but she stayed standing and after a moment she turned and she looked at me and she said:

"Thank you very much for shouting my name in my ear when I wasn't really here but right now I have to run back out there and drown myself in the open ocean."

And Esther Martin was off again in a bright yellow blur as she ran down into the great waves again only this time she kept right on going all the way out and into the open ocean and I saw her yellow dress was beginning to billow out around her in the water like a bloated yellow lemon rind so I ran right out after her again and I made my way through the great waves until I caught up with her and I grabbed at her arm and I began to pull her on backwards with me through the bursting surf until we got all the way back up on shore again only this time I made sure she sat down on the dry sand and then I asked her why the hell she was trying to drown herself out there in the open ocean and after a long pause Esther Martin said it was because her angel voices told her to do it and I said I thought those angel voices weren't talking to her anymore and she didn't say anything to that and just then I caught a quick glint of moonlight reflecting off something up in a window on the second floor of the hotel and I knew it was Ted Wylie watching us through his set of field binoculars so I told Esther Martin I was going to get her back up to her room and I reached down and I lifted her up in my arms and she felt as light as a tiny bird that had just fallen out of the night sky and I carried her across the narrow strip of beach and on up the porch stairs and in through the hotel lobby where Jose was sitting at the reception desk reading page 163 of *The Banana Factor* by Ted Wylie and I carried her onto the ancient elevator and it went up to the second floor where I set Esther Martin down dripping wet in the hallway outside her door and she unlocked the door and she went in and she slammed the door shut in my face so I stood there for a long moment wondering what the hell was going on and then I

153

turned and I went back to the ancient elevator and I went up to the third floor to my room where I threw my wet clothes off and I fell across the bed and I went to sleep.

This is the end of chapter seven of this lousy novel and here's the quiz I said I'd be giving you to see if you were paying close attention to all the opening chapters and you should be able to answer 4 out of 5 of the following questions right:

1. *What did Mary Wilde write about?*
2. *Who wrote the short story about the high school English teacher who throws herself over a rushing waterfall?*
3. *What 3 angels did Esther Martin write about?*
4. *What state of the country did Dr. Frank R. Brainard come from?*
5. *Who did I tell Ted Wylie was the greatest influence on my own writing?*

That's the quiz and if you were paying close attention to all the opening chapters then you should be able to answer 4 out of 5 of the questions right but if you can't then that means you have to go back to chapter one and begin reading the whole thing all over again but if you answered 4 out of 5 of the questions right then that means you can keep reading these lines that I am trying to write right now.

eight/Friday

And I woke up about 7:00 AM and I lay in bed thinking how weary
I was of this corny boring writers conference and I began toying
with the idea of packing my bag and walking right out of the San
Marcos Hotel this morning and getting a bus and going to the airport in Santa Barbara and flying back to New York where I'd
phone Cindy Stevens and ask her to marry me and we'd both go live
in a little cabin in Vermont where I'd write my own writing all day
and Cindy would go out walking in the woods and screw around
with the squirrels all day until it was time for us to stay up all night
making love and in about 5 years I'd have 4 or 5 of my own novels
behind me and then I could make them all into stage plays so Cindy
could play in them and they'd be a hell of a lot better for her than
that sick play she was about to play on Broadway because I'd write
parts for her where she could keep washing her hands scrub scrub
scrub every time she was onstage and everyone would see she was
one of the outstanding actresses of our time but as I lay there day-
dreaming all these things I suddenly remembered that Ralph Perry
never paid anyone until after the writers conference was all over so

I couldn't afford to walk out of here until Sunday afternoon so I got up and I got dressed and I went down to the dining room where I got a cup of coffee and I sat down at a corner table and I began to sip at my coffee when Laura Perry came over and she asked me brightly if I minded some company at breakfast and I said brightly not at all so she sat down and she pulled her long shawl around her shoulders and she asked me how I liked the writers conference this year and I said gosh I thought it was swell and then she asked if I was coming to hear Miriam Morse give the poetry program this evening and I said I was so tired I hadn't been planning on it and Laura Perry said:

"If you're so tired then Miriam Morse's poetry program is just what you need because her little poems are like fine tiny jewels of supernatural stillness so do try to come because it would mean so much to Miriam Morse to know that you were there and after all this is the last evening program before the farewell banquet."

And I said I'd try to make it and then Laura Perry leaned forward toward me and she said:

"I had a manuscript conference yesterday with that lovely Esther Martin who always wears those delightful daffodil dresses and she told me you had been so very helpful with her short stories and I think her poems are exquisite and lyrical and I'm going to nominate her to receive the poetry award for this year."

And I said that would be fine because Esther Martin needed to have some recognition for her work and then as I got up to leave Laura Perry called out after me:

"I'll tell Miriam Morse that you'll be coming to her poetry program this evening."

And I walked out of the dining room and through the hotel lobby where Jose was sitting behind the reception desk reading page 167 of *The Banana Factor* by Ted Wylie and I kept walking out onto the porch and down the wooden stairs and along the narrow strip of beach and as I walked I was thinking about the fiction class I was going to teach later on in the morning because I knew it would be the last writing class I would ever teach for the rest of my life so I wanted to think about what I was going to say because I wanted to cut through the phony nonsense of this writers conference and talk about the real hell of trying to write your own writing and how there are times when it feels like your whole life is a lie and you have some sort of a dehydration of the heart or a polio of the soul or a cancer of the understanding and it feels as if your insides had been taken out and set aside on dry ice and I knew no one here wanted to hear any of this because most of the people here had managed to make their own writing into a semi-interesting hobby but as I stood there watching the great waves that were on their way to burst into surf I knew this was what I wanted to talk about because I wanted to tell them how it feels to be so close to the sore at the source of the soul and when I thought that thought then I turned and I walked back up to the hotel and through the lobby and on down to the main hall where Ralph Perry was just finishing up his last marketing lecture and I stood outside the door and I heard him say:

And for gosh sakes do be sure to write your own writing the way the publisher tells you to write it because he's the one that has to sell it and he knows what the readership wants to read and after all publishing is selling and that's what real writing is all about—

And I felt sick at the thought of all those students in there copying down this idiocy in their notebooks so I waited for the marketing class to finish and for Laura Perry to wheel in her little cart and serve up her crumby cookies and her insipid iced tea and then I went in and over to the old oak desk and I sat down there and I looked out over the great vacancy of faces that were all waiting for me to begin talking to them and for an instant there I began to taste the empty space between me and all those students and I began to eat whole areas of air and for a long moment I was frozen motionless but then I began to talk about writers and writing and I said I had told them in the first class that when you are really writing it is the easiest thing in the universe because it feels like you are listening to a distant brook that keeps on babbling to itself about itself but I said that was a lie because I said real writing is the hardest thing in the universe and sometimes you can listen to the distance all you want to and you won't hear anything and so I said it takes a lot of time and it takes a lot of patience and faith to try to write your own writing and I said you also have to have an instinct for bullshitlessness so you won't lie to yourself about yourself and you also have to have the courage to go through long dry periods of not writing your own writing and sometimes these dry periods can go on for some 5 years at a time but I said even so you still have to keep trying to write your own writing because you know in your own mind that it is the only kind of worthwhile life that you can ever live and when I said that I looked out over the class and I saw no one was taking any notes on what I was saying because Betsy Childs had stopped doodling stick figures in her open notebook and Ted Wylie had stopped fixing his beady eagle eye on me and Esther Martin had stopped staring straight ahead in the air and all the other conferees were beginning to shift around in their seats and they were trying to keep their eyes aside so I said okay I'll sum it up for you and I said real writing is and always has been and always will be one of the loneliest lives that you can ever live and no amount of writers conferences or fiction classes or individual manuscript conferences can ever lessen the awful loneliness of a writer who has been brought face to face with writing his own writing but I said this awful loneliness can teach you more than any writing teacher can ever teach you because I said the only way to learn how to write is to write and when I said this I paused and no one said anything so I got up and I walked out of the main hall and I went down to the dining room and I thought now I've blown the whistle on their whole silly scene so now I'll never be invited back to another writers conference for as long as I live and suddenly I began to feel pretty good about myself and when I sat down to eat my lunch I noticed the tuna salad tasted pretty good and the iced tea tasted pretty good and just then the conferees began coming into the dining room and some of them looked over in my direction but I noticed that no one sat on my side of the dining room except for Ted Wylie who came right over and he sat down next to me and he leaned forward toward me and he said:

"Listen to me Morrison that was nothing but a lot of diddletwat because you don't know how to teach anyone anything and you don't even know how to screw one of your stupid writing students because what the hell did you think you were doing with Esther Martin out there on that narrow strip of beach last night and if I'd wanted her to go drown herself in the open ocean I'd have told you that was what I wanted for my new novel but I told you I wanted you to screw her ass off so I could watch the 2 of you doing it through my field binoculars but no you just kept chasing each other in and out of those great waves and now I don't have time to crap around with you so at 10:00 PM tonight I'll expect you to be upstairs outside Esther Martin's door and I'll be there also to go right in with you because I am going to watch as you make love to her and this time you'd better do exactly as I say."

And I sat there listening to Ted Wylie's latest mad plan and it sounded like he was losing his mindless mind so I just waited until he was done and then I said quite quietly that I was tied up tonight and when I said that Ted Wylie began shouting out at me:

"You'd better be there at 10:00 PM tonight Morrison or I swear to God I'll spread the word around the whole publishing industry that you're bad news and you'll never get another book of yours published for as long as you live!!"

And Ted Wylie got up and he stalked out of the dining room so I just sat there sipping at my iced tea and then I lit a cigarette and I blew some beautiful blue fumes in the air and I watched as they formed all sorts of curious configurations and I thought I still felt pretty good about myself and then I got up and I walked out of the dining room and through the lobby and down to the reading room where Douglas Mercer was waiting for me and I sat down and I took out his short story and this is what it was about:

A young boy is playing touch football all afternoon with his friends and then as he walks back home he begins to daydream about how he is the star quarterback for the New York Giants football team and he sees himself fade so far back he loses sight of all possible pass receivers so he stands there in an instant of air as he waits for the crush of muscle that will send him collapsing backwards still holding on to that damn ball and when he gets home he takes a bath and his father's electric shaver drops down splash into the warm bath water and the boy is killed in a blinding flash of blue lightning.

And I said this was interesting but I wasn't sure what the point was and Douglas Mercer shrugged and he said he wasn't sure anything really had a point because he said life itself was sort of senseless and I said maybe so but I thought there were better ways of dealing with its senselessness than just writing a senseless short story and Douglas Mercer shrugged and he said maybe so and then he began to gather up his short story manuscript so I asked him what he thought of all the things I'd been saying in the fiction class this morning and Douglas Mercer looked at me and he said:

"You want to know what I thought of all the things you were saying in the fiction class this morning and what can I say man except you are in big trouble."

And I asked him what he meant by that and Douglas Mercer said:

"You are in big trouble man because you really believe all those things you were saying to us about how writing your own writing is the hardest thing in the universe and that's why you are in big trouble man because you shouldn't even be here at this corny boring writers conference because you should be off somewhere writing your own writing and you should leave all that phony baloney stuff to dudes like Ralph Perry because he's much better than you are at farting up a storm because that man don't believe in nothing he ever says and that's cool but man you believe in everything you say and that's why it hurts just listening to you and that's why you are in big trouble man."

And I asked Douglas Mercer if he'd gotten anything at all out of this writers conference and he said:

"Yeah and I got this one thing out of the writers conference because there is a sweet lady here named Betsy Childs and she carries a notebook around with her that is all filled with stick figures who are fucking each other in all sorts of oddball positions and I think I might like to try and write about what a neat sweet lady she really is."

And I said that sounded okay and I wished him luck with writing about her and then Douglas Mercer got up and he wished me luck with writing my own writing and he left the reading room and just then Dorothy Kingsley came in and she was an older woman with a beautiful sane face and fierce gray eyes and I took out her novel manuscript and this is what it was about:

A mountain climber takes a group of tourists to the wrong ledge of a sheer rock glacial gorge and he leaves them there to die of exposure and as the tourists lie all huddled together there for 3 long days and nights it comes out that one of them is the long lost brother of the mountain climber and 20 years ago this brother swindled the mountain climber out of the family fortune and that's why the mountain climber left all the tourists up there on the wrong ledge to die of exposure and when the other tourists find out who the long lost brother is they pick him up and they toss him to his death down the sheer rock glacial gorge.

And I told Dorothy Kingsley that I thought this was the best written manuscript I'd seen here at the conference and when I said that she clapped her hands together and she said:

"Oh I'm so glad because I spent the last 3 years working on this novel manuscript and I wasn't quite sure that it came off because I tried a reversal of the usual whodunit formula since here you know it's the mountain climber who dunit but you don't know who he dunit to because you don't know which of the tourists is the long lost brother or at least you don't find out until the very last chapter."

And I said yes that was certainly a good way of reversing the usual whodunit formula and then Dorothy Kingsley leaned forward toward me and she asked:

"Did you guess who the long lost brother was?"

And I tried to remember who the long lost brother was but my head was swimming in a sea of all those other student manuscripts I'd been reading over this past week and I thought maybe the long lost brother was the young boy who wanted to be star quarterback for the New York Giants football team but I thought no that was Douglas Mercer's short story so then I thought maybe the long lost brother was the millionaire baseball owner who hits all those home runs but I thought no that was Joseph Baum's novel manuscript so then I thought maybe the long lost brother was the R.A.F. pilot who crash-landed on the Arabian desert and lived happily ever after with Fred the camel but I thought no that was Roberta Heite's novel manuscript and I saw Dorothy Kingsley was still leaning forward toward me with her fierce gray eyes and she was waiting for me to tell her who I thought the long lost brother was and suddenly I couldn't remember if I'd even finished reading through her novel manuscript and just then Dorothy Kingsley said:

"Did you think it was Reverend Smyth who kept talking about how he was his brother's keeper?"

And I thought ah good she's going to give me a few clues so at least I'll have a 50-50 chance if I answer yes or no and I figured she wouldn't give me the right answer right away so I decided to go with a no answer and I said no and Dorothy Kingsley clapped her hands together and she said:

"Good because I didn't think you'd fall for anything as obvious as that because Reverend Smyth was such a fuddy duddy and he couldn't have swindled his own grandmother out of her knitting needles but then did you think the long lost brother was Harry Edwards the insurance salesman from Chicago?"

And I began to sweat as I thought she's probably leading up to the right answer slowly and I don't think she'd give it to me this soon so I'd better say no again and I said no and Dorothy Kingsley clapped her hands together again and she said:

"Good because I can see how you might have thought it was Harry Edwards with all his talk about swindling as many people as he could but that's just because he's an insurance salesman from Chicago so then did you think the long lost brother was Kurt Duryea the former fighter pilot?"

And my stomach began to tighten as I braced myself for the wrong answer I knew I was going to give but I thought the first 2 names she gave me were wrong so maybe she's going to give me the right name now and so I should probably say yes so yes I said and my heart was going like mad and yes I said yes it was Kurt Duryea the former fighter pilot yes yes yes and Dorothy Kingsley practically fell off her chair in triumph as she clapped her hands together and she said:

"I knew you'd think it was Kurt Duryea the former fighter pilot but don't you remember at the end of chapter 5 when Harry Edwards the insurance salesman from Chicago asks Kurt Duryea how many insurable relatives he has and Kurt Duryea says he has 4 and they are his wife and his 2 children and his sister who lives in St. Louis so that means Kurt Duryea couldn't possible be the long lost brother of the mountain climber!"

And I felt myself collapse in a heap of broken nerves as Dorothy Kingsley sat there gloating over me and she said:

"Everyone who's ever read my novel manuscript has said it was Kurt Duryea the former fighter pilot but of course you knew that was wrong when you read the final chapter."

And I wanted to ask Dorothy Kingsley who the long lost brother was but I thought I'd better leave it alone so I just nodded my head and I said yes she had certainly taken me in completely and Dorothy Kingsley began to gather up her novel manuscript and she said:

"I wanted you to be good and surprised when you found out there was no long lost brother because there was no family fortune because the mountain climber was a criminal psychopath who had escaped from an asylum in Geneva and he just liked to go around leaving tourists on the wrong ledges of sheer rock glacial gorges but then of course you know all about all that because you read the last chapter of my novel manuscript.''

And Dorothy Kingsley went breezing out of the reading room in triumph as I sank dead weight down in my chair and suddenly I wondered if there was no long lost brother then who did those tourists toss off the ledge to his death and I almost went running after Dorothy Kingsley to find out but then I said to hell with it and I sat there thinking my christ it will take me weeks to get all these images out of my mind from reading through so many student manuscripts and it felt as if I had sat through 3 dozen bad movies over the last week or else it felt as if I had drunk 3 dozen cases of stale root beer and all of a sudden I wanted to vomit up all that stale root beer bad movie imagery but just then I looked over and I saw Marianne Roseblatt was at the door with her 2 ball-point twinkle eyes and I thought thank god here comes my last individual manuscript conference and I felt like Hercules must have felt when he had finished cleaning almost all the bullshit out of those Augean stables and he looked over in a corner and he saw there was one last small pile of steaming bullshit left for him to deal with and I smiled at Marianne Roseblatt as she came in and she sat down and I took out her novel manuscript that was titled *A Tribute to Ted Wylie Based on My Reading of The Banana Factor* and this is what it was about:

A man has a BF score of 99 percent and this the largest Banana Factor ever recorded so he decides he has nothing to lose and he begins to marry as many women as he can until he has 50 wives and there is one wife in every state of the union and he begins to sign over property from one wife to another and pretty soon he has amassed a considerable fortune and every year he spends one week with each wife and he takes 2 weeks off in August to go vacation in the Bahamas all by himself and this goes on for 17 years until one day the man goes to his local readout center and he discovers his BF score has dropped down to a respectable 34 percent so now his only problem is how to get rid of all those wives and he does this by buying up a lot of air time on all the major TV networks and he holds a press conference where he announces that he is no longer legally married to anyone and then he goes out and he falls in love with a 10 year old girl who is busy blowing bubble gum and popping it in the air and they live happily ever after.

And I told Marianne Roseblatt she'd come pretty close to the totally mindless style of Ted Wylie's novel and Marianne Roseblatt just blinked her 2 ball-point twinkle eyes at me so then I asked her if she admired Ted Wylie so much then why hadn't she signed up for an individual manuscript conference with him instead of with me and she said:

"I wouldn't dare walk up to Ted Wylie and hand him an imitation of his own writing style because he's such a vicious cynical critic but then I thought if you wrote a note on the back of my manuscript saying you liked what I had written then I could show it to him."

And I said I didn't think Ted Wylie would pay any attention to anything I said because he'd be insulted by any writing that didn't come out of his own mindless mind and just as I said that my own mind went completely dead the way a car battery will suddenly go completely dead and I tried switching my mind's ignition key on and off a few times but there was no response so I knew my mind had come to a dead stall and it was lying idle and lifeless but Marianne Roseblatt was eyeing me with her 2 ball-point twinkle eyes so I thought I'd better say something and I tried forming a few words but it was like pushing a lot of cotton wads out of my mouth and just then I heard Marianne Roseblatt say she would take her manuscript to Ted Wylie anyway and she picked it up and she walked out of the reading room and I sat there feeling as if my brain had just been raped by a herd of wild cabbages and I knew I was dangerously close to the sore at the source of the soul so I told myself I had to get up out of the chair and start moving around the room because otherwise I might stay stationary in the chair and I would remain frozen motionless forever and then Ralph Perry would come and he would put a plaque across my back that said I was a memorial to the Unknown Writing Teacher and every year writing students from all over the world would make a pilgrimage to pay tribute to my stone cold lonely soul and they would all lay their manuscripts at my feet and then they would step back and they would whisper to one another all about how I used to tell them how to rewrite their writing and I thought my god I've got to get up and out of this chair before that happens to me so I began to lift myself up very slowly and I began to walk around the reading room and I went out through the hotel lobby where Jose was still sitting behind the reception desk and he was getting giddy with dizziness over page 169 of *The Banana Factor* by Ted Wylie and at that exact same instant Maureen Talbot was walking into Ralph Perry's office and she began to tell Ralph Perry that he had to hire her as a full time faculty member next year or else she'd walk right out of his office and never see him again and Ralph Perry swung around in his swivel chair and he said:

"But if you were a faculty member what the heck would you teach?"

And Maureen Talbot said:

"I'd teach all the fiction classes because Eliot Morrison won't be coming back here next year and as for Ted Wylie the only reason he ever agreed to come here in the first place was because I promised to put out for him."

And when Maureen Talbot said that Ralph Perry was so shocked and outraged that he almost fell off his swivel chair and he said:

"Do you mean to tell me you had to promise to let Ted Wylie take advantage of you just so he'd come here this year and wait until I have a talk with that man because I'll tell him a thing or 2 about the way we do things around here and that does not include his compromising the virtue of our Assistant Director."

But Maureen Talbot began to motion for Ralph Perry to calm down and she said:

"Don't go making such a big fuss about it because believe me he wasn't that much to put out for so all you need to do is tell me whether you'll let me teach the fiction classes next year."

And Ralph Perry looked out the window at the great waves as

they came breaking against the slippery glistening rocks and he said:

"I'd better think about it because gosh knows I've got to be sure I'm doing the right thing for the San Marcos Writers Conference."

And Maureen Talbot said she'd give Ralph Perry 24 hours to think it over and then she turned and she stalked out of his office and into the hotel lobby where she ran right into me and she said:

"Do you know what Ted Wylie told me to do with all my notebooks and he told me to toss them all onto a raging bonfire and I am not going to do any such thing because I will not waste all those years and years of taking notes and making love to all those writing teachers because I am going to use those notebooks to write my own novel that will tell everyone everything there is to tell about writers and writing."

And I said that sounded like a fine idea and then Maureen Talbot leaned forward toward me and she whispered in my ear:

"And did you know that Ted Wylie is writing a new novel and he is using you as one of the characters in it?"

And I said I wasn't going to be just one of the characters in his new novel because I was going to be the single central character in it and Maureen Talbot kept right on whispering to me:

"And did you know Ted Wylie has all sorts of things in this new novel about how the 2 of us made love when we were together 5 years ago and I think that's obscene and indecent for anyone to go writing that sort of thing about anyone else and besides he copied it all out of my own notebooks and he's not even giving me any credit for it."

And I said it sounded like Maureen Talbot was mad because Ted Wylie had beaten her at her own game and Maureen Talbot kept right on whispering to me:

"And did you know Ted Wylie has things in there about how you used to like for me to suck on your nuts and oh I feel so ashamed for telling him all those things."

And I said Maureen Talbot shouldn't worry about it because

she was the best nut sucker I'd ever known and I said I'd be happy to write that out in a dust jacket statement she could use for her own novel and just then the ancient elevator arrived so we both got on and we went up to the second floor where Maureen Talbot got off and then I went up to the third floor where I went down to my room and I threw myself across the bed because my brain was racing because I knew I was still dangerously close to the sore at the source of the soul and I thought my christ what if I had a heart attack in front of one of my writing classes and I began to spit blood all over the laps of the students in the front row as I went lurching out of my chair and flailing my arms as my stark heart kept clenching and unclenching like an angry fist inside my rib cage and all those students would probably think it was just some sort of a writing exercise so they would start writing stream of consciousness in their open notebooks as I fell forward on all fours coughing out my consciousness all over the classroom floor and I would have an advanced case of aphasia so all I could do would be to lie there on the rock-hard hospital bed with a lot of plastic tubes poked up my nose and taped on my arms and stuck in my anus and as I lay there all these writing students would line up beside my bed and they would file by me and smile and say something polite and they would all lay their manuscripts on my stomach and the pile would grow higher and higher and heavier and heavier until my rib cage was suddenly crushed to mush and as I thought all these things I tried to calm myself down and I told myself I would never face a writing class again for as long as I live because I was through being a writing teacher because I was going to try and write my own writing for the rest of my life but all the while I was thinking these things my brain still kept racing all the way into a deep sleep where I dreamed a marathon dream that was a mad scramble of all the manuscripts that I'd read over the past week and this was the dream:

> A girl kills her parents so she goes to Canada where she meets this camel named Fred who owns a baseball team and they fall in love and they hit a lot of home runs and then they sit down

to eat a lot of roast beef dinners and then they walk down by a
bridge that overlooks a rushing waterfall and they make love
but one day Fred the camel goes off to the college of his choice
and the girl writes him a lot of sickening saccharine sentimental letters but she never gets any answer to them because thank
god camels can't write so the girl goes out and she gets laid by a
lot of Canadian cadets in a tank and on top of a helicopter and
inside a missile silo and under a pup tent but then she holds a
press conference and she announces that she is no longer legally married to anyone and then she marches all the cadets on
up a sheer rock glacial gorge hup hup hup hup and she leaves
them all on the wrong ledge there and she keeps climbing up to
the top of the mountain where she can see to the very ends of
the earth and while she is up there she drops a great huge mahogany cabinet down on top of all the cadets and their guts
gush pus and custard and it oozes on down all over the sheer
rock glacial gorge and then the girl goes home and she takes a
nice warm bath and as she is lolling around there in the bathtub
she watches the water buoy up her beautiful 2 boobs and she
begins to think about Fred the camel with that big sexy hump
on his back so she begins to diddle with her deedee right there
in the bathtub and suddenly her father's electric shaver drops
down splash into the warm bathwater and there is a blinding
flash of blue lightning and the girl is off in hee haw country
where there is no knowing her—

And as I was dreaming this dream Sylvester Appleby was sitting outside the hotel in the small enclosure that housed the garbage
pails and he was writing in his small pocket notebook what Harry
Holton had told him the night before and this is what he wrote:

Harry Holton says if a girl turns her back on you and you come
up behind her and you put your hand on her shoulder while her
back is turned to you then that really makes her want to get
laid.

And just then Harry Holton came out of the kitchen and he
told Sylvester Appleby that it was high time for them to make their
move with Esther Martin because he said:
"She has a room on the second floor and you won't have any

trouble at all man so just go knock on her door tonight and you'll be in bed with her in no time at all."

And Sylvester Appleby gulped a big gulp because he had no idea he was going to have to do this one all by himself so he said:

"Won't you be coming with me?"

And Harry Holton said:

"No dumbbell because she'd get suspicious if she saw the 2 of us standing out there in the hall and besides she's probably already seen me reading all her secret sexual signals in the dining room so you'll have to be the one to make the first move but like I told you man you won't have any trouble at all because she is definitely and unquestionably wide open and so once you get inside then I'll sneak in and then all 3 of us will have ourselves a ball."

And that seemed to make sense to Sylvester Appleby although he still didn't know what the hell he was supposed to do so he said:

"What do I say to her when I knock on her door?"

And Harry Holton said:

"You should use the really direct approach man so when she comes to the door just come right out and say you want to fuck her and you can bet she'll zap herself out of that yellow dress and she'll pop down on the bed where you can hop right on top of her."

And Sylvester Appleby gulped another big gulp and he looked sideways at Harry Holton because he was thinking this was his last chance to make up for that dumb mistake he made last night when he began that goofy stupid gagging on his iced tea up at Betty's Diner just as Harry Holton was edging his right elbow on into the left thigh of the waitress because now Harry Holton was giving Sylvester Appleby one last chance to show that he did believe in the secret sexual signal system and Sylvester Appleby didn't want to screw things up again so he said:

"Okay Harry I'll do it."

And just then I woke up from my dream and I looked at my wristwatch and I saw it was 8:00 PM and time for the poetry program downstairs and I had promised Laura Perry I'd be there so I jumped off the bed and I changed my shirt and I ran to the ancient elevator and I went down to the lobby and into the main room where I found a place in the last row next to Cleveland Mason who stood up and shook hands with me and he said he would be giving me something by the end of the week and I said that was fine and just then Laura Perry went up to the podium and she began adjusting her long shawl around her shoulders as she introduced Miriam Morse:

> This is the seventh year that our dear Miriam Morse has been with us at the San Marcos Writers Conference and aside from all her duties here she is also editor of the *Poets Nook* column for the San Marcos *Times* and she is also moderator of the KSMC program *Readers Riches* and she has also published 3 volumes of her own verse with Advantageous Press and these books are *Held in His Hands* and *What Pain What Joy* and *Prism of Love* and who knows what other treasures of creativity our dear Miriam Morse may be preparing for us there in the warehouse of her heart and I know we are all in for a delightful treat because her little poems are like fine tiny jewels of supernatural stillness so it gives me great pleasure to introduce Miriam Morse to you.

And the audience applause was like the patter of spring rain as Miriam Morse came up to the podium and she was wearing a grotesque bouquet of plastic flowers and large lavender hat and after a few nervous bird chirps Miriam Morse said she would begin by reading a poem from *Prism of Love* and this is the poem she read:

> Of field and tree
> And sky and sea
> And fancy free
>   I sing—
>
> Of swan and duck
> And hens that cluck
> And babes that suck
>   I sing—
>
> Of heart and hand
> And wind and sand
> And this glad land
>   I sing.

And Miriam Morse chirped her way through the poem as if she were giving an imitation of a slightly deranged sparrow and Laura Perry sighed a long sigh in the front row as she rearranged her long shawl around her shoulders but Douglas Mercer was sitting a few rows ahead of me and he turned his head around and he began rolling his eyes skyward in mock ecstasy and I was afraid to laugh for fear I would fall forward on the floor so I just sat there thinking what the hell did this diddletwat have to do with trying to write one's own writing because one's own writing keeps happening each instant of one's inner life and it happens imperceptibly like daylight breaking through gray haze and it happens haphazardly like a lot of tiny globules of mercury that keep forming and reforming themselves into infinitesimal fine tiny beads as if the brainlake itself were made up of so many magic moieties and it happens hypnotically like great waves that keep coming in to break against the slippery glistening rocks and anything less than trying to write one's own writing was like nothing was happening at all so I began to look along the back row of seats to see how many pairs of feet I would have to step over to get out the door and I counted 6 pairs of feet so I knew there would be 6 pairs of angry eyes glaring up at me as I began to step over their feet but I thought what the hell I can't sit through any more of this bird chirp stuff so I stood up and I excused myself to Cleveland Mason who stood up also and he shook my hand and said he would be giving me something by the end of the conference and I said that was fine and I stumbled on and mumbled an apology to Dorothy Kingsley and I stumbled and mumbled over the feet of Mary Anne Berre and Susan Restnor and Roberta Heite and Mary Wilde until I had reached the end of the row and I ducked out the door and I ran through the hotel lobby and on out to the porch where I gulped in a lot of huge lungfuls of fresh air as if I had suddenly come up out of a deep-sea dive and as I stood there on the porch I began to wonder where Esther Martin was because I hadn't seen her at the poetry program and I thought that was odd because Laura Perry said she was going to nominate Esther Martin for the poetry award this year and as I stood there wondering where

Esther Martin was just then Ted Wylie was getting on the ancient elevator from the second floor because he was on his way down to the hotel lobby where he was going to put through an important long distance collect phone call to Dr. Max Wittgenstein in New York City so he pushed the button for the lobby and the ancient elevator closed its door and it began wheezing its way down but then Ted Wylie looked at his wristwatch and he saw that it was almost 10:00 PM and that was the time he had told me to meet him outside Esther Martin's door so he could go in and watch me make love to her so he pushed the button on the ancient elevator for it to turn around and go back up to the second floor again and this was more than the ancient elevator could handle so it lurched upwards for a moment and then it settled into a stubborn stall halfway between the hotel lobby and the second floor and it began to emit a sick sweet acid scent and then a thin wisp of blue smoke began to rise from the wiring overhead and then there was nothing but dead air and downstairs in the hotel lobby Jose was sitting behind the reception desk and he was getting giddy with dizziness over page 171 of *The Banana Factor* by Ted Wylie when all of a sudden he heard a muffled clubbing that was coming from inside the elevator shaft and Jose dropped his paperback book and he darted around the reception desk and he ran over to the ancient elevator where he began to press the lobby button but that only made another thin wisp of blue smoke begin to rise from the wiring overhead and the ancient elevator began to emit more sick sweet acid scent and the muffled clubbing from inside the elevator shaft got much louder and just then Mr. Ruiz appeared and he told Jose to run up the backstairs and press on the second floor button and Mr. Ruiz said he would stay downstairs and press on the lobby button and maybe between the 2 of them something good would happen so Jose ran up the backstairs to the second floor where he began to press on the button up there but that only made another thin wisp of blue smoke begin to rise from the wiring overhead and the ancient elevator began to emit more sick sweet acid scent and then the muffled clubbing from inside the elevator shaft stopped and there was silence in the dead

173

air because Ted Wylie had curled himself up into a small body ball on the floor of the elevator because he was remembering something that had happened to him a very long time ago when he was a small child and his mother tossed him into the bathroom of their house with a few tuna salad sandwiches and some iced tea and a huge bunch of bananas and then she locked the bathroom door and she went off to Atlantic City for 17 days and little Teddy Wylie had to stay locked up in there all by himself so he curled himself up into a small body ball on the cold tile of that bathroom floor and when his mother came back and let him out he wandered around as if he were in some other air and right now as Ted Wylie was curled up in a small body ball on the floor of the ancient elevator he felt almost as awful as little Teddy Wylie had felt so long ago and just then the ancient elevator let out a dismal pneumatic sigh and then it began to emit one last sick sweet acid scent and **then** it sent one last thin wisp of blue smoke that rose from the wiring overhead and it began to lurch its way on upwards to the second floor where it shuddered to a halt and when the door opened Jose was standing there in the hall and Jose looked inside the ancient elevator and he saw there was a small body ball that was lying on the floor and then he saw this small body ball begin to roll its way slowly out of the ancient elevator and into the hallway of the second floor and right on up to where Jose was standing so Jose reached out his hand and he tried to touch the small body ball but just then Ted Wylie sprang upright like a gigantic jack-in-the-box and he swatted Jose clear across the hall where he went sprawling up against the wall and just then Mr. Ruiz came running up the backstairs to the second floor and Mr. Ruiz began wringing his hands and dancing up and down in front of Ted Wylie and he said:

"I phone for someone come see elevator but is no worry because is only once in while so is only nuisance."

And Ted Wylie whirled around and he roared:

"You are the fucking nuisance with your broken-down San Marcos Hotel and your pukey tuna salad and your pissy iced tea

and your creepy cretin people like this little illiterate who sits be-
hind the reception desk!!"

And Jose sensed that Ted Wylie was saying something about
him so he began to nod and smile but Ted Wylie whirled around
and he swatted Jose clear across the hall again where he went
sprawling up against the other wall and then Ted Wylie turned and
he ran down the backstairs and through the hotel lobby where he
slammed himself into the pay phone booth and he dialed the operator and he shouted out at her:

"Get me person to person in New York a Dr. Max Wittgenstein
and tell him it's a collect call from Ted Wylie in California and
make it snappy."

And Ted Wylie sat there in the pay phone booth as the operator made the connections across Utah and Kansas and Indiana and
Pennsylvania to New York City where Dr. Max Wittgenstein was lying sound asleep in his bed and when the phone began to ring beside
his bed he reached out his hand in the dark and he picked up the receiver and he said:

"Zo?"

And the operator said he had a person to person collect call
from Mr. Ted Wylie in California and Dr. Wittgenstein said:

"Kollekt from Kalifornia?"

And Ted Wylie's voice broke in and he shouted out:

"Oh for Christ's sake Max accept the fucking charges and I'll
pay you when I get back to New York."

So Dr. Wittgenstein sat up in bed and he said:

"Fery vell operator und I vill axcept de chargez."

And Ted Wylie said:

"Listen Max I'm in big trouble because my mother tossed me
in the bathroom with a few pukey tuna salad sandwiches and some
pissy iced tea and a huge bunch of bananas and then she locked the
bathroom door and she went off to Atlantic City for 17 days and I
had to stay curled up in a small body ball on the cold tile of that
bathroom floor and that's why I don't know who I am as a writer

or as a human being so I've got to see you when I get back to New York next week before I lose my mindless mind."

And Dr. Wittgenstein switched on the night light and he said: "Yez vell you call me ven you get in und ve zet up a time."

And Ted Wylie said:

"Tuesday?"

And Dr. Wittgenstein said:

"Yez Tuezday und you call ven you get in."

And then Dr. Wittgenstein hung up the phone and he laid his head back on the pillow and he thought:

"Zo Ted Vylie haz come back to me und dot meanz he haz an 86 perzent chanz uf going marblz."

And Dr. Wittgenstein began groping with his hand in the wastebasket for his copy of *The Banana Factor* by Ted Wylie that he had tossed in a few days ago but it wasn't there because the cleaning woman had fished it out and she had taken it home and right now she was reading it in her fourth-floor rented room in Brooklyn and she was beginning to get giddy with dizziness and at that same instant Ted Wylie stood up in the pay phone booth and he began to push at the door to open it but it was stuck so he began to kick against it but nothing happened so he began to rock the whole pay phone booth back and forth until its wooden thighs began to grate against the floor and Jose was back sitting behind the reception desk reading page 172 of *The Banana Factor* by Ted Wylie when he looked up and he saw the pay phone booth was swaying back and forth in the hotel lobby like a Mexican jumping bean only this time Ted Wylie was the helpless worm trapped inside so Jose began clapping his hands together in beat to the rhythmic swaying of the pay phone booth but then it swayed a little too far over in one direction and it stayed suspended endlessly in mid-air for an instant and then the whole thing toppled over and it smashed with a terrific crash all over the lobby floor and Jose stopped his clapping as he saw Ted Wylie leap like a giant moth out of the wreckage of the pay phone booth as if he were bursting out of a huge cocoon and Ted Wylie flew right past Jose and he ran on up the backstairs and Jose just sat there gaping at this weird sight because if Jose had known that this huge moth of a man who had just flown out of the pay phone booth was the same Ted Wylie who had written the words that were right there on page 172 of *The Banana Factor* by Ted Wylie then Jose would have had a few things to figure out about the nature of art and reality but since Jose had no idea that books were written by real people who leaped like giant moths out of the wreckage of pay phone booths then he could just shrug his shoulders and go back to reading page 173 of *The Banana Factor* by Ted Wylie and all the while this was happening I was still standing outside on the hotel porch breathing in the clear night air and wondering whether I ought to go up to Esther Martin's room and find out if she was all right and at that exact same instant Esther Martin was sitting at her desk in her room and she had been there since 8:00 PM and she was holding her pen suspended in mid-air over a blank piece of paper because she was waiting for her angel voices to come tell her what to write but nothing was coming to her so she sat there for an hour or so until there was a knock on the door about 9:00 PM when she set her pen down on the desk and she got up and she walked over to the door and she opened it and there was Sylvester Appleby standing out in the hall with his hair falling all over his face and he gulped a big gulp and he said:

"Hi there my name is Sylvester Appleby and I work in the kitchen and I was just wondering if you'd like me to come in and fuck you."

And there was a long moment of silence as Esther Martin stood there in her own air and then she stepped backwards and she said:

"Thank you very much but I'm waiting for the angel Gabriel."

And then Esther Martin slammed the door in Sylvester Appleby's face and she turned and she walked back to her writing desk and she sat down and she held her pen suspended in mid-air over the blank piece of paper on the desk and she stayed that way for another half an hour until there was a knock on the door about 9:30 PM when she set her pen down on the desk and she got up and she walked over to the door and she opened it and there was Joseph

Baum standing out in the hall with his fly wide open and his cute little cock was sticking right out there in the air and he said:

"You want watch me hit home run?"

And there was a long moment of silence as Esther Martin stood there in her own air and then she stepped backwards and she said:

"Thank you very much but I'm waiting for the angel Gabriel."

And then Esther Martin slammed the door in Joseph Baum's face and she turned and she walked back to her writing desk and she sat down and she held her pen suspended in mid-air over the blank piece of paper on the desk and she stayed that way for another half hour until there was a knock on the door about 10:00 PM when she set her pen down on the desk and she got up and she walked over to the door and she opened it and there I was standing in the hall with my shaggy hair and my crumpled coat and the dislocated look in my eyes and I said I was just wondering why Esther Martin wasn't at the poetry program this evening and there was a long moment of silence as Esther Martin stood there in her own air and then she stepped backwards and she fainted dead away and she fell down in a neat small body heap of bright canary yellow and I knelt over her and I felt for her pulse and it was going lickety split so I reached down and I lifted her up in my arms and I carried her over to the bed and I set her down there and I whispered her name in her ear Esther Martin and I told her she should come back from wherever it was she was right now and after a moment or so Esther Martin opened her large dark startled eyes and she lay there staring up at me and so I smiled and I said hi but Esther Martin let out a quick cry of surprise as if I were a creature from the overworld and she said:

"You've come to tell me what to write."

And I thought oh my god she thinks I'm the angel Gabriel and Esther Martin kept staring up at me and asking me to tell her what I wanted her to write so I said okay I am the angel Gabriel and I've come to tell you that all of us angels got together last night and we had ourselves an angel writers conference and we decided it was high time for you to try to write your own writing out of your own voice and so that means none of us angels will be coming to tell you what to write anymore but I said that's okay because you can do it on your own now only be sure you give your stories a little more of a point and then I asked Esther Martin if she understood what I was saying to her and there was a long pause and then she said:

"If that's what you want for me to do then I'll try to do it."

And I said I had to be on my way now because us angels had a lot of skywriting to do and I got up from off the edge of the bed and I told Esther Martin to get some rest and I did not lean over and I did not give her a quick passionless benediction kiss on the lips because I just turned and I walked out of her room and I went back upstairs to my room where I lay down on my bed and I fell asleep.

This is the end of chapter eight of this lousy novel and by this time if you don't like the book then you should have tossed it over your shoulder a long time ago and gone on to other things unless of course you were being paid to read this whole thing all the way through to the end like some book reviewers are paid to read books all the way through to the end so then they can write a lot of phony longwinded book reviews or else maybe you're paying someone else to make you read this whole thing all the way through to the end like students in a half-assed literature class who will have to take some dumb midterm exam that asks them to write a lot of asshole essay questions on what this lousy novel is all about and if that's the way it is with you I mean if you are paying someone else or if you are being paid by someone else to keep reading this whole thing all the way through to the end then I guess you have no choice because you have to keep reading these lines that I am trying to write right now.

nine/Saturday

And I woke up and I lay in bed thinking thank god this is Saturday so nothing much will happen today and all I have to do is go through the phony closing ceremonies and pick up my paycheck tomorrow and then head back to New York so I stretched out and yawned and then I got up and I got dressed and I went down to the dining room where I got a cup of coffee and I sat off at a corner table and just then Marianne Roseblatt came over and she sat down next to me and her 2 ball-point twinkle eyes looked like small bloodshot dots and I asked her if she'd shown her satire Banana Factor short story to Ted Wylie and she picked up a small plastic fork and she began to jab a lot of sharp hard jabs into the plastic tablecloth and she said:

"Yes I showed it to that faggoty bastard and he took 17 seconds to glance through it and then he tore the whole thing into fine tiny pieces and he tossed them over his shoulder onto the floor and then he began to stomp around on all the pieces until he had ground them into the floorboards and then he shouted out at me that I should give up writing completely and go in for manslaughter or sodomy or horse torture or something really useful and then he yelled for me to get the hell out of his room and never speak to him again for as long as I lived."

And I said that didn't sound like Ted Wylie thought so highly of her writing and Marianne Roseblatt just kept jabbing a lot of sharp hard jabs with her small plastic fork and she said:

"That son of a bitch can go fuck himself with his crappy Banana Factor because I'm going to go off and write a novel that will be one hundred times better than anything that beady-eyed ego could ever write."

And I said I thought Marianne Roseblatt could do it easily if she really set her mind to it and just as I was saying that Sylvester Appleby was sitting down outside in the small enclosure that housed the garbage pails and began to sob as Harry Holton stood over him and he was slapping his fist in his hand because he was trying to figure out what had gone wrong when Sylvester Appleby went up to Esther Martin's room last night and Harry Holton said:

"All the secret signals said that Esther Martin was definitely and unquestionably wide open so you must have made some goofy stupid mistake so tell me what the hell did you say to her?"

And Sylvester Appleby stopped sobbing and he gulped a big gulp and he said:

"I took the really direct approach like you said I should and I said hi there my name is Sylvester Appleby and I work in the kitchen and I was just wondering if you'd like me to come in and fuck you and Esther Martin just stood there in her own air and then she stepped backwards and she said thank you very much but she was waiting for the angel Gabriel and then she slammed the door right in my face."

And Sylvester Appleby started to sob again as Harry Holton began shaking his head in disgust and he said:

"No wonder she slammed the door in your face because you shouldn't have told her that you work in the kitchen because she sure as hell wasn't going to go fucking any dumb slob that was nothing but kitchen shit for christs sake so listen to me now because when you go back up there tonight you should knock on her door and when she opens it you should tell her you're really a hotshot writer from the writers conference and the only reason you told her you were working in the kitchen was so you could get some background material for this big deal novel you're writing about writers and writing and you just wanted to test her last night to see what she'd say when you told her you work in the kitchen and all but she passed your test okay so now you're going to write her into your big deal novel as one of the leading characters and as soon as the novel is published it's going to be made into a major motion picture and you'll get a famous movie star to play her part and when you tell her all these things then you can bet she'll be flopping all over you in no time at all.''

And Sylvester Appleby gulped so hard he almost began gagging at the thought of having to go back up to Esther Martin's room tonight so she could slam the door in his face again and he said:

"Harry please let me off this one time please because I'll admit it was my own goofy stupid fault that I screwed things up last night because I can't do anything right and it has nothing to do with the secret sexual signal system because that works fine all the time only please don't make me go back up there tonight please.''

And Harry Holton shook his head in disgust and he began thinking my god am I going to have to put up with this whining chickenshit kid all the way down to Mexico City at the end of the summer but Sylvester Appleby picked up on that thought and he said:

"Listen Harry if I went up to Esther Martin's room again tonight you can bet she'd complain to Mr. Ruiz and then he'd fire both of us and then I couldn't pay both our ways down to that real Mexican whorehouse.''

And Harry Holton thought my god the kid has a point so he reached down and he picked up a pebble and he tossed it out over the gravel driveway and then after a long pause he said:

"Okay but you'll be missing a really great lay with Esther Martin but that's your own loss and anyway we're going to do that waitress up at Betty's Diner later on tonight because she's even more wide open than Esther Martin is so are you with me on that?"

And Sylvester Appleby nodded his head that he was with Harry Holton on that so Harry Holton said:

"Okay then after the farewell banquet tonight we'll race through cleaning up everything so we can scram-ass out and drive up to Betty's Diner because we're going to take that waitress out and we're going to ball her right in the back of the pickup truck."

And just then I was finishing my coffee and I got up and I wished Marianne Roseblatt good luck on writing her own novel and then I walked out of the dining room and down to Ralph Perry's office for the 10:00 AM staff meeting and when I got to the door I saw Laura Perry and Miriam Morse and Maureen Talbot and Ted Wylie were already all in there sitting around on chairs and they looked like a lot of fish that were lying half alive on dry ice and Ralph Perry was sitting in his swivel chair and he was chuckling to himself and sucking on his pipe as he looked out the window at the great waves that came in to break against the slippery glistening rocks and when he saw me he motioned for me to come in and sit down and he said:

"Well now everyone is here so we can begin to choose the writing awards for the best student manuscripts in fiction and nonfiction and poetry and you all know I'll be giving these out at the farewell banquet tonight and these writing awards mean an awful lot to the students here and they're also swell free publicity because the students always put them down on their résumés and that way we always get a lot of indirect advertising for the San Marcos Writers Conference."

And I thought what a weird way to see writing awards but Ralph Perry kept on going and he said:

"I've already decided to give the nonfiction writing award to Roberta Heite for a really swell article she did on the mating habits of camels in the Arabian desert and the award book I'll be giving her is a signed manuscript copy of my unpublished novel on the War of 1812."

And there was a murmur of approval around the room and then Ralph Perry asked Miriam Morse if she had chosen the poetry writing award and Miriam Morse perched up in her chair and she said it should go to Esther Martin for her exquisite and lyrical angel poems and Laura Perry bobbed her head up and down in strong agreement so Miriam Morse handed Ralph Perry an inscribed copy of *Prism of Love* for him to give to Esther Martin at the farewell banquet and then Ralph Perry swung his swivel chair around so he was facing Ted Wylie and he said:

"Well now we've got the nonfiction and the poetry writing awards all taken care of so who will be getting the fiction writing award for this year?"

And Ted Wylie fixed his beady eagle eye on Ralph Perry and he said:

"I haven't seen a damn thing here that deserves any award because the writing at this place wouldn't win honorable mention in a garbage dump."

And Ralph Perry looked over at me like a drowning puppy who was in desperate need of rescue so I said I thought Dorothy Kingsley's novel about a mountain climber who leaves a group of tourists on the wrong ledge of a sheer rock glacial gorge was about the best thing I'd seen so Ralph Perry beamed and he said:

"Fine then we're all agreed that Dorothy Kingsley will get the fiction writing award and the award book will be an autographed copy of *The Banana Factor* by Ted Wylie."

And Ralph Perry handed Ted Wylie a paperback copy of *The Banana Factor* for him to inscribe for Dorothy Kingsley but Ted Wylie tossed the book right back at Ralph Perry and he said:

"I'll be damned if I'm going to inscribe one of my own books for some menopausal broad whose work I've never even seen."

And Ralph Perry held the book in his hands and he said:

"Well now I can understand your feelings Mr. Wylie so perhaps I'll just inscribe it myself as Director of the San Marcos Writers Conference."

And Ralph Perry scribbled something on the flyleaf of the

book and then he put it on his desk with all the other award books and then he leaned back in his swivel chair and he looked out the window at the great waves that were coming in to break against the slippery glistening rocks and he said:

"Now let's keep these writing awards a secret until this evening's farewell banquet and gosh all I can say to all of you is that it's been such a really swell conference this year and I've always said this is such a great place to hold a writers conference because you can practically feel the creativity coming up from the floorboards and I always tell all the conferees if they can't write here then they can't write anywhere . . ."

And Ralph Perry's voice began to trail off and then he fell silent and he sat quite quiet in his swivel chair and it looked as if he might have slipped off on us and there was an embarrassed silence in the office until Laura Perry began to motion to us that the meeting was over and we should all leave so one by one we all got up and we filed out of the office but before I made it through the door I heard Ralph Perry's hoarse voice call out to me:

"Did you get a chance yet to read through my World War Two novel manuscript guy?"

And I turned around and I went back over to where Ralph Perry was sitting in his swivel chair and I said I hadn't had a chance to look at his manuscript yet but I would get to it this afternoon and I'd write out a statement he could use on the dust jacket of his book and Ralph Perry looked up at me and he patted my elbow with his hand and he thanked me and then I turned and I walked out of his office and Ted Wylie was waiting for me outside in the hall and I knew he was going to ask me about whether I had made it with Esther Martin last night like he told me to so I didn't wait for him to say anything but I asked him where the hell he was because I said I was waiting for him outside Esther Martin's door at 10:00 PM like he told me and I said finally I couldn't wait anymore so I went on in to Esther Martin's room and I said all sorts of glorious things began happening in there and I began rolling my eyes skyward with a mock ecstasy expression on my face and then I walked right past

Ted Wylie who just stood there in the hall looking as lost as a lost child who has just been told he was left out of a field trip to an amusement part and I keep on walking through the hotel lobby and into the dining room and I sat down at a corner table where I ate my lunch alone and then I lit a cigarette and I leaned back and I thought here it is Saturday so perhaps if I can stay sane I'll find out what happens on Saturday night at San Marcos and then I got up and I walked back through the hotel lobby where Jose was at the reception desk reading page 189 of *The Banana Factor* by Ted Wylie and I went out on the porch where I stood and looked up at the afternoon sky where there were these great gray rain clouds were gathering in the west and I saw the wind was beginning to whip the heads of the great waves and I knew that in a little while those skies would start cascading down terrific sheets of rain that would pelt hell out of all the shrubbery and underbrush along the coastline of San Marcos and then I turned and I went back into the hotel and up to my own room where I tossed my clothes off and I threw the manuscript of Ralph Perry's World War II novel down on my bed and I lay there reading through it and it didn't take me long to realize it was a disaster of writing because the entire novel kept telling what kind of buttons a rear admiral wore on his uniform and what kind of instruments were in his cabin and what kind of weather reports he got over his short wave radio and there wasn't one word about where the rear admiral was going or what he was supposed to be doing on the ship and instead there were lots of line drawings of the different insignias on his buttons and all the different barometer readings he recorded every day and the whole novel was the biggest collage of trivia I had ever seen and after a while I lay back on my bed and I wondered what kind of a dust jacket statement I could write about this hopeless manuscript that would make an old man happy and then I reached over and I opened a notebook and I wrote out this statement:

Who but Ralph Perry would put so many buttons and barometers and weather reports into a war novel and who but Ralph

Perry would care more about insignias and instruments than about a lot of vague issues like life and death and who but Ralph Perry would serve for 7 years as Director of the San Marcos Writers Conference that is dedicated to teaching student writers how to write books like this book?

And I thought that's the best I can do with it so I got up and I got dressed and I slipped the statement inside the black plastic cover of the novel manuscript and then I went downstairs to the hotel lobby and I went into the dining room where I saw Laura Perry was busy placing colorful paper frills at each place setting and Ralph Perry was bustling around all the different tables straightening the paper tablecloths and occasionally he would call out to Mr. Ruiz for gosh sakes to be sure there were enough paper napkins to go around and Mr. Ruiz was standing over by the kitchen door and he was immaculately dressed in a pin-striped suit with cameo cuff links and he couldn't have cared less about whether there were enough paper napkins to go around and I went over to Ralph Perry and I handed him his novel manuscript and I showed him the dust jacket statement I had written about it and Ralph Perry stood there reading through the statement and then his eyes began to well up with tears and he said:

"Aw gosh that's awful darn good of you guy."

And Ralph Perry called Laura Perry over to his side so she could read the statement and her eyes also began to well up with tears as she pulled her long shawl around her shoulders and I left the dining room and I went out onto the porch where the wind was blowing now against the windows of the hotel and making them shake and rattle in their frames and there were bits and chips of debris being blown along the narrow strip of beach and the shrubbery and underbrush were shaking hard with the pounding down of the wind and it was getting so rough I wondered if the old hotel would hold together for the night and just then Cleveland Mason came out on the porch and he said he would have something to give me by tomorrow morning and I said that would be fine and he shook my hand and he walked away and I went back in the hotel lobby where all the conferees were going on into the dining room for the farewell banquet so I went along with them and I sat at a table with Joseph Baum and Susan Restnor and Mary Wilde and Dorothy Kingsley and I saw Harry Holton and Sylvester Appleby were both dressed in white starch uniforms and they moved around the various tables with huge platters of steaming tuna salad casserole and large plastic cannisters of iced tea and everyone began to eat and talk about who they thought was going to win the writing awards this year and then when everyone had finished eating Ralph Perry stood up at his table and he began to clink with a plastic fork against an empty plastic cannister and everyone quieted down and Ralph Perry began to say a few words about what a really swell writers conference it was this year and how you could feel the creativity coming up from the floorboards and if you couldn't write here then you couldn't write anywhere and then he said he was awful gosh darn proud to announce the San Marcos Writers Conference writing awards for this year and everyone was silent as Ralph Perry read off the names of Dorothy Kingsley and Roberta Heite and Esther Martin and then everyone let out loud shouts of delight as the 3 conferees got up and they went over to Ralph Perry and they shook his hand and they got their book awards and then they went back to their seats and then Ralph Perry said:

"Now we have a special surprise for all of you in honor of our distinguished faculty member Mr. Ted Wylie."

And Ralph Perry motioned for the kitchen boys to carry in a huge cake with yellow frosting and the whole thing was in the shape of a giant banana and it had the words BANANA FACTOR spelled out across the top of it in little chocolate chips and everyone began to laugh and applaud as Harry Holton and Sylvester Appleby set the cake down right in front of Ted Wylie and they also placed a stack of paper plates in front of him so he could cut the cake in pieces and they could pass them round to all the conferees but Ted Wylie stood up at his table and he glared around at everyone and all the conferees thought he was going to make a speech so they quieted down and there was a long pause and then Ted Wylie said this was the sickest exhibition of philistinism he had ever seen and he turned and he stalked out of the dining room and there was dead silence in the dining room until someone asked what philistinism was and someone else said they thought it must be some sort of exotic venereal disease and then everyone began to pass around pieces of the giant banana cake and after a while the farewell banquet broke up and the conferees began to leave the dining room so I went up to my room where I fell down on my bed and I lay there trying to decide whether I should quit teaching all my writing classes back in New York City so I could spend the rest of my life trying to write my own writing and outside it was beginning to rain a steady heavy rain and downstairs in the dining room Harry Holton and Sylvester Appleby went racing around the various tables scooping up the paper plates and cups because they were hurrying to scram-ass out of there and drive up to Betty's Diner off Route One so they could make it with the waitress there and Sylvester Appleby asked Harry Holton if they shouldn't wait and do it some other night when it wasn't raining so hard because he didn't know anything about how to get laid in the rain but Harry Holton said:

"Not a chance man because all the secret signals say tonight is the night for that waitress."

And Sylvester Appleby gulped a big gulp and he said okay and they finished throwing all the paper plates and cups into the large plastic garbage pails out back and they stacked up the empty plastic cannisters in the kitchen sink and they took off their white starch uniforms and they got dressed in T-shirts and jeans and then they made a mad dash out the door across the gravel driveway to the San Marcos pickup truck and Sylvester Appleby sat by the window and Harry Holton sat in the driver's seat and he turned on the ignition and the windshield wipers and the lights and he began driving out onto Route One and as they drove along Harry Holton said:

"Don't forget that thing I told you about putting your hand on a woman's shoulder while her back is turned to you and how that really makes her want to get laid."

And Sylvester Appleby said he would not forget that thing and just then they drove into the parking lot of Betty's Diner and the 2 of them got out and they ran through the rain up to the diner and when they stumbled through the door they walked right into some pretty heavy sexual signals that were going on just then between the chef and waitress there because waitress had just refused to do something chef had asked her to do because chef had asked her to pose nude with her legs spread far apart so chef could get some photographs of a basset hound going down on her and waitress had said she would do no such thing and it wasn't as if waitress were all that modest about showing off her vagina because she had already posed nude for chef dozens of times and chef had taken hundreds of photos of her which he used in his private business which was running an underground correspondence club which he advertised in all the national sex magazines and the paid ads that chef wrote ran something like this:

Eager to correspond with well hung young stud who wants a lot of hot action and no phonies please but if you've got a rock-hard situation on your hands then write me right away and I can take a load off your mind.   Betty Smith   Box 127

And as soon as someone wrote in to one of these paid ads chef would send off a short answer that ran something like this:

Dear well hung young stud:

Thanks for your letter and I like your style a lot and I really want us to get our things together but gosh darn I have to have this little operation but as soon as that's over then we can meet and ball our brains out so meanwhile how would you like to see some nude photos of me and my moist pussy so you can stay hot for me and send $5 to cover the cost of printing these photos up because they're so far out I have to have them done privately and I can't wait to feel your throbbing cock inside of me.

Sincerely yours,
Betty Smith   Box 127

And chef always wrote these letters in the diner kitchen while the fried eggs sizzled and the hamburger patties spit on the griddle and he wrote with one hand as he used the spatula with the other hand to flip the hamburger patties and land the eggs once over lightly and you might say chef was the ideal writer because writing was the only thing he really enjoyed doing and he made the griddle sing as he wrote out all his phony Betty Smith letters and then he would mail them off to the correspondents all over the country and he would wait a week or so and sure enough the correspondents would write back with $5 so chef would mail them off 4 or 5 photos of waitress posing nude in various states of sexual readiness and there would be one photo of waitress touching her tongue to the top of her nose and another photo of waitress slipping her fingers in and out of her vagina and another photo of waitress with her eyes clouding over in vague appeal and there was one especially gross photo of waitress spreading her rear cheeks far apart to show off the small pink rim of her tiny tight asshole and these were the photos that would go off to all the correspondents who sent in their $5 and along with the photos there would also be a second letter that ran something like this:

Dear well hung young stud:

Here are the nude photos of me and I hope they show you how red hot I am for you and how I'd like to feel your rock-hard cock throbbing inside of me but gosh darn that mean old doctor says I can't ball anyone for another 2 weeks and isn't that a drag so listen if you send me another $5 to cover the costs then I'll send you some really far out shots of me in action with this boyfriend I used to go with and they'll show you how I can make your juices flow when we finally do get our things together.

Sincerely yours,
Betty Smith   Box 127

And chef wrote this letter with one hand while his other hand crumbled some heads of lettuce and then he tossed the lettuce shreds in with a lot of sliced tomatoes and cucumbers and onions and green peppers and he mixed all these things together in a large bowl all the while he finished writing the second letter about another batch of photos that showed waitress and chef balling each other and there would be one photo of waitress sucking on chef's enormous dong and another photo of waitress taking chef's cock up her ass and another photo of waitress being sucked off with all sorts of ecstasy expressions on her face and another photo of chef about to slide his rock-hard throbbing cock into waitress's moist pussy and these photos were all taken by the local high school English teacher who did photography as a hobby and this English teacher developed the film and he ran off 100 contacts of each shot and as payment after each photo session and upon receipt of all the contact prints then chef would let the English teacher ball the waitress and this letter-writing racket had been going on for about a year now and by this time the daily mails brought in about 35 letters a day and each letter had a $5 bill in it so that ran to about $175 a day or about $1050 a week or about $4200 a month or about $50,400 a year and that was pretty good money for a writer and all chef had to do was come up with a few new fuck photos to keep the correspondents happy so from straight nude shots he went on to photos of waitress balling chef and then he went on to sado-masochistic shots of chef and waitress going at each other and there would be one photo of chef whipping waitress and another photo of waitress whipping chef and another photo of both of them whipping each other and another photo of chef and waitress clubbing each other with a lot of boots and chains and waitress said she liked these photos the best because somehow they got to the heart of something in her relationship with chef and for the first year or so that was as far as any of the correspondents would go with their $5 bills because after they got their third gosh darn letter from Betty Smith they figured this broad had no intention of ever balling them because all she really wanted was to push her sappy fuck photos at them so after the third letter all the well hung young studs would go elsewhere with their letter writing but during the last month or so chef began to notice more and more letters were coming in with $5 bills for a fourth batch of photos and maybe it had something to do with the growing alienation of the times and chef wouldn't know about that because he was no philosopher because he was only a writer so he began to cook up a fourth Betty Smith letter in the diner kitchen all the while he was grilling 5 hamburger patties and 3 grilled cheese sandwiches and chef was a dance of hands as he wrote out the new letter and it ran something like this:

Dear well hung young stud:

Gosh darn and that mean old doctor says I can't take any action for another 2 weeks and isn't that a waste of good screwing time but meanwhile I've something to keep you good and hot for me because you won't believe this latest batch of photos where I let a basset hound go down on me and slobber around my pussy and there's this one photo of him sticking his slippery red rod right into me all the while he keeps wagging his dumb stump tail and there's this other photo of me licking his big basset hound balls all the while he's squirting me all over with a lot of thick jets of dog gyzm so send me $5 to cover the costs and I'll send you these photos to keep you horny until we can get together and do our own dog thing.

Sincerely yours,
Betty Smith   Box 127

And chef finished writing this fourth letter and he scooped up the hamburger patties and the grilled cheese sandwiches and he did a casual pirouette with his left foot all in the same movement and then he went around the counter to the pay phone and he called the high school English teacher and he told him to set up a photo session for later on that evening and the high school English teacher said:

"Okay chef and what are we going to be doing this time?"
And chef said:
"Dog fucking."
And the high school English teacher said:
"Oh boy dog fucking far out!"

And chef said:

"Yeah well we've given them everything else because we had nude shots and balling shots and S&M shots and so the only thing left for us to give them is dog fucking shots."

And there was a long pause so the high school English teacher thought he might try to be helpful so he said:

"Hey chef what about lesbians?"

And chef said:

"What about what?"

And the high school English teacher said:

"Yeah lesbians you know dyke types and I've got a couple of them in my composition/literature class and they'd be glad to do it for you chef and you could have one of the girls sucking off waitress while the other one was pushing her pussy into waitress's face and that would make for some really great photographs."

And there was another long pause and then chef said:

"Cut the shit man because what the hell do you take me for some kind of pervert or something?"

And chef was about to slam the receiver down when the high school English teacher began talking very fast and he said:

"Okay chef okay no lesbians and no dyke types because that's too sick and twisted and you're running a straight operation here and you don't want waitress exposed to anything that weird or perverted so listen chef what time do you want me to come by and set up the dog fucking shots for tonight?"

And chef said:

"Two AM as soon as we close down the diner and bring all your cameras and lights and stuff and hey listen you know that basset hound of yours?"

And the high school English teacher said:

"Yeah?"

And chef said:

"Okay now listen very carefully to what I am saying to you because I want you should go out and buy a nice big piece of raw red beefsteak and I want you should feed it to that basset hound of yours tonight and then I want you should give him a good hot bath and use lots of soap all over him and then I want you should rinse him off real good and dry him down real dry and you understand what I am saying to you?''

And the high school English teacher said:

"Yeah sure chef first I feed him a nice big piece of raw red beefsteak and then I give him a good hot bath with lots of soap all over him and then I rinse him off real good and then I dry him down real dry and then I drive him over to Betty's Diner at 2:00 AM.''

And chef said yeah and then he hung up the phone and he went back into the diner kitchen and he called waitress to come back there and he told her he had just set up a photo session for her to pose nude at 2:00 AM and waitress said okay and then she asked chef what was it going to be this time and chef said she was going to screw around with the high school English teacher's basset hound and that was when waitress said hell no because she said she wasn't going to let any stupid basset hound go slobbering around her pussy and it wasn't that she had anything against basset hounds as a breed or anything but it was just that she didn't like the idea of any kind of dog screwing around with her down there because she said who knows maybe she might get rabies or else she might get pregnant with a lot of stupid baby basset hounds and besides she said she'd heard stories about how dog fucking can be dangerous because the dogs get so excited that they nip away at a woman's clit and chef said that was a lot of chickenshit and waitress said chickenshit or not she wasn't going to let any stupid basset hound have a go at her and chef said what the hell if she didn't like basset hounds then he'd call up Rodrigo because he had a German shepherd and waitress said she was not going to go dog fucking any dog no matter its nationality and that was that and chef said yes she was and waitress said no she wasn't so chef lifted the back of his hand and he took a swat at waitress but waitress ducked under chef's arm so chef began

shouting out at her that she was nothing but a dumb cunt and waitress said if chef started calling her names she'd get on the phone to
her mother in Kansas City because she said:

"Mother would be out here like a shot because if there's one
thing she will not stand it's people calling other people disrespectful
names."

And when waitress mentioned her mother chef got so pissed
that he grabbed a large kitchen knife by the handle and he held it up
over his head and he was about to skim it through the air at waitress
when just then Harry Holton and Sylvester Appleby came stum-
bling through the diner door out of the night rain and for a split instant chef was frozen motionless with the large kitchen knife over
his head and then he slowly lowered it and he began to chop at some
hard-boiled eggs and he kept chopping away at them until they were
in a lot of fine tiny pieces as Harry Holton and Sylvester Appleby
went over to sit down in a corner booth and waitress came over to
them and she flopped 2 menus down on the table and then she stood
there waiting to take their orders and she began to tilt her head sideways and Harry Holton nudged Sylvester Appleby under the table
for him to notice and Sylvester Appleby began nodding his head so
hard his hair fell all over his eyes and then Harry Holton said he
wanted a tuna salad sandwich and a glass of iced tea and Sylvester
Appleby said yeah he'd have the same so waitress wrote their order
down on her pad and then she scooped up the menus and she went
away and Harry Holton leaned forward toward Sylvester Appleby
and he whispered:

"Hey man did you see the way she was tilting her head sideways at us?"

And Sylvester Appleby said yeah he'd seen that and Harry
Holton said:

"I'm telling you man she is definitely and unquestionably wide
open so as soon as I give you the signal I want you to take the check
on over to the counter and ask the chef how come it's as much as it
is and while you're doing that I'll grab the waitress and take her on
out to the pickup truck and then you get your ass out fast and we'll

all take off and drive along Route One a long way and once we're out of sight then we'll stop and we'll all have ourselves a ball."

And Sylvester Appleby gulped a big gulp and he said:

"Are you really and truly sure that waitress will want to go along with us in the pickup truck?"

And Harry Holton scowled a dark scowl at Sylvester Appleby and he said:

"What the hell do you mean man because didn't you see the way she was tilting her head sideways at us?"

And that seemed to make sense to Sylvester Appleby and just then the waitress brought their 2 tuna salad sandwiches and their 2 glasses of iced tea and she set them down and then she went over to the other end of the diner by the pay phone where she stood tilting her head sideways and Harry Holton whispered to Sylvester Appleby:

"She's thinking about fucking both of us tonight."

And actually the waitress was thinking about dog fucking because she was thinking how did she know getting it on with a basset hound would be all that bad unless she gave it a try and just then Harry Holton called out for the waitress to please bring them some more iced tea so she went and she got the large plastic cannister of iced tea and she brought it over to the booth and she filled up both their glasses and then she stood there writing out their check and while she was doing this Harry Holton began nudging his right elbow on into her left breast but waitress was so spaced out she didn't even notice what he was doing because she was thinking maybe she might like having her clit licked by a basset hound and she began tilting her head sideways as she thought about that and in the diner kitchen chef was chopping up some cucumbers with his large kitchen knife and he was thinking about how he was going to club shit out of waitress as soon as those 2 punk kids got the hell out of there and just then Harry Holton picked up the check and he handed it over to Sylvester Appleby and that was the signal for them to make their move so Sylvester Appleby gulped a big gulp and he got up and he took the check on over to the counter and the chef came out through the swinging doors and he was still carrying the large kitchen knife in his right hand and chef began ringing up the check on the cash register but Sylvester Appleby asked him how come the check was as much as it was and chef looked down at the check and he said:

"What the hell do you mean how come it's as much as it is because it says here you had 2 tuna salad sandwiches and 4 iced teas."

And Sylvester Appleby shook his head and he said:

"No sir because we had 2 tuna salad sandwiches and 2 iced teas and the other 2 iced teas were only refills."

And just then Harry Holton slipped his arm around waitress and he made a mad dash with her on down to the diner door and the 2 of them went flying out into the night rain but fast as a flash chef was over the counter with the large kitchen knife in his right hand and he kicked the diner door so hard that it stayed open and he ran out into the night rain where he collided with Harry Holton and the waitress and he made a sideways swipe at both of them with the large kitchen knife and waitress let out a quick yelp and she ducked under chef's arm and she ran back into the diner where she dashed over to the pay phone and she reached in her pocket and she pulled out a dime and she began dialing the operator to put through a long distance collect phone call to her mother in Kansas City and by that time Harry Holton was in the pickup truck and he had locked both the doors and he got the lights on and the engine running and the windshield wipers wiping away the night rain as chef jumped onto the running board and he began jabbing down at the cab roof with the large kitchen knife so he made a lot of huge holes in the cab roof and the rain began coming right through on Harry Holton who began honking on the pickup truck horn and he rolled his window down half an inch and he began shouting out for Sylvester Appleby to forget about the waitress and just get his ass out of there fast and into the pickup truck so they could both take off but Sylvester Appleby was still inside the diner and he was watching waitress yell into the pay phone and she was shouting out:

"That's right mother it's really true he wants me to have sex

with a basset hound so he can take pictures of me dog fucking and then he's going to mail these photos all over the country to a lot of weird perverts and that's not all mother because he's also swinging at me with this large kitchen knife and he just made a sideways swipe at me with it and listen to this mother as if that weren't bad enough he's also calling me a lot of disrespectful names!!"

And while waitress was yelling this into the pay phone Sylvester Appleby was standing there telling himself this was one time he was going to show Harry Holton how much he believed in the secret sexual signal system because he was remembering how Harry Holton had said that if you put your hand on a woman's shoulder while her back is turned to you then that makes her really want to get laid and so he walked over to where waitress was standing and yelling into the pay phone and he reached out his hand and he put it on her shoulder while her back was turned to him but when waitress felt Sylvester Appleby's hand on her shoulder she dropped the phone out of her hand and she turned around and she shot a cold hard hate ray stare right through Sylvester Appleby and she said:

"You get your lousy fish hand off my shoulder you plain faced creep because I don't like being touched by someone who's as homely and boring and stupid looking as you are!"

And when waitress said this to Sylvester Appleby it came as such a cold shock blow to him that he slowly took his hand from off her shoulder and then he began backing away from waitress all the while her words kept burning their way into his brain and the hot awful tears were beginning to stream on down his cheeks and for a long moment Sylvester Appleby was frozen motionless and he kept staring straight at waitress's face and for the first time in his life he was aware that Harry Holton had been lying to him all along about the secret sexual signal system because here he had just put his hand on a woman's shoulder while her back was turned to him and she didn't look as if she really wanted to get laid any more than Esther Martin had looked as if she really wanted to get laid back there at the San Marcos Hotel just before she slammed the door in Sylvester Appleby's face and that meant the whole thing was nothing but a lot of bullshit lies and Sylvester Appleby had bought every bit of it like a dumb jerk and he had even written it all down in his small pocket notebook and he had tried to learn it all by heart so when the time came for him to make it with a woman he would know all there was to know about getting laid but now here he was standing face to face with this waitress and she had just shot a cold hard hate ray stare right through him and she had also called him a plain faced creep and she had also said he was homely and boring and stupid looking and that didn't sound as if she really wanted to get laid and so the whole thing was nothing but a lot of bullshit lies and suddenly it felt as if Sylvester Appleby's whole life was a lie as if he had some sort of a dehydration of the heart or a polio of the soul or a cancer of the understanding and it felt as if his insides had been taken out and set aside on dry ice and just then Harry Holton began honking on his horn again and shouting out in the night rain for Sylvester Appleby to get his ass the hell out of there fast and back into the pickup truck and so Sylvester Appleby began to back his way slowly backwards away from waitress on his way out of the diner and he began to stumble backwards through the open diner door and just then chef was backing his way slowly backwards away from the San Marcos pickup truck and he was still holding the large kitchen knife in his right hand as he began to stumble backwards through the open diner door and suddenly Sylvester Appleby and chef bumped backs right there in the open diner door and when chef felt Sylvester Appleby's back bump his back he whirled around fast as a flash and he plunged the large kitchen knife right into Sylvester Appleby's back and when that happened Sylvester Appleby just stood there frozen motionless for a long moment because it felt as if a sudden bolt of bright blue steel had passed right through his body parts and as a matter of fact that is exactly what happened because right now the large kitchen knife was deeply embedded in Sylvester Appleby's back and for a long moment there it felt as if there were ice behind Sylvester Appleby's eyes and there was silence inside Sylvester Appleby's mind and then there was a dissolving of consciousness like a lozenge and a collapsing backwards into a lot of black holes that were eating all his light alive until he got so giddy with dizziness that his whole head began to feel awash in a conceptual stew and his toes began to tingle and his ears began to ring with a million long distance collect phone calls and there were a hundred million live flies copulating inside his braincave as he felt the fresh fruit juice loony foolishness that is all around us always and in that instant Sylvester Appleby began to eat the air of everything he ever felt or thought or saw and he began to taste the acid sadness of his entire life and all the trouble in his bloodstream and the flood of all those bullshit lies that had ever made him believe that he could be at all lovable and then he felt his eyes begin to glaze over and he heard himself let out a long low moan and he knew his nose was bubbling blood and he watched himself try to turn himself around in the open diner door and he began to lurch forward on distant feet out into the night rain as he staggered forward toward Harry Holton who was still honking on the pickup truck horn but suddenly Sylvester Appleby felt his whole body crumple in on itself as it fell down on the ground and its head hit hard against the wet asphalt parking lot pavement and then that was all there was to that and just then chef came running over to where Sylvester Appleby's body was lying in the night rain and chef stood there for a long moment looking down at it and then he wheeled around and he ran back into the diner and he slammed the diner door shut and he locked it tight and then he ran over to where waitress was standing and she was on the pay phone again only this time she was yelling at the State Police that there was big trouble over at Betty's Diner off Route One and she was shouting out:

"That's right officer there are these 2 punk kids out here and one of them just put his lousy fish hand on my shoulder while my back was turned to him and who knows maybe he thinks that's some new way of making me really want to get laid or something and the other punk kid is outside right now in a pickup truck and he is honking on the horn so you'd better send a state police car out here quick—"

And chef grabbed the phone from out of waitress's hand and

then he ripped the whole pay phone off the wall and he heaved it across the counter where it went crashing up against a glass display of cheese danish and waitress let out a quick yelp as she tried to duck under chef's arm but he grabbed her and he slapped her hard across the mouth and then he dragged her through the diner kitchen and out the back door to where chef kept his own car because he wanted them both to get the hell out of there before the State Police car came and just then Harry Holton unlocked the door of the pickup truck and he jumped out and he ran through the night rain to where Sylvester Appleby's body was lying on the wet asphalt parking lot pavement and he reached down and he began to shake at Sylvester Appleby's shoulders and he began to yell for him to get his ass up fast and get on into the pickup truck but Sylvester Appleby's body just kept lying there in the night rain so Harry Holton grabbed it and he began to drag it across the parking lot to the pickup truck where he pushed it on up and into the cab and then Harry Holton got in behind the steering wheel and he slammed the door shut and he locked it tight and he began to rev the engine and that was when he looked over to see how Sylvester Appleby was doing and he saw Sylvester Appleby's head was tilted sideways and his eyes were wide open and staring straight ahead in the night air and his nose had been bubbling blood and that was when he saw there was a large kitchen knife sticking out of Sylvester Appleby's back and Harry Holton said:

"Oh Jesus."

And Harry Holton began to wail a long low wail of pain and panic as he took the brake off and he began to back the pickup truck around in the parking lot so he could get out onto Route One but at that exact same instant there was another bright pair of headlights coming off Route One and into the entrance of the parking lot and this was the high school English teacher's car with a camera and tripod and lights and a freshly bathed basset hound sitting on the backseat with its big pink tongue lolling out of its mouth because in its own dog way it was looking forward to all the fun things the high school English teacher had been talking about as he was scrubbing the dog clean in the sudsy bathtub and Harry Holton began honking on the pickup truck horn for the high school English teacher to get the hell out of the way so Harry Holton could drive out onto Route One but at that exact same instant there was another bright pair of headlights coming around the other side of the diner and this was chef in his car with waitress sitting beside him and she was saying she didn't see why chef was in such an awful hurry to get the hell out of there because waitress had been thinking the whole thing over and she'd changed her mind about the basset hound because as waitress put it to chef:

"How do I know dog fucking is all that bad unless I give it a try?"

But chef yelled at waitress to shut her dumb cunt mouth and he began honking on his horn and yelling at Harry Holton and the high school English teacher for them both to get the hell out of the way so chef could get out onto Route One and at that exact same instant there was another bright pair of headlights coming off Route One into the entrance of the parking lot and this was a State Police car and its eerie overhead red lights were rotating and inside the car were State Trooper Emerson Quaid and State Trooper Paul R. Stevens and they both saw there were 3 cars there blocking the entrance to Betty's Diner and they were all honking on their horns and the first car was the San Marcos pickup truck with Harry Holton at the wheel and Sylvester Appleby slumped over on himself with the large kitchen knife sticking out of his back and the night rain was raining in on them through the huge holes in the cab roof and the second car had chef and waitress and waitress was saying as a matter of fact she was really sort of curious to find out what dog fucking was all about and chef was yelling at her to shut her dumb cunt mouth and the third car had the high school English teacher with his tripod and lights and camera and a freshly bathed basset hound sitting in the backseat which was looking forward in its own dog way to slobbering its big pink tongue around the pussy of a beautiful naked woman and as soon as all 3 cars saw the State Police car with its eerie overhead red lights rotating they all stopped their honking and just then chef spun his steering wheel around and he slammed his foot down hard on the accelerator and his car went roaring up over the parking lot curb and it sideswiped the high school English teacher's car and as they went flying by the waitress caught sight of the freshly bathed basset hound in the backseat of the high school English teacher's car and she leaned her head out the window of chef's car and she began waving wildly at the basset hound who began jumping up and down and peeing a lot of quick hot spurts of dog pee all over the backseat of the high school English teacher's car and it started barking loud dog barks out the back window at waitress and the 2 of them were barking and waving wildly at each other because they knew that now they would never get together on this night or on any other night as chef's car landed with a crash on the state highway and it roared north along Route One and back in the pickup truck Harry Holton looked over at the large kitchen knife that was sticking out of Sylvester Appleby's back and he let out another long low wail of pain and panic and then he spun his steering wheel around and he slammed his foot down hard on the accelerator and the pickup truck went roaring up over the parking lot curb and it sideswiped the high school English teacher's car on the other side as it went flying by and landed with a crash on the state highway and it roared south along Route One and just then State Trooper Paul R. Stevens opened the door of the State Police car and he got out and he walked through the night rain to the one remaining car in the parking lot which had the high school English teacher and the freshly bathed basset hound in the backseat and Trooper Stevens leaned in against the front window of the car and he said:

"All right you 2 you're both under arrest."

And the freshly bathed basset hound began barking loud dog barks at Trooper Stevens as the high school English teacher said:

"But officer why are we under arrest?"

And Trooper Stevens said:

"You're both under arrest for putting your lousy fish hand on the shoulder of the waitress inside Betty's Diner and also for honking on your horn out here in the parking lot."

And the high school English teacher said:

"But officer you don't want us because you want THEM!!"

And the high school English teacher pointed south along Route One where Harry Holton had just gone roaring off in the San Marcos pickup truck although actually the high school English teacher didn't know what the hell was going on but he had seen chef and waitress go roaring north along Route One and he didn't think it would be such a hot idea to send the State Police car after them so instead he pointed south and that was where Trooper Stevens looked for a long moment and then he told the high school English teacher to wait right there in his car until he got back and he ran back through the night rain to the State Police car and he got in and he told Trooper Emerson Quaid that the person who had put his lousy fish hand on the waitress had just headed south along Route One and Trooper Quaid said they'd better turn on their siren and head after him so they turned on their high whining siren and they began driving at 85 miles an hour south along Route One and after about 4 minutes Trooper Stevens caught sight of the taillights of the San Marcos pickup truck just as it was turning into the gravel driveway of the San Marcos Hotel and Harry Holton drove the truck right up to the small garbage enclosure where he slammed on the brakes and the truck went sliding sideways and it dug up an enormous trenchful of gravel in its wake as it came to a dead halt and Harry Holton turned off the windshield wipers and he turned off the lights and he switched off the ignition and then he looked over at Sylvester Appleby's body that was lying under the dashboard now with his eyes wide open and staring straight ahead in the air and Harry Holton let out another long low wail of pain and panic as the State Police car came roaring into the gravel driveway with its high siren whining and it pulled up behind the pickup truck and its siren cut off in a long dying whine but its eerie overhead red lights kept rotating and they turned the whole side of the San Marcos Hotel into a slow motion light show as Trooper Stevens and Trooper Quaid jumped out of the State Police car and they both went running over to where Harry Holton was sitting in the pickup truck and Trooper Quaid looked in the front window and he saw the great huge holes that had been jabbed in the cab roof and then he looked over and he saw Sylvester Appleby's body lying under the dashboard so he yelled at Harry Holton to open the front door and get his ass out of there fast so Harry Holton unlocked the door and he got out as Trooper Quaid reached in and he unlocked the door on the other side and Trooper Stevens opened that door and Sylvester Appleby's body went spilling out onto the gravel driveway and it lay there with the large kitchen knife still sticking out of its back and Trooper Quaid reached down and he tried to take Sylvester Appleby's pulse but after a long moment he stood back up and he began to shake his head very slowly and then he went over to the State Police car and he switched on the police radio and he made this report:

Car 17 at the San Marcos Hotel off Route One and we've got a young kid down here got killed back at Betty's Diner and we're here with the body so you'd better send an ambulance right away—

And I was still lying upstairs in my own room trying to decide whether I should quit teaching all my writing classes back in New York City and spend the rest of my life trying to write my own writing when I heard the high whining siren die down outside so I got up off my bed and I went over to the window and I looked out and I saw the eerie red lights rotating all over the gravel driveway and I thought I might as well go downstairs and see what's happening on Saturday night at San Marcos and everyone else in the hotel must have thought the same thought because one by one all the other conference people began going outside and by the time I got there they were all standing around the gravel driveway and they were all staring at Sylvester Appleby's body which was lying there with the large kitchen knife sticking out of its back and Trooper Stevens was standing next to the body and he began shouting out:

"Don't nobody touch nothing."

And everyone was frozen motionless except for Harry Holton who was wailing his long low wail of pain and panic so I went over and I took him by the arm and I led him on over to the edge of the grass and I made him sit down there where he began to shiver and whimper like a lost puppy and by this time the rain had let up to a light misty drizzle in the night sky and I looked over to the other side of the gravel driveway and I saw Ted Wylie who looked as if he had just been let out of a locked bathroom and he was wandering around as if he were in some other air and Maureen Talbot was standing a few feet away from him and she was writing furiously in an open notebook all about how Sylvester Appleby's body looked with the large kitchen knife sticking out of it and just then Trooper Quaid came over to where Harry Holton was sitting on the grass and he told him to hand over his driver's license and Harry Holton kept on shivering and whimpering as he took his wallet out and he handed his driver's license over and just then Ralph Perry came down the steps of the porch and he walked over to Trooper Stevens and he said he was the Director of the San Marcos Writers Conference and he asked what had happened here and Trooper Stevens shrugged and pointed down at Sylvester Appleby's body and Ralph Perry shook his head and said what a gosh darn shame and just then Laura Perry came out on the porch and she stood there at the top of the stairs pulling her long shawl around her shoulders and she closed her eyes and she began to say a silent prayer to all the misty drizzle that was overhead and I looked around and I saw all the other writers conference people were huddled together there and there was Marianne Roseblatt and Cleveland Mason and Dorothy Kingsley and Joseph Baum and Robert Ingersoll and Mary Wilde and Roberta Heite and Mary Anne Berre and Susan Restnor and Mildred Manson and off to one side Douglas Mercer was standing with his arm around Betsy Childs and just then Miriam Morse came out of the hotel and she was wearing her grotesque bouquet of artificial flowers and she stood there for a moment perched on the top of the porch stairs and she looked down and she saw Sylvester Appleby's body and she let out a nervous bird chirp and she turned and she hopped back into the hotel and just then Esther Martin came to the top of the porch stairs and she was wearing a bright canary yellow dress and she looked down with her large dark startled eyes and she saw Sylvester Appleby's body with the large kitchen knife sticking out of the back and Esther Martin began to listen for what her angel voices had to say about this but her angel voices didn't have anything to say about anything because all Esther Martin could hear was the sound of the misty drizzle in the night air but she kept standing there for a long moment and then she began to hear her own voice saying something very softly under her breath so no one else could hear but she was saying it and this is what she said:

"Goodbye Sylvester Appleby and I'm sorry I slammed the door in your face last night because maybe a part of me did want you to come in and fuck me."

And just then Mr. Ruiz came out on the porch and he stood there immaculately dressed in his pin-striped suit with cameo cuff links and he was thinking about all those years when the San Marcos Hotel was almost torn apart by all the fistfights and knifings and drownings on the beach and now here was one of his own kitchen boys lying there on the gravel driveway with a large kitchen knife sticking out of his back and it was just like old times only Mr. Ruiz didn't like it one bit and just then upstairs on the fourth floor of the San Marcos Hotel a dark hand was slipping its long slender fingers between the curtains of a window and 2 sharp dark eyes stared down at where Sylvester Appleby's body was lying on the gravel driveway and Mrs. Ruiz said a rapid prayer in Spanish for the dead kitchen boy and just then there was a loud shout from inside the hotel and suddenly the front door burst open and Jose came sailing out over the porch stairs and he seemed to stay suspended for an instant in mid-air before he fell down and landed smack flat on his face in the gravel driveway because Jose had just finished reading the last page of *The Banana Factor* by Ted Wylie and now he was drowning in an ocean of dizziness and his toes were tingling and his ears were ringing and there were a hundred million live flies copulating on the inside of his braincave as Jose lay there on the gravel driveway and then he sat up and he closed his eyes and he began reciting his full name:

"Jose Pancho Villa Jimenez Francisco Miguel Pedro Moya Don Carlos Manuel Garcia Humphrey Bogart Mendez Jesus Rodriguez."

And then Jose picked himself up and he began running around bumping into people and he bumped into Ted Wylie who swatted him aside and that sent him careening off the front fender of the San Marcos pickup truck and Jose bumped into State Trooper Paul R. Stevens who drew his service revolver and he shouted out for Jose to freeze right there so Jose froze right there over the dead body of Sylvester Appleby and Jose gazed down into Sylvester Appleby's wide open eyes that were staring straight ahead in the night air and in that instant it was eyes into eyes as Jose suddenly remembered how he was once a small child running up and down the aisles of the scenic tour buses selling all those hand printed lists of all the whorehouses in Mexico City and what their going rates were and Jose had no way of knowing that the only reason that Sylvester Appleby was working at the San Marcos Hotel was so he could go down to a real Mexican whorehouse at the end of the summer with his friend Harry Holton and now he would never get to go down there and even though Jose could not have known any of this Jose still felt all the fresh fruit juice loony foolishness that is all around us always as he stared down into Sylvester Appleby's wide open eyes and that was when Jose fainted dead away and he fell down in a neat small body heap right next to Sylvester Appleby's body and I looked around at all the other writers conference people who were still standing frozen motionless by the gravel driveway and then I walked up to where Sylvester Appleby was lying and

I stood there looking down at him for a long moment and then I said:

"Goodbye Sylvester Appleby and you were enormously likable in your unassuming stupidity and now you're off in hee haw country where there's no knowing you."

And then I turned around and I walked past all the other writers conference people and I climbed up the porch stairs and I went into the hotel lobby and I got on the ancient elevator and I rode up to my room and I went in and I sat down at the desk and I opened a notebook and I began to write the opening lines of this lousy novel that you're reading right now.

ten/Sunday

And I kept writing this lousy novel right through the night and I knew I was really writing because it was the easiest thing in the universe because it felt as if I were listening to a distant brook that kept babbling to itself about itself or else it felt like the bright light of childhood when I was so alive with life or else it felt like an unseen inner energy that was spooky and delusional and it kept on coming up with worlds that were more real than any words that I was trying to write in my notebook so all I had to do was write out everything I heard with my own inner ear and before I knew it the page was a play place where I could create great shapes that were the images of all those ghosts that come and go far in the darkness of the heart and one of these images was Sylvester Appleby lying on the gravel driveway with the large kitchen knife sticking out of his back and another image was Esther Martin running along the narrow strip of beach on her way out to drown herself in the open ocean and another image was little Teddy Wylie curling himself up into a small body ball on the cold white tile of his bathroom floor and another image was Clarence in that instant of air when he sees a shell is slipping through his fingers and he knows he is about to be blown apart and another image was that great aged elk that was trying to die in the shrubbery and underbrush with its milky eye seeing only autumn leaf and the distant disinterested sky and I had no idea where any of these images were coming from or what they were all about but I knew they were all out there in the air and they were all so real that they were beginning to be absolutely unbearable so once or twice I even tried closing my eyes to see if they would go away but they were still being absolutely unbearably real inside my mind so I kept writing my own writing through the night and sometimes all these images were so real that it felt as if I might be going crazy so from time to time I looked out the window and I could see there were all those millions of stars that were up there in the night sky and they were shining light in that great vacancy of space and I could hear the great waves as they came in to break against the slippery glistening rocks or else they burst into surf along the narrow strip of beach and then it felt as if all those stars and all those waves and all that bursting surf were all just as unreal as I was since they were also just as endless as I was as I kept writing my own writing through the night and sometimes all these images were so real that I began to wonder whether this lousy novel was ever going to go anywhere or was it just a lot of unconscious nonsense on my part but then I saw the night sky was beginning to fade into daylight and it began to be dawn in all its early morning glory and I saw that I had already filled up 4 notebooks with my night writing so I opened up a fifth notebook and I thought now that makes one notebook for each of the years that I was not really writing and I kept writing my own writing until I felt my wrist was beginning to ache and my eyes were beginning to blur and my head was beginning to get heavy so finally I tossed my pen down on the desk and I closed the notebook of my own accord and I knew I had written as much as I could write in this one night so I stood up and I stretched my arms as far as I could stretch over my head and I felt all the blood begin to leave my braincave but I still stayed sane and clear so I decided to go downstairs and get some early morning air and I looked at my wristwatch and I saw it was 6:30 AM so not that many people would be up but even so I didn't want to leave all my writing behind me so I took all the pages out of the notebooks and I folded them over into one large wad and I shoved it all into my coat pocket so it would be close to me and then I left my room and I went down to the hotel lobby where I saw Jose was slumped over on the reception desk and he was sound asleep with his head resting sideways on page 2 of a paperback copy of my first novel *A Dream of Clarence* that Ralph Perry must have given to him and I thought Jose didn't get very dizzy over my first novel because it just put him to sleep so I made a mental note to send Jose a copy of this lousy novel I am writing right now so then he could read about how dizzy he gets when he gets giddy with dizziness and maybe that would make him even more dizzy and then I went out on the porch and I stood there as the wet sea air hit my face and I felt like someone who has just come out of some dark underground cave after 5 long years of wasting away in the darkness and suddenly he sees the sunlight for the first time and it feels amazing to face the day and just then I noticed that there was someone else that was also standing out there on the porch and I saw it was Esther Martin who was wearing a bright canary yellow dress so I walked over to her and I said good morning and I wanted to go on and tell her how I had stayed up all night writing about how she had gone running along the narrow strip of beach on her way out to drown herself in the open ocean but then I thought I'd better not mention that to her and I noticed she was holding a book in her hands and I saw it was a copy of *Prism of Love* by Miriam Morse and when she saw I saw it she opened it to the flyleaf and she showed me what was written there and this is what it said:

This poetry writing award book is given to Esther Martin
for her exquisite and lyrical angel poems
with all best wishes from Miriam Morse
The San Marcos Writers Conference

And I told Esther Martin I was glad she had won the poetry writing award because she certainly deserved the recognition and I was only sorry the prize was such a silly collection of bird chirp verse and when I said that Esther Martin held the book in her hands for a moment more and then with a quick flick of her left hand she sent it skimming out over the porch railing and down through the air into the open ocean where it landed plop on top of a great wave that was on its way in to break against a glistening slippery rock and for a split instant the wave seemed to raise itself up and it began turning the pages of the book as if it were trying to read the silly bird chirp verse that was there on the pages and suddenly the wave seemed to shudder in disgust and it slammed the book up against a large hard rock with such force that the binding of the book was torn apart and all the pages began to drift off in different directions and they all began to sink on down to drown in the sweet peace of the deep sea and I looked over at Esther Martin and I asked her why had she tossed her poetry writing award book into the open ocean and she kept staring straight ahead in the air as she said:

"I always win a poetry writing award book at all the writers conferences I go to and they always say my work is exquisite and lyrical but the truth is my poems are nothing but a lot of sick dictation by imaginary angels and that's nothing to give anyone an award for and so I always throw all my writing award books away."

And I looked out at the open ocean where an occasional page from the poetry book came floating up to the surface and a sea gull would swoop down and it would pause for an instant in mid-air as if it were reading the bird chirp verse on the page and then suddenly the sea gull would fly skyward letting out loud raucous cries of disgust and Esther Martin turned to me and she said:

"The angel Gabriel came to me 2 nights ago and he told me all the other angels had an angel writers conference and they decided it was high time for me to try to write my own writing out of my own voice and so the angel Gabriel said that none of my angel voices would be coming to tell me what to write anymore but he said that was okay because I could do it on my own now only he said I should be sure to give my short stories a little more of a point so I stayed awake all last night trying to write my own writing out of my own voice and after a long while I did finally write this short piece of writing.''

And Esther Martin took a piece out of her blouse and she handed it over for me to see and this is what it said:

Once upon a time there was a kitchen boy named Sylvester Appleby and he came knocking at my door and he said he was wondering whether I wanted him to come in and fuck me but I was listening for my angel voices to come and tell me what to write so I slammed the door in his face and the next time I saw Sylvester Appleby he was lying on the gravel driveway and there was a large kitchen knife sticking out of his back and I know the angel Gabriel said I should be sure to give my stories a little more of a point but I don't know what point there is to slamming a door in Sylvester Appleby's face and then sticking a large kitchen knife in his back and maybe that's why my angel voices have gone away because they know there isn't that much point to anything and if that's the way it is then I'm just as glad they've gone away because there's much more point in my trying to write my own writing out of my own voice because I can do it on my own now even though there's not that much more of a point to it.

And I gave the piece of paper back to Esther Martin and I said it was better than anything her angel voices ever told her to write and I said she should keep writing her own writing out of her own voice and then I reached into my own coat pocket and I took out the large wad of notebook pages I had written last night and I showed them to Esther Martin and I told her this was the first real writing I had written in 5 years and I said we should both celebrate our writing our own writing so I said why don't we get together for a few days down in Santa Barbara after the conference is over and when I said that Esther Martin stared at me with her large dark startled eyes and after a long moment she said:

"Thank you very much but what would the 2 of us do in Santa Barbara?"

And I said there were a lot of things we could do in Santa Barbara because I said we could go feed the seals and talk to all the old people and visit the Franciscan Mission but after another long moment Esther Martin said:

"Thank you very much but the angel Gabriel told me to keep writing my own writing out of my own voice and that means I have to keep going to all my other writers conferences and my bags are already all packed to go to the Arizona Writers Conference this next week and then to the Santa Fe Writers Conference and then I have to go back and see Dr. Nesbitt at Hope Valley."

And I said Esther Martin had my address in New York City and as soon as she had a collection of her short stories together that she had written out of her own voice then she should send it to me and I would show it to my agent Marcia Masters and she could try and find a publisher for it and when I said that Esther Martin said:

"Thank you very much but I'm afraid it will take me a long time to get a collection of short stories together that are all written out of my own voice and I'm just grateful that I'm writing anything at all right now and I have you to thank for that."

And suddenly Esther Martin came forward toward me and she kissed me a quick passionless benediction kiss on the lips and then she turned and she was off the porch in a bright blur of yellow and so I stayed out there and I watched the great waves come in to break against the slippery glistening rocks and I thought how odd it all is how very odd and my god I am such an oddball among oddballs and then I turned and I walked into the hotel where I saw the weirdest woman I had ever seen in my entire life and she was wearing a black dress all buttoned up to the neck and a black skirt that went all the way down to her ankles and she had on black stockings and black shoes so she looked like a giant black bird that had just flown through the front door of the San Marcos Hotel to hunker around in the lobby and this giant black bird was Mrs. Ruiz who had come downstairs from her fourth-floor room and she was standing over at the reception desk trying to shake Jose awake and her eyes were tiny pinpoints of black light that were smoldering like candles smolder when you have just snuffed them out and Mrs. Ruiz had all her bags packed and they were piled high in the lobby and inside one of the bags there was the epic novel she had just finished writing about 17 generations of a noble Spanish family that went through blood duels and misty castles and exquisite senoritas with the chaste gaze of the Latin Catholic Christ that was a fierce archangel sunlight blazing down on the white hot sandstone and Mrs. Ruiz stood there at the reception desk trying to shake Jose awake but Jose was off in a deep sleep inside a glass dome where he was dreaming about how his 17 older brothers and sisters used to form a great long chain line across the dusty dirt road so they could stop the scenic tour bus and climb on board and run up and down the aisles selling all their various wares to the American tourists and after a few more shakes Mrs. Ruiz gave up on Jose and she turned and she walked into the dining room where she shouted out an order in Spanish but there was no one in the kitchen except a lot of empty plastic cannisters stacked up in the kitchen sink so Mrs. Ruiz turned and she came back out into the hotel lobby and she went over to the pay phone so she could call a taxi but there was nothing left of the pay phone booth except a lot of splintered wood and wire and broken glass so Mrs. Ruiz turned and she went out the front door of the hotel where she walked right into Mr. Ruiz who was standing outside the door and he was immaculately dressed in a pin-striped suit with cameo cuff links and Mrs. Ruiz yelled at Mr. Ruiz for him to call her a taxi but Mr. Ruiz said all the taxis would be coming along very soon to pick up the conference people so Mrs. Ruiz turned around and she went back into the hotel lobby where she began to gather up her bags and she began to carry them out through the front door but when Mr. Ruiz came over and tried to help her with the bags Mrs. Ruiz spit at Mr. Ruiz a quick bitter spit and just then a taxi drove into the gravel driveway so Mrs. Ruiz walked toward it and she opened the back door and she began piling in all her bags on the backseat and then she was about to get into the taxi herself but suddenly she paused for an instant and she turned and she walked over to the place where Sylvester Appleby had been lying on the gravel driveway last night and there was only a faint dark area there now but Mrs. Ruiz stood over the place for a moment and then she fell down on her knees and she leaned forward toward it and she bent her face down so she could touch her lips to the faint dark area and she said some thing very softly in Spanish under her breath so no one else could hear but she was saying it and what she said was god rest your soul forever and then Mrs. Ruiz got back up on her feet and she walked on over to the taxi and she got in and she slammed the door shut and then she rolled the rear window down so she could spit one last quick bitter spit at Mr. Ruiz and then she rolled the window back up and she shouted out something in Spanish at the driver and the taxi drove out of the gravel driveway and it turned right onto Route One and Mr. Ruiz stood there in the open door of the hotel and he watched Mrs. Ruiz disappear down the state highway and at that exact same instant I was walking down to Ralph Perry's office to pick up my paycheck for the conference and I was also going to tell Ralph Perry that I wouldn't be coming back to San Marcos next year and when I came to the door of his office I saw he was sitting in his swivel chair and puffing away on his pipe as he read *The San Marcos Sunday Times* and when he saw me he motioned for me to come in and sit down and he handed me the newspaper for me to see the front page where there was a double column news item and this is what it said:

PALO ALTO YOUTH IS KILLED
OUTSIDE SAN MARCOS DINER

Sylvester Appleby of Palo Alto died early Sunday morning of a knife wound he allegedly received outside Betty's Diner off Route One and the 16 year old youth was pronounced dead on arrival at the San Marcos Hospital.

State Troopers Emerson Quaid and Paul R. Stevens pursued a speeding pickup truck to the San Marcos Hotel at 2:27 AM where the dead Appleby youth was discovered with his 19 year old companion Harry Holton of North Atherton.

Police are searching for the whereabouts of the chef and waitress of Betty's Diner who are tentatively identified as 46 year old Anthony Porter and 21 year old Elizabeth Page be-

cause police say these 2 did the alleged stabbing and then fled
north along Route One.

Officials say they have confiscated a large quantity of ex-
tremely revealing and highly relevant photographs of the 2
suspects and these documents have been taken to the State
Police barracks in San Pedro where they are being examined by
State Troopers but officials would not release any of these
photographs for publication in *The San Marcos Sunday
Times*.

State Police say they also apprehended 28 year old Jeremy
Newton who teaches Senior English at the San Marcos High
School on a charge of reckless endangerment for falling asleep
at the wheel of his car at the entrance of the parking lot of Betty's Diner at 5:30 AM long after the Appleby youth was discovered dead and police are also questioning Newton to find out
how both sides of his car got sideswiped on the night of the
alleged stabbing.

A basset hound belonging to Newton was remanded to the
town pound until officials could determine its role in the chain
of events that took place on Saturday night at San Marcos.

And I handed the newspaper back to Ralph Perry and I said
whoever had written this news article did it pretty fast as the whole
thing happened only a few hours ago and I said I was sorry about
Sylvester Appleby and when I said that Ralph Perry began shaking
his head in dismay and he said:

"It's such a darn shame because those 2 kitchen boys were only
trying to come to the rescue of that poor waitress because the chef
there was trying to take advantage of her but all that Appleby boy
got in the way of thanks for his gallantry was a kitchen knife in the
back and my gosh what is this world coming to and this morning
Mr. Ruiz told the Holton boy to pack up his bags and get the heck
out of here and that's not the worst of it either because Ruiz came
down to see me and he's steaming mad about the bad publicity he
says this will bring down on his hotel and he blames it all on our
writers conference because he says we stir people up in crazy ways
and he says it's also our fault that the pay phone booth got wrecked
out there in the lobby and he says it's also our fault that the old
claptrap elevator got stuck between floors the other evening and so

he says we'll have to forfeit our $1000 bond and I already owe him $5000 rent for the week and Ted Wylie's Thursday evening lecture cost me another $500 and that special banana cake cost me another $50 and I guess I'll just have to dig into my life savings and pony it up if this writers conference is going to go on."

And Ralph Perry sighed a long sigh and then he fell silent so I said even so it had been an okay conference this year and so I didn't see any need for me to come back here next year because I'd made up my mind I was going to spend the rest of my life trying to write my own writing and when I said that Ralph Perry suddenly sat bolt upright in his swivel chair and he said:

"What the heck are you talking about Morrison because of course you'll be coming back here next year and gosh knows the San Marcos Writers Conference couldn't get on without you."

And I said I was sure the conference could get on without me and then Ralph Perry lowered his head and he looked up at me the way a small puppy will look at you when it wants permission to go pee on the carpet and he said:

"Aw say you'll do it for me please guy because we could create a special position for you here as our writer in residence and you could just sort of hang around and write your own writing and you wouldn't have to teach any fiction classes if you didn't feel like it because maybe I might be able to talk Maureen Talbot into taking them and you could get an awful lot of your own writing done right here because gosh knows you can almost feel the creativity coming up from the floorboards and I've always said if you can't write here then you can't write anywhere."

And I knew Ralph Perry was just trying to con me into saying I'd come back next year so he could put my name on the brochures and try to pull in a few more registrations from some of the old faithful students but I shook my head and I said I'd made up my mind and it was final so Ralph Perry lowered his eyes again only this time he was staring straight down at all those old floorboards as if he were trying to see if any of that phony creativity was really coming up out of them and apparently he didn't see any because after a moment he looked back up at me and he sighed a long sigh and he said:

"Okay guy and I think I see what you're saying because maybe I might be saying the same thing if I were in your place because just look over there at that shelf with all those black plastic bound manuscripts of all my unpublished war novels and there they all are lying idle and lifeless and that's an entire lifetime of my writing and I know gosh darn well no one will ever publish any of them because I never had the time to sit down and figure out what the heck was wrong with them because I was always so busy bustling about setting up schedules and getting people for the next San Marcos Writers Conference so now it's going to use up the last of my life savings to publish all those war novels myself and that's a pretty awful thing to have to do."

And I said publishing his own war novels wasn't such a bad thing to have to live with but Ralph Perry waved that away and he went right on:

"What I'm trying to say to you guy is maybe you're right to get the heck out and stay away from all these writers conferences while you still can so you can go off and try to write your own writing before you end up a tired old man who has nothing to show for a lifetime of writing but a lot of unpublished stuff on the shelf."

And Ralph Perry reached into his desk drawer and he pulled out an envelope that had my paycheck in it and he handed it over to me and I thanked him and I got up and I shook his hand and I turned and I walked over to the door and I half expected Ralph Perry to call out after me the way he usually did but this time he didn't so I turned and I looked back at him and I saw his head had slumped forward on his chest and one arm was hanging down the side of the swivel chair and his pipe was lying on the floor and it was curling up a thin life line of beautiful blue fumes and I thought maybe this was Ralph Perry's last writers conference also but there was nothing I could do about that and I just knew I had to get the hell out of there fast and get back to New York so I could keep writing my own writing so I left the office and I went to the hotel lobby to get Maureen Talbot to come see how Ralph Perry was doing but as I passed the reception desk Cleveland Mason came up to me and he smiled a shy sheepish smile as he handed me an envelope and he shook my hand and he thanked me and then he turned and he walked away and I opened the envelope and I took out a piece of paper and this what it said:

A WORTHWHILE LIFE by Cleveland Mason

When our first child was born the doctors told me there was severe brain damage and the child would never be able to get any better so we ought to send him away to an institution where he could be taken care of for the rest of his life but I talked it over with my wife and we agreed to keep the child with us and see if we could live a worthwhile life together and that was 17 years ago and we have never once regretted our decision although god knows it has not been easy for us and it has not been easy for Bobby either and for a long time now I have wanted to write about all this because who knows there may be other persons out there who may also be trying to live a worthwhile life and maybe I might be able to say something that might be helpful to them and I owe it all to Mr. Eliot Morrison at the San Marcos Writers Conference because he told me to go ahead and try to write my own writing so I did and now I can go on and try to write about the life I have lived with my wife and with our young son Bobby because it is the only kind of worthwhile life that I could ever live.

And I stood there in the hotel lobby holding Cleveland Mason's paper in my hands and I thought well what the hell and maybe this corny boring writers conference wasn't such a total waste of time after all and then I looked around and I saw the lobby was filling up with conference people who were all carrying suitcases and just then Maureen Talbot came running up to me so I began to tell her to go down and see how Ralph Perry was doing but she cut me off and she said:

"Ralph Perry says that as long as you and Ted Wylie won't be coming back here next year then I can teach all the fiction classes and give all the individual manuscript conferences."

And I said that was fine but if she really wanted a San Marcos Writers Conference next year then she'd better get her ass down to Ralph Perry's office fast and see how he was doing because when I left him a few moments ago he wasn't in such hot shape and when I said that Maureen Talbot stood there wide-eyed for an instant and then she let out a sad gasp and she turned and she ran down to Ralph Perry's office and just then Betsy Childs came up to me and she threw her arms around my neck and she kissed me on the lips and then she whispered in my ear that I was a major event in her life and now she was going to go off and write about how she had always wanted to fuck her own father and then she ran over to Douglas Mercer and they put their arms around each other and they went out through the front door and just then Mildred Manson came over to me and she said she was going to go home and rewrite her short story *Forsaken Heart* one more time so it would be a little less sickening saccharine sentimental and then she went out the front door and just then Robert Ingersoll came through the lobby looking gray and tanned and vested and I thought if this guy is a plainclothes Jesuit then I never writ nor no man ever loved and he looked over at me as if he'd never seen me before and I thought I just hope he's not on the same plane I'm taking back to New York and by that time all the other conference people were in the lobby and they were standing around and saying goodbye to one another and promising to write long letters to one another and just then I saw there were 2 gangster types standing on the other side of the lobby and they were wearing black leather trench coats and black leather hats pulled down over their foreheads and they were holding black leather bags and they were the first arrivals for the next conference at the San Marcos Hotel which was THE NORTH AMERICAN STUDY OF DEMOCRATIC INSTITUTIONS and that was a cover for a Los Angeles syndicate that laundered dirty money in Mexico City and sent it back up through Miami Beach and Mr. Ruiz ran over to greet these 2 men and he shook their hands and one of the men grunted a gross animal grunt and then they all went over to the reception desk where Jose was still sound asleep over a paperback copy of my first novel *A Dream of Clarence* and Mr. Ruiz picked up a ball-point pen and he began jabbing Jose in the ear with it and Jose woke up with a loud shout and he stared straight ahead into the shifty gaze of one of the gangster types so Jose whirled the register around and he shoved it forward toward the 2 men for them to sign it and just then Laura Perry came running through the hotel lobby and she was adjusting her long shawl around her shoulders and as she passed me she said something about how Ralph Perry needed her and I left the hotel lobby and I went out onto the porch for one last long look at those great waves that were making their way to break against the slippery glistening rocks but I saw Ted Wylie was also standing out there so I just kept walking toward the stairs that led down to the narrow strip of beach but Ted Wylie called out to me:

"Morrison I want you to tell me where you're going to be going when you leave here in case I want to ask you any more questions for the new novel I'm writing about you."

And I turned and I said I'd be at my place in New York but I said I would be trying to write my own writing so I wouldn't be able to help anyone with any other writing and when I said that Ted Wylie walked over to where I was standing and he began speaking to me in a suspiciously solicitous voice and he said:

"Listen to me Morrison because you probably think I'm a pretty cold son of a bitch but that's not true because I'm really quite a nice guy behind my razor face and my beady eagle eye and I could be the best friend you ever had and that's right Morrison I could be a real buddy to you because I could help you write your own writing and then I could help you get it published with any publisher you want to publish with and what do you say to that Morrison?"

And this was such a phony pitch that I couldn't keep from reaching into my coat pocket and pulling out the large wad of notebook pages that I had written last night and I showed them to Ted Wylie so he could see that I was really writing again so I was no longer a writer who was not really writing and that meant that his own novel about me was already hopelessly outdated and kaput and

Ted Wylie glanced at the first page of this lousy novel manuscript and this is what he read:

> I began writing this lousy novel at a corny boring writers con-
> ference out in California where a lot of lost souls go to be told
> how to write their own writing and I hadn't been really writing
> anything myself for the last 5 years but that didn't seem to
> bother anyone else out there so long as I taught the fiction
> classes and gave the individual manuscript conferences and
> helped the conferees write their own writing then nobody gave
> a good god damn whether I was really writing or not but I gave
> a good god damn because I can tell you it's hell to be a writing
> teacher at a writers conference when you're not really writing
> anything yourself—

And Ted Wylie took 17 seconds to glance at this first page of my lousy novel manuscript and then he fixed his beady eagle eye on me and he snorted a short snort of scorn and he said:

"So you think this is really writing is that it Morrison and I can tell you it's not because it's nothing but a lot of rotten tedious non-writing so that still makes you nothing but a writing teacher who's not really writing."

And I said that wasn't true either because I was also going to quit teaching all my writing classes as soon as I got back to New York City so I could spend the rest of my life trying to write my own writing and when I said that Ted Wylie said:

"Listen to me Morrison you're just trying to screw up my new novel about you because I've already written that you're nothing but a writing teacher who's not really writing and that's the way you're going to have to stay until I finish writing my new novel so I'm going to take these notebook pages of yours and I'm going to toss them over my shoulder so they will all fall down there in the open ocean."

And Ted Wylie snatched the notebook pages from out of my hands and he began to toss them over his shoulder but fast as a flash I slammed him hard and I grabbed back the notebook pages and I stuffed them into my coat pocket and Ted Wylie stood there in a dazed state for a long moment as his razor face began to turn beet red and his beady eagle eye began to leak real tears and then he began to shout out loud at me:

"God damn it to hell Morrison don't go giving me any shit about how you are a writer who's really writing because I'm telling you you're nothing but a sad laugh in the air and a weak fart in the breeze and that's all you are and all you ever will be and that's why you're not even worth my trying to write a best selling novel about!!"

And Ted Wylie turned and he ran off the porch and on into the hotel and I stayed there looking out at the great waves that were coming in to break against the glistening slippery rocks and I thought my christ what are we writers anyway except a lot of pre-historic tree creatures who keep lacerating our selfish asshole selves so we can keep hacking out a lot of thin life lines on the bare walls of our braincaves and if that's the way it is then this is one caveman who is going to keep on keeping on with trying to write his own writing for the rest of his life and that means no more weird dizzy spells and no more desperation panic states and no more corny boring writers conferences and just as I thought that thought I heard a loud crash of shattering glass and I looked up and I saw Ted Wylie's set of field binoculars was flying through the air out of his second-floor window and I watched them fall down down down through the air down into the water where they splashed dead weight down into the depths of the unseeing sea and that was when I knew that was the end of Ted Wylie's trying to write his new novel about how I was a writing teacher who was not really writing and just then I heard the high whining siren of an emergency vehicle on its way into the gravel driveway of the hotel and I turned and I walked into the lobby and I got on the ancient elevator and I went up to my room and I threw all my things into my suitcase and I closed it and I carried it down to the hotel lobby where I saw there was an ambulance standing outside on the gravel driveway and there were 2 men dressed in white starch uniforms at the reception desk with a portable stretcher and they were trying to shake Jose awake by poking at him with a stethoscope so they could ask him where they could find Ralph Perry and I went up to them and I pointed them on down the hall to Ralph Perry's office so they took their portable stretcher and they went down there as I tossed my room key onto the reception desk and then I closed Jose's copy of my lousy first novel *A Dream of Clarence* so he'd lose his place and he'd have to go back and begin reading the whole thing all over again and then I walked through the lobby past Mr. Ruiz who was busy ushering some more gangster types into the hotel and I went out the front door and I saw there was a taxi that was driving out of the gravel driveway and Esther Martin was sitting in the backseat and she was wearing a bright canary yellow dress and she was on her way to the Arizona Writers Conference and I stood there and I began waving like crazy for the taxi to stop because I wanted to ask Esther Martin to spend a few days with me down in Santa Barbara but I saw the taxi turned right onto Route One and I watched it disappear down the state highway so I picked up my suitcase and I began to walk along the gravel driveway past the ambulance and out onto Route One where I stood there and I waited for a bus to come take me to the Santa Barbara airport and when I got on the bus I must have fallen asleep because the next thing I knew I was at the airport and I got off the bus and I boarded the plane for New York and I found a seat by a window and I sat down and I looked around and I saw there was no one from San Marcos on the plane so I leaned back and I tried to relax as the plane began to rev its jet engines and I felt the shudder of a sudden terrific roar forward as the plane began its headlong racing down the runway and then I could feel my body being buoyed upwards in the liftoff and then I could feel a yielding into empty air as the plane climbed slowly higher higher skyward and then it began to glide through cloud banks and I could see a lot of smoke wisps begin to cut across the wing of the plane and then I began to think about this lousy novel that I am trying to write right now and I thought about all the things that would probably happen to this novel once it was finally finished and I thought first there would be the whole bullshit agent trip with Marcia Masters because she would read through the novel manuscript and she would probably loathe most of it because she'd say darling it has far too many characters in it and it has far too many plot summaries in it and it has far too many words in it and then she'd say darling the whole idea of trying to write a novel about a writer who's trying to write a novel about a writer who's not really writing is hardly a very marketable idea and then she'd say darling the whole thing is too much like *A Dream of Clarence* because there is also a young kid who gets killed and this kid also tastes the acid sadness of his entire life and he also eats the air of everything he ever felt or thought or saw and so this new novel is just about as dopey as the old one but then she'd say darling of course she'd handle it out of loyalty to me so then she'd send the lousy novel manuscript around to all the major publishers in town who would send it right back to her so then she'd send the lousy novel manuscript around to all the minor publishers in town who would also send it right back to her so then she'd go groping around in trashcans and behind garbage dumps until she located some broken down publisher who was looking for a fast tax loss and this broken down publisher would agree to publish my lousy novel manuscript and maybe he'd even agree to pay me a pitiful small pittance out of loyalty to Marcia Masters and I thought then there would be the whole asshole editor trip because the broken down publisher would probably assign this lousy novel manuscript to some asshole editor who worked out of a cramped rat hole office and he would read through the novel manuscript and he would probably loathe most of it and he would want to make a lot of changes in it and that began to bother hell out of me because I thought how can I stop that asshole editor from cutting a lot of things out of this lousy novel manuscript and just then I thought maybe one way to beat that asshole editor would be for me to put in one senseless sentence that would be so god-awful that anyone in his right mind would want to cut it out of this lousy novel manuscript and so I opened up my notebook and I began to write out the most god-awful senseless sentence I could write and this is what I wrote:

Somewhere there is a great aged elk that is trying to die right now in the shrubbery and underbrush and its milky eye sees only autumn leaf and the distant disinterested sky.

And I thought there that's about as god-awful a senseless sentence as I can write so if that asshole editor wants to cut anything from this lousy novel manuscript let him cut that out but just as I thought that thought I heard a phone was ringing in the back of my braincave so I picked it up and I said hello and I heard a voice on the other end of the line and it said:

"Hi there Eliot Morrison I'm your asshole editor at the broken down publisher and I just read through your lousy novel manuscript and I loathe most of it but there's one part that I like very much."

And I asked him what part he liked very much and the asshole editor said:

"Well that one god-awful senseless sentence about the great aged elk that's trying to die is quite exquisite and lyrical."

And I said thanks a lot and then the asshole editor said:

"Of course there are certain other parts that will have to be cut if we're going to go anywhere with this lousy novel manuscript because there are parts of it that are so grotesquely overwritten and anecdotal and there are other parts of it that are in such monumental bad taste that no one will want to keep reading the whole thing all the way through to the end so first we'll have to cut a few of the characters that might offend certain areas of readership like Jose the desk clerk who might offend a lot of Mexican American readers and we'll also have to cut Mr. and Mrs. Ruiz who might offend a lot of Latin American readers and we'll also have to cut Douglas Mercer and Emerson Quaid who might offend a lot of black American readers and we'll also have to cut Marianne Roseblatt and Joseph Baum who might offend a lot of Jewish American readers and we'll also have to cut Robert Ingersoll and Esther Martin who might offend a lot of Roman Catholic readers."

And I asked the asshole editor if there was anything else that would have to be cut and he said:

"Well we'll also have to cut the characters of Cindy Stevens and Maureen Talbot who might offend a lot of feminist readers and we'll also have to cut all those State Troopers who might offend a lot of law enforcement readers and we'll also have to cut that bit about the secret sexual signal system which might offend a lot of Stanford University readers and we'll also have to cut Dr. Julian Nesbitt and Dr. Max Wittgenstein who might offend a lot of readers who are undergoing psychoanalysis."

And I asked the asshole editor if there was anything else that would have to be cut and he said:

"Well Jesus man there are so many kinky things in this lousy novel manuscript like Ted Wylie's tacky voyeurism and all those weird sex games with 10 year kids and all that incest and homicide and bestiality in the student manuscripts and incidentally you make your fellow writers out to be such a bunch of silly philistines and dilettantes and you're not helping yourself much with the publishing industry either the way you keep calling me an asshole editor."

And I asked the asshole editor if there was anything else that would have to be cut and he said:

"Of course I realize now I'm getting into the area of personal opinion but I'd say we should also cut that bit about the fuck photos at Betty's Diner because that comes awfully close to hard core pornography and after all this broken down publisher does have a reputation to worry about and I'd say we should also cut the characters of Harry Holton and Sylvester Appleby because no one would believe a couple of kids could be so stupid and retarded about sex in this day and age."

And I asked the asshole editor if there was anything else that would have to be cut and he said:

"Well I don't much like the title *Saturday Night at San Marcos* because it sounds too pretentious and literary and who the hell is going to go into a drugstore in Peoria and pick up a paperback with a title like *Saturday Night at San Marcos*?"

And I said I wasn't about to get paranoid about Peoria and when I said that the asshole editor said:

"Now you're talking good titles Morrison because Paranoid About Peoria has a good ring to it and I can see the front cover with this naked woman lying on her side all gaunt and haunted and this animal hand is reaching out of the shadows and is about to strangle her and written in bright red blood across her 2 nude boobs are the words PARANOID ABOUT PEORIA and I like it Morrison I like it and now I think we're beginning to get somewhere with your lousy novel manuscript."

And I asked the asshole editor if there was anything else that was wrong with my lousy novel manuscript and he said:

"Well and as for your nonstop writing style I don't understand why you have to keep using all these run on sentences and all these endless paragraphs one on top of another and you also tend to pile up all your prepositions and do you realize there's not one comma in your entire novel manuscript?"

And I said I knew all about all that but it was just the way the whole thing came out and the asshole editor said:

"That may be all very well for you to say Morrison but if we published this lousy novel manuscript the way it is right now you'd make us the laughingstock of every English department in this country and after all we do have the academic readership to think about."

And I asked the asshole editor if there was anything else that was wrong with my lousy manuscript and he said:

"Well and if you really want me to level with you Morrison I'd say there is this one huge technical flaw that runs through your entire novel because you're writing the whole thing in the first person so how the hell can you know so much about what other people are saying and doing behind your back when you're not even there because what have you got some kind of second sight or something?"

And I said it wasn't second sight as much as it was an idea I had about how everything is always telescoped together in one single instant of air and I said I've experienced time like that a lot of times and I said that's all explained in chapter 5 of this lousy novel and when I said that the asshole editor said:

"Listen Morrison don't go giving me a lot of shit about how you think everything is always telescoped together in one single instant of air because that's why that phony longwinded book reviewer called you such a fishy mishmosh of paranoia."

And I said I'd rather be a fishy mishmosh of paranoia who was trying to write his own writing than be some asshole editor who worked out of a cramped rat hole at some broken down publisher and when I said that I slammed the phone down in the back of my braincave and I sat there on the plane looking out the window at all the beautiful blue air that was out there and suddenly I felt pretty damn good about myself and just then the stewardess stood up in the front of the plane and she told us we were coming into Kennedy airport and would we please fasten our seat belts and the plane was already lowering lowering lowering and then it began to fly level along the late afternoon water and then it lowered some more until it looked as if it were going to skim the tops off the great waves of water with its wings and then there was the flat strip of earth rushing under us and the landing gear touched down and the plane bumped and screeched and it began to shudder as the jet engines raced backwards to brake the speed and then we were rolling along smoothly now at a steady ground speed past the brilliant runway lights and then we came to a dead halt beside the passenger terminal and I unfastened my seat belt and I stood up and I took my suitcase and I got off the plane and I walked through the airline terminal and I got on a bus that was going into Manhattan and I went on in to my apartment and I opened my mailbox and I pulled out all the mail that was crammed in there and I saw there were lots and lots of bills and lots of student manuscripts and there was a note from Marcia Masters and I ripped it open and this is what it said:

Darling:

Hy Kantor at Central Studios sent back *A Dream of Clarence* because he said he didn't see any way he could make a feature film out of a young kid who gets killed and how he eats the air of everything he ever felt or thought or saw but he said maybe it might make an interesting animated cartoon and he wished you luck with it and I'm sorry darling but I do hope you had fun at your ridiculous writers conference.

Marcia Masters

And I crumpled up the note and I tossed it over my shoulder and I went on upstairs and I heard the phone was ringing inside my apartment so I unlocked the door and I went in and I picked up the phone and I said hello and there was a pause and then I heard a voice on the other end and it said:

"Hello there shitface and how many of those cute little chickeepoos did you screw out there this time?"

And I said hello Clara and I told her that I only screwed one of them out there this time and Clara said:

"Oh so you only screwed one of them out there this time and was she such a hot lay that you just kept balling her all week long?"

And I said that wasn't the way it was because this student was an okay screw but I only made it with her once and the rest of the time I was deciding I would quit teaching all my writing classes here in New York so I could spend the rest of my life trying to write my own writing and when I said that there was a long pause on the other end of the phone and then Clara's voice was soft and low the way it was ice ages ago when she was a gentle tender soul who cared very much about me and she said:

"Thank god Eliot at long last you're going to try to write your own writing and so of course I forgive you for screwing that one student out there and now I'll leave you alone only promise me I'll be the first one to read whatever it is you're writing when it's finally done."

And I promised Clara she'd be the first one to read this lousy novel manuscript when it was finally done and then I got off the phone and I sat down and I said to myself my christ it is true I am really writing again but when I thought that thought I began to go into one of my desperation panic states and I knew I had to see Cindy Stevens one last time so I reached out for the phone and I called Cindy and she didn't sound too pleased when she answered the phone and found out who it was calling her and she said:

"Jesus Christ Eliot Morrison and we both agreed last time that this time it was final and we both agreed we would never be in touch with each other not ever again after last time."

And I said I knew all about all that but this time it was urgent because this time it was an emergency because I was beginning to go into one of my desperation panic states because I was just back from this corny boring writers conference in California and I needed to see Cindy one last time and I pleaded with her please to come down and see me please for one last time and when I said that Cindy said:

"Eliot Morrison you're always saying you need to see me one last time and you know damn well if I came down there tonight we'd just keep this sick thing going and we've both agreed it's no good for either of us because you're not really writing and my own show opens in 2 weeks and I don't even have lines yet and how the hell do you expect me to do good work at rehearsal tomorrow if I stay up all night at your place?"

And I said I wouldn't keep her up all night and besides I said I was writing a new novel now and I said Cindy was in the opening and closing chapters and I said the whole thing would be made into a play someday and Cindy would get to play herself onstage and I said that would be a hell of a lot better than playing in sick plays like the play she was in right now and then I asked her did she get my letter where I told her what Ted Wylie said about how she was supposed to be playing in his sick play and Cindy said:

"Yeah I got your letter and he said my action is to watch but that's no help because how can I play someone who wants to watch some zombie author take notes on how 17 chipmunks kill 45 guinea pigs before I fuck him right there onstage in front of an enormous mirror just so everyone in the audience can get to see us do it double?"

And I said if Cindy came down right away tonight then I'd explain the whole thing to her and then she could go to sleep and she'd

234

never have to see me again not ever for the rest of her professional life only I asked her to come down now please come because I needed her and there was a long pause at the other end of the phone and then Cindy said:

"I hope you know what you're doing to yourself Eliot Morrison because you're bullshitting yourself and my analyst says something in you refuses to believe that you could ever be at all lovable so that's why you keep telling yourself all these bullshit lies like how you're writing a new novel now and how the hell can I buy that when I know perfectly well you haven't really written anything for the last 5 years and you shouldn't lie about a thing like that not even as a cheap way of getting me into the sack with you."

And I told Cindy she was just trying to bring me down with all her helium highs and asshole lows and all her sick bitch quick switch mind life criticism and how the hell was I supposed to be really writing anything when all I could ever think about was whether she was off fucking someone else and I said she was such a hopelessly childish child that I didn't need her anymore because now I was trying to write my own writing and when I said that Cindy said:

"Oh shit."

And I asked her did oh shit mean that she was coming down to see me and she said she'd be there in half an hour so I got off the phone and I spent the next half hour pacing up and down in my apartment until I heard the doorbell ring and I ran over and I opened the door and there was Cindy standing there with her bright gold hair and her loose full breasts and her 2 ice blue tiny iris eyes so I put my arm around her and I led her right on into the bedroom and I took off all her clothes and I put her down on the bed and I lay down next to her and I began playing with the stiff little tips of her nipples and then when I got on top of her and I eased myself on into her she suddenly threw her arms around my neck and she cried out aloud:

"Oh god darling I've missed you and I've needed you and I've missed you so fucking much!"

And suddenly there I was looking down into her 2 pinpoint pupils that opened out onto another universe as I kept thrusting away inside of her and she began to let out these small whimpering puppy noises under me and I kept pumping and pumping and pumping away inside of her until suddenly I felt myself beginning to let go and that was when I thrust as hard as I could thrust on in and up and ah god I was gone in an explosion of composure and it was like an ocean flowing over me and then I felt myself collapsing backwards in a blackout as I rolled over on my side beside her and I went swimming in an underwater duckpond where there are these centuries of sand and large dark shapes that keep darting in and out in their slow motion going and for a long moment I was floating all alone down there in the sweet peace of sleep.

This is the end of the last chapter of this lousy novel and by this time you must be feeling pretty damn good about yourself because you just finished reading the whole thing all the way through to the end but that's nothing because just think of how I'm feeling pretty damn good about myself because I just finished writing the whole thing all the way through to the end and now here we are on the last page of this lousy novel and if you're holding this book in your hands then that means some broken down publisher did go ahead and publish it and if there's that one god-awful senseless sentence about the great aged elk that's trying to die then that means the asshole editor didn't make any cuts or changes at all and so that means that right now I'm probably off somewhere else trying to write another lousy novel and that new novel will also show a tiny bit of all the fresh fruit juice loony foolishness that is all around us always but that new novel is not written yet so that means it is still up there in the air because all real writing is always up there in the air because that's where all rare fair things always are up there in the bright areas of air.